BEYOND STALINGRAD

Also by
Geoffrey Sambrook

**Tarnished Copper
Czar Rising**

Rooney, I hope you enjoy it!

13:04:24

BEYOND STALINGRAD

by

Geoffrey Sambrook

Geoff

Beyond Stalingrad © Geoffrey Sambrook 2020.

Geoffrey Sambrook has asserted his rights under the Copyright Designs and Patents Act 1988 to be identified as the author of this work.

All rights reserved. No part of this work may be reproduced or stored on an information retrieval system (other than for purposes of review) without the prior permission of the copyright holder.

Published in Great Britain by Twenty First Century Publishers Ltd.

A catalogue record of this book is available from the British Library.

ISBN: 978-1-904433-78-1

This is a work of fiction. Names, characters and incidents are the product of the author's imagination or are used fictitiously, and any resemblance to actual persons, living or dead, is entirely coincidental.

This book is sold subject to no resale, hiring out, loan or other manner of circulation in form other than this book without the publisher's written consent.

Cover design: painting by Fred Piechoczek.

AUTHOR'S NOTE

This is a work of fiction. While the backdrop is the history of the middle of the twentieth century, I have made use of that history to suit the development of my own plot and characters, and where real characters or events are used, there should be no suggestion that they behaved or unfolded as I have portrayed them.

However, the story of Armin Kuhlmann and his family in the years leading up to the Battle of Stalingrad is based on fact. His disappearance there in January/February 1943 mirrors what my grandparents, mother, aunt and uncle had to face; their son/sibling disappeared. The letter in the text from a former comrade is - subject to necessary minor (and name) changes - a translation of one received by my grandfather in 1950. The name of my uncle (as he would have been) does indeed feature on the memorial at Rossoschka, although it is not Armin Kuhlmann.

The story post battle is entirely my own imagining of how the aftermath of that dreadful encounter may have played out. I would not suggest it is an accurate, historical account of the way the Gulag system worked, and any resemblance between events and people portrayed is entirely fortuitous.

You may try to join the dots, but in the end I would suggest that is a futile activity. This is a piece of fiction.

January 1943 - Russia

Chapter One

Cold. Bitter, unforgiving, mind-sapping, agonising, deadly cold.

Armin Kuhlmann squinted out through the slit in the front of his concrete pillbox. In the middle distance, he could see the smouldering fires still burning in the ruined city of Stalingrad. A thin mist of snow was falling, and he shrugged his clothing closer around his shoulders to try and warm his body; it didn't make any difference. Although he wore a heavy greatcoat over his black Panzer uniform and had a scarf and balaclava wound around his head, he hadn't been warm for weeks. He was cold, hungry, frightened and a long way from home. He scratched at his shoulder, through the clothing; he was lice-ridden as well. When he was a boy, back in Germany, snow had meant fun. It had meant playing in the big garden of the beautiful house in Aue, throwing snowballs at his brother and sisters, and then chasing their father through the drifts until they all fell in a heap, laughing. And then there had been the New Year holidays at Garmisch; the skiing, the parties, the bright, twinkling fairy-lights in the streets and such a sense of pride in his Papa, seeing how the other adults deferred to his views and opinions. He was a man of substance. Those had been good times, the snow his friend and a source of such fun. Here in the Stalingrad Kessel - the cauldron, in which day by day the Germans were getting more and more squeezed - it was a bitter enemy, the only saving grace that while it was falling, the poor visibility at least kept the Stormoviks grounded at their airfields to the east of the city, so the relentless bombing and strafing stopped temporarily. That was the good bit. But it was so bitter, sitting in the snow in this place. It sapped the will to live. The lethargy created by the cold, just as much as the enemy fire or the starvation or the disease was crushing the 6th Army to death.

And why was he here? He had no love for the uniform he wore. He loathed the regime it represented; his family were all in England, for God's sake, on the other side. The last news he had had, months and months ago, was that his brother Franz was in the British army and the elder of his two sisters was engaged to a British officer. But he sat here, surrounded by the Red Army, bombed and strafed by their aeroplanes, blasted by their shells and rockets. And he knew he would die here. At this stage of the battle, with the Russians tightening their grip on the Kessel every day, there was hardly a man apart from the diehard fanatic Nazis who hadn't been infused with the fatalism of a defeated army.

He wiggled his toes in the Russian felt boots he wore in another futile attempt to get warm as he lit his last cigarette. There was a scuffling noise behind him, and he looked round to see his sergeant dropping in through the narrow slit in the roof of the pillbox.

"Morning, Schulz," he said.

"Morning, Sir. 'Fraid there's no room service breakfast today. Ivan wouldn't let me send out to the shop for supplies."

Kuhlmann couldn't help but smile. He had come to have a great affection for the wiry, indomitably good-humoured Berliner who had been with him since the previous summer in Ukraine.

"That's all right, Sergeant, I'm on a low-intake diet."

The sergeant grinned back. He had no illusions about some of the officers, but Kuhlmann was one of the best. The men not only respected him, they liked him. He didn't shirk anything, unlike some of the others. They knew he was as frightened as they were, but he shared everything with them – the patrolling, the sentry duties, the work parties; and he always made sure they had their rations before taking his own. Most of them had been with him since they first hit Russia, still in their tanks then, eighteen months ago. But their numbers were dwindling rapidly.

"How was it last night?" Kuhlmann asked, knowing the sergeant would have been around the company's positions before coming to report.

"Relatively quiet. No attack on the front lines, but pretty constant fighting out on the perimeter all night." That brought Kuhlmann up with a start. He was so used to the constant background firing, he hadn't even been aware of it; if he'd been asked, he'd have said it was quiet outside. The sergeant continued. "Three more men frozen to death overnight, though, so if – or when – the Russkis do attack, we'll be even more thinly spread. It's still snowing at the moment, but it's getting lighter. Should think it will lift soon. There's a bunch of high-ups waiting on the runway; they must be expecting a plane in and they want to be on it on the way out. I'm just waiting for the colonel to give me my first-class ticket."

Kuhlmann smiled wanly as he clapped the NCO on the shoulder. "No ticket out for us, Sergeant, this is where we're going to die. To get out, you need more gold braid; or a pair of lightning-flashes on your collar."

Beyond Stalingrad

"Too true."

Neither man concealed his indifference to the Party or the regime, at least between themselves.

"I'll spell you here for a while, Sir, if you want to get out for a bit. There's no incoming fire at the moment."

"Thanks." Kuhlmann slung his machine-pistol over his shoulder and squeezed out through the narrow slit opening. Outside, the cold took his breath away. Schulz had been right; as he looked, he could see the air becoming clearer as the snow lifted. Smoke rising from the city obscured the eastern horizon with a black stain. Here and there the flames were also visible.

Kuhlmann's company was dug in along the perimeter of the Pitomnik airstrip, right in the centre of the Kessel; some of their positions were concrete strong-points, like the one he had spent the night in, others were no more than shallow trenches scraped in the frozen earth. He calculated as he walked. Three more dead. His company strength should have been a hundred and eighty; with those three more gone, he had sixty-seven men left to hold on to his sector. It was never going to work. If they wanted, all the Russians had to do was to sit and wait while the 6th Army starved or froze to death; then they could just walk over and take back their land.

He heard the crackle of aero engines bursting into life and looked across the airfield to see two of the remaining 109s taxing on to the runway. Presumably, they were heading off as the weather improved to escort in whatever transport planes were expected. Perhaps this time they'd be lucky and get them in before the Russian fighters arrived. It was getting more difficult, though, since the Luftwaffe had lost the crucial aerial dominance in December. The fighter pilots did what they could, nobody could deny that, but the arrival of the Yak-9 had further compromised their efforts, with its clear superiority over the 109. Still, Kuhlmann envied the fighter pilots; as long as they had petrol in their tanks, they knew they had a way out to the west. The ground troops were stuck; they were never going to get home.

The crackle of small-arms fire and the crump of the mortars was a constant background as he plodded on. Ahead of him, he could see the bunker that served as the HQ, with behind it the hospital, if you could call that charnel house a hospital. He'd been in it a few times to visit some of his men. It was a nightmare vision, the wounded crammed together, most simply lying on the floor. The doctors and medical orderlies did what they could, but the cold, the lack of supplies and the ever-increasing numbers of wounded made their task nigh-on impossible. Very few of the men who went in there made it out alive.

"Hey, Armin! How goes it?" A figure clambered out of a slit trench and fell in alongside him.

"Klaus, good morning. I'm just taking a morning constitutional before Ivan comes visiting again. Walk with me for a bit."

Klaus Müller fell into step with his friend. He was half a head shorter; even though they were wearing every bulky piece of clothing they could find, both men were frighteningly emaciated. "Relatively quiet last night," he said.

"Yes, I only lost three more men frozen to death. No incoming shellfire, so I suppose overall that counts as quiet." He looked seriously at the other man. "It can't go on much longer, though. There are sixty-seven men left in this company. There should be a hundred and eighty. And those sixty-seven are freezing and starving." He jerked his thumb savagely towards the hospital. "There are the ones in there as well, I suppose. No doubt the Führer would expect them to come out and fight for his glory." He laughed bitterly. "What the Hell are we doing here, Klaus? God knows how many men have already died in this mess and there's thousands and thousands more here who won't get out. What's the point?"

"Careful, Armin. There are still zealots here who would report you for that as spreading alarm and despondency. They still believe the Führer will rescue them. Only yesterday that SS pillock Schneider told me that Manstein was within range with his armoured column and would break the Russian siege within a day or two. He'll still believe we'll soon be sweeping on to Moscow the day he gets a Russian bayonet through his guts."

They walked on together over the frozen ground. At least here at the airfield, away from the front line, they could walk upright, unthreatened by the snipers who were a constant presence amongst the ruined buildings of the devastated city and lay camouflaged out in the snow on the steppe beyond the front line. They'd been in the street fighting in the city before Christmas, part of the desperate struggle over the Tractor Factory. That had been weeks of sheer terror, twenty-four hours a day. It was even worse in there now, as the Luftwaffe's superiority had been taken from it. Now there were no Stukas to come to the rescue of the beleaguered infantry; the Russian gunners had the German positions firmly in their sights and just kept pounding away at them. Casualties were dreadful, cartloads of wounded arriving in a constant stream at the hospital every day. In contrast to that, out here at the airfield the major concern was trying to keep warm and dodge the bombs and strafing runs of the Stormoviks. At least the anti-aircraft guns clustered round the HQ bunker still had sufficient ammunition.

They knew their turn would come again to go back into the front line. They'd been at Pitomnik for about ten days; while it was no holiday camp, it did afford a modicum of relief from the unrelenting awfulness of the street-fighting in the city ruins. Kuhlmann was a talented artist, and he spent a lot of his time drawing, sketching the tight, drawn faces of his

Beyond Stalingrad

comrades as they huddled in their shelters. It was such a contrast to the happy days of his childhood, when his sketching had produced picture books for his little sisters and bright landscapes done in the peace of the countryside around the Erzgebirge.

They reached the HQ bunker, where, as Sergeant Schulz had reported, there was a group of senior officers anxiously scanning the western horizon. The distinctive black uniforms of the Waffen-SS were prominent amongst them and scattered around them on the ground were various bags and bits of kit. The adjutant of the battalion saw the two walking towards the bunker and called them over "Ah, Kuhlmann, good. I was about to send a runner to your position. I must congratulate you. We have just this morning received your promotion to Captain. This is recognition that as you have been doing the job of company commander for so long now, it is right that you should hold the appropriate rank. And on the bottom of the signal, there was a personal message of congratulation from the Führer!"

Kuhlmann knew what he really wanted to say; instead, he came to attention, saluted and said, "Thank you, Sir. I shall treasure that message from the Führer as long as I live."

The adjutant looked suspiciously at him, as Müller bit back a chuckle. "Yes, well, you'd better get back to your company. Carry on, gentlemen." And he scurried off, back into his bunker.

As the other two turned to walk back to their positions, Müller said: "You know what that's about, don't you? They're sure that a personal message like that from the Führer will stiffen your resolve, make sure you don't surrender."

"You may be right, but it makes no difference. We're all going to die here anyway, whatever the Führer says about it. You have only to look at the ruins of the city over there to know the Russkis won't be taking any prisoners. And even if you only believe a tenth of the rumours about what the SS and the Einsatzgruppen have been getting up to behind us, you know we'll see no mercy. You were the historian at university, Klaus; I was just an art student. But even I can tell you that this is one of, if not the, most catastrophic military campaigns of all time. So do I care about a personal message from the man who orchestrated it? And anyway, cynic that I am, I suspect that my personal message is but one of many thousands written by an aide, comfortable in an office in Berlin with absolutely no idea what it is like here."

"Well, Captain Kuhlmann, as I must now call you, that smacks of defeatism. I put it down to your Britishness. Only someone who is half British could be so pessimistic. Where is your faith that our Führer will save us?"

Kuhlmann smiled at his friend, then turned serious. "Klaus, this is a total fuck-up, isn't it? What are we doing here? Why are we fighting this war? I don't want to. Frankly, I don't really care about the Russians, but my family are all in England. My brother's in the British army, for God's sake. All I want to do is to go back home, finish my studies and see if I can really make it as an artist."

"Ah yes; you and Adolph, potentially the two great German artists of the twentieth-century. You're keeping good company, Armin." Müller chuckled as he said it.

Suddenly, from the east, they heard the drone of aero-engines. Looking that way, trying to see through the haze of thick black smoke from the city, they finally picked out the vee formation of three Stormoviks heading their way at about fifty metres altitude. As the anti-aircraft batteries all opened up together, creating a cacophony of noise, the two dived into the nearest slit trench. The higher-ups were already sprinting for the shelter of the bunker.

The Stormoviks flashed over, machine guns chattering, targeting anything they could see. As they pulled up over the perimeter fence, the bombs they had dropped exploded. This time, they completely missed their target, the runway. One of the bombs went off close to the hospital, showering it in debris, and the other two exploded harmlessly outside the perimeter. As the Stormoviks climbed, the anti-aircraft gunners hit one; it exploded in a sheet of flame. There were no parachutes. The other two turned to the east and headed off at full throttle. As Kuhlmann and Müller climbed out of their trench, the reason for their departure became clear. Streaking in from the west came the two 109s, in hot pursuit of the Russian aircraft. Behind them, dipping as it prepared to land, came a Junkers Ju 52, the old workhorse transport they had been escorting in. After touching down, it taxied off the runway and rolled to a halt alongside the HQ bunker. The pilot cut the engines as the group of senior officers re-emerged and moved towards it. At the same time, the Feldgendarmerie troops who had been lurking around the bunker moved forward and surrounded the aircraft, their weapons at the ready, keeping a close eye on the ordinary soldiers who surged forward towards it.

"Look at that," said Müller, bitterly. "They're already at the door. I bet there's no supplies on it, either; it's just come in as a way to get the boys out."

"Not those boys, though," said Kuhlmann, pointing to the ordinary soldiers, sullen-faced under the watchful gaze of the Feldgendarmerie. "They're going nowhere. They're just cannon-fodder, like us."

They looked across. The ordinary troops were grey-faced and cadaverous. They shambled along like automatons, eyes downcast. The smart Wehrmacht uniforms of 1941 had gone, replaced by the standard Kessel mixture of German and Russian kit, all in an attempt to ward off the cold. The lucky ones wore felt boots, ripped off a Russian corpse. The German leather boots some were still left with were one of the most obvious examples of the lack of effective planning by the German High Command – the leather rotted quickly in the constant wet and freezing conditions, leading to agony for the wearers. They looked better polished on a parade ground than the Russian ones, but the Kessel was no parade ground.

"Look at that, Klaus; that's what defeat looks like. And look there" – he pointed at the Junkers – "no supplies, no ammunition, nothing coming out of it. An empty aeroplane, burning fuel we desperately need – just so those rats can leave the sinking ship." He spoke with bitterness and contempt. "Why did they even bother to stop the engines? They're out of here so fast."

Sure enough, as the last of the group of brass-hats climbed aboard and slammed the door behind him, the propellers began turning again, one after the other. The pilot ran up the three engines and taxied out to the end of the runway. The engine note reached a crescendo, and the lumbering machine started rolling. As it reached take-off speed and lifted slowly into the air, a higher-pitched sound blotted out the noise of its engines. As Kuhlmann and Müller turned to the east to see what it was, two Yak-9s came in low over the airfield boundary. The Ju 52 had barely climbed to a hundred metres when they opened up and hosed it very deliberately from tailplane to cockpit. The Ju 52 was a robust old machine, but there was no way it could withstand the concerted attack from the two interceptors. The end was inevitable. The pilot desperately tried to avoid the cannon fire, but with a blast audible over the engines of the Yaks, the machine burst into an orange fireball and dropped about half a kilometre from the end of the runway.

Kuhlmann and Müller looked at each other. "Well," said the former, "they may have been on our side, but actually I take my hat off to the Russkis for that one. Rats sinking with the ship, for a change."

They made their way back to the pillbox that served as the company headquarters; stepping though the doorway, they were plunged into gloom. As their eyes adjusted to the darkness, they made out the pitiful flame under the billycan of greasy liquid the men were clustering around. Glancing up and seeing the officers, one of the men plunged a metal cup into the pan and handed it to Kuhlmann. "Breakfast, Sir." Kuhlmann nodded his thanks and sipped the unappetising liquid. After so long here, he didn't ask what was in it; it was at least warm. The thought did cross his mind as to whether his taste buds would ever recover from the assault they'd borne here; then he shook his head. Futile even to think of it; he'd probably never eat proper food again.

He gestured to the pan. "Take that around to the sentry posts. That's all they're going to get today. I'll make my rounds in about half an hour."

Two of the soldiers nodded and picked it up, then manoeuvred themselves awkwardly through the narrow doorway. There was no salute, no heel-clicking; discipline by now was wafer-thin. The senior officers may try to deny it, but they all knew that some of the corpses found overnight were junior officers with slit throats. Nothing was said, and they were thrown into the same mass grave as all the others, but some of the men were determined to exact vengeance on those they blamed for their situation and the platoon officers were the nearest representatives of the command. Not so Kuhlmann, though; his men trusted him absolutely. They knew he'd never asked them to do anything he wasn't doing himself; he'd helped them through all the worst of the fighting. They all knew it wouldn't be long, though, and were living in an almost trance-like state, the relative calm of the airfield almost like a half-way house between life and death.

A battalion runner squeezed through into the pillbox. He saluted. "Captain Kuhlmann, the major would like to see you at headquarters immediately, please."

"OK, tell the major I'll be right there." Wearily, Kuhlmann stepped out into the cold again. Stupid, stupid people, he thought. I've just been over there; they saw me. Why do they want me to traipse over there again?

Müller followed him out. "I'd better get back to my platoon. I'll see you later, Armin."

Kuhlmann acknowledged him with a wave and set off back across the airfield. He had gone two or three hundred metres when he heard the rushing, roaring sound of an incoming salvo of Katyushas. Immediately, instinctively, he threw himself to the ground. The Russians hadn't got the range right, and most of the rockets went harmlessly beyond the far perimeter. One fell short, though, and scored a direct hit on the pillbox he had just left. As he stood up again, he could see there was nothing remaining of it but a smouldering hole in the snow. Over to his right he saw another figure rising from the ground; Müller waved to show his friend he was all right; Kuhlmann waved back and they both continued on their way. We must have charmed lives, he thought; if we'd left two minutes later, or if the Russians had fired a couple minutes earlier, we'd be dead in that hole. Looking about him, he realised the irony of the thought of a 'charmed life' in the Stalingrad Kessel.

Chapter Two

Kuhlmann stepped into the HQ bunker and saluted the major. "You wanted to see, me, Sir?"

"Ah, Kuhlmann, yes. We have a new command for you." He stepped across to the map of the positions on the wall. "You're to go to the northern perimeter, here" – he jabbed his finger on the map – "and take command of a company holding the front line in that sector. They're HIWIs, and their officer was killed yesterday; the fighting up there has been tough." He looked up, and saw the expression of dismay on Kuhlmann's face. "What's the matter? Do you have a problem with HIWIs? Well, tough. None of us gets what he wants in this place. Now, get up there straight away. Müller can take over your position here."

"Sir." Kuhlmann saluted, turned and left the bunker. The truth was, he did have a problem with HIWIs. They were Hilfswillige, 'volunteers'. But not ordinary volunteers. They were Russians, Ukrainians, Latvians and others who had chosen, for whatever reason, to fight for the Germans. Many of them were anti-communist zealots, others were captured Russian soldiers who preferred to serve with their enemy than to go into a prisoner of war camp, and some were just peasants swept into the Wehrmacht as the Panzers had rolled through in the early days of the invasion. Whatever their motivation, Kuhlmann knew what their fate would be when the Russians captured them. The chances of survival caught as a German were low enough; to be taken amongst a company of renegades didn't bear thinking about.

He wandered back - again - across the airfield to pick up the few meagre possessions he had left; the only thing he really cared about was the leather case holding his drawings. That had been with him for the whole Barbarossa operation, from the heady early days when they had swept forward through the Russian resistance to the River Don, to the vicious street fighting around the Tractor Factory. Even if he lost everything else, he'd fight to protect that.

As he came out of the pillbox, he saw Schulz just returning from a tour of the positions.

"Schulz, this is goodbye," he said. "You'll be going on without me. I'm being sent to a company of HIWIs up on the perimeter front line. They've lost their officer."

Schulz looked serious." HIWIs, Sir? Don't get captured with them. Not popular with the Russkis."

"Yes, I know. Still, nothing I can do about it. Look after the men, Schulz. Lieutenant Müller will be taking over as company commander."

"You look after yourself, Sir. We'll miss you. It's a long time we've been together."

"It is indeed. A long time and a lot of thousands of kilometres. I'll miss you too, Schulz." He shook the man's hand – an unusual gesture between officer and NCO. "But Klaus Müller's a good man. He'll do his best for the men."

He turned and set off. Schulz looked after him. If only there were a few more like him, he thought, and less of the crazies; then perhaps we wouldn't be in this mess. He kicked at the snow in annoyance and swung down into the pillbox. He knew Klaus Müller was a good man, but the men would feel a lot more exposed without Kuhlmann there.

Kuhlmann started off on foot for the northern perimeter. He knew where he was going, although the last time he'd been there it hadn't been a front line position, it had been part of the reserve lines. That was an indication of the power of the Russian advance. He caught up with a cart pulled by an emaciated pony, hardly able to stand between the shafts. A brief conversation with the driver established they were going in the same direction, and he gratefully accepted a ride, swinging himself up onto the back of the cart among a pitifully small number of ammunition boxes. The poor pony was slipping and staggering; it clearly wouldn't be long before it found itself on the plates of the troops. Kuhlmann found himself hoping its last journey would end at his destination. It was thin, but it was meat.

The cart bumped on over the snow-covered ground. He sat on the back, hugging his arms around his body to try and at least create an illusion of warmth. The landscape was unutterably bleak, pockmarked with shell holes and scarred by the burned-out carcasses of wrecked tanks. The land was flat, featureless and devoid of trees or any vegetation. Here and there the remains of a cottage or some farm buildings still stood, mostly providing some sort of shelter for groups of soldiers. Since the most recent Russian onslaught had begun on 9th January, the area inside the Kessel was being squeezed smaller and smaller. There were about 235000 men caught in the trap, rapidly running out of food, ammunition and fuel. The Russians kept up a constant stream of firing at the perimeter, and the rattle of machine guns and the crump of mortars had become the backdrop to daily life. Like most of the men in there, Kuhlmann was able to shut out the sounds of battle, and the pitching and rocking of the cart was almost soporific, setting his mind drifting off into memories of the past.

He remembered Christmas 1938, the last time he had seen his beloved family. He could see the twinkling candles in the tree, he could almost touch the bottle of wine on the table and the smell of the goose that

Beyond Stalingrad

Papa was about to carve beckoned him across the years. They were all in London by then, of course, and he imagined he heard the excited chatter of his brother and sisters, in their peculiar mix of German and English. He'd been home for his university vacation, from Hamburg, and the girls had been so happy to see their big brother. Then he could hear the two of them, their pure voices soaring in "Stille Nacht", the carol with which the Kuhlmanns always began their Christmas celebrations. The ties of blood ran deep in that family, and in his mind he found a momentary peace from this freezing, frightening, lice-ridden hell. Tears formed in his eyes, as the cart gave a violent lurch and he was brought back to the reality of January 1943 in the Stalingrad Kessel.

The gunfire was louder now, and he ducked instinctively as he heard the roar of the Katyushas flying overhead. Then he settled back against the ammunition boxes again, and another memory came unbidden, this one less welcome. It was January 1939 and he was sitting in Papa's study the day before he was due to go back to Hamburg. Papa was pacing the room, agitated. "Armin, you can't go back. It makes no sense, it's too risky."

"Papa, I have two terms left until I finish my degree. It would be crazy to give up now. I'll be back here by the end of June, all finished, and then I'll probably stay in England. Look, I know you're worried about the Nazis, but I think you exaggerate the risk. All the people I know think they're just a bunch of crazies and that they won't last."

"I'm sure all the people you mix with do think that; they're all like you – decent, educated, liberal-minded students. But you're not the majority. Those same Nazis who you say won't last are the people who forced us out of Germany. That was four years ago, so they've already lasted that long. And they're not going to allow an election, so how will they be got out? Armin, the way it's going, there will be another war. They are not going to stop until they are forced to; first it was Austria, then Czechoslovakia, next it will be somewhere else. And the British are the ones who will have to stop them. This country and our homeland will be at war. Do you want to be there when that happens?"

"Papa, the Germans are sensible people. This is just an aberration. They remember what happened last time; do you really believe the whole population want to see that again? Have some faith in your countrymen."

"I'm as proud to be a German as you are. I did my duty in 1914, even though that duty led us to disaster. But this is not just an aberration, as you say. This time, the country has taken a bad turning and it will not end well. A monster has been created which will end by consuming the nation.

"Look, there are lots of good universities here in England; why not finish your studies at one of them?"

"No, you know how much this course in Hamburg means to me. I must finish it."

"Well, if I can't persuade you, I can't. I think you're being stupid and selfish. But at least promise me and your mother that if the situation gets worse, then you will come back here straight away."

And he'd gone back to Hamburg having made that promise, fully intending to keep it if necessary. It hurt, though, with a deep pain, that the last real conversation he had had with his father had ended like that, with Papa calling him stupid and selfish. But events had spun out of his control, and within a few months, travel restrictions had been brought in which prevented him leaving Germany, as he was of military age. That's when he realised, with a chilling certainty, that Papa had been right and he'd been wrong. The crazies were not going to be ousted before they had wreaked a dreadful havoc on Europe. There was nothing he could do; along with his classmates, he'd received his conscription papers and walked in to the Wehrmacht training barracks on the outskirts of Hamburg. That had led him inexorably to here, the killing fields on the Russian steppe.

The cart lurched again, shaking him out of his reverie. Even Papa had never imagined it would be this bad. He scratched again at the lice. Which would get him? The cold, the hunger, the disease or the Russians? That was now the only existential question left to him and the others trapped there. The driver halted the cart, and Kuhlmann looked around him. They were out on the featureless steppe, the horizon flat and distant. The only visible objects were the burned-out tanks; then he saw a figure emerge from a trench dug in the shelter of a group of three of the wrecks. The man was wearing what at this stage of the battle was standard Wehrmacht uniform on the front line – a heavy grey German overcoat with Russian quilted battle-jacket over it. The head was covered with a scarf and balaclava and the feet shod with Russian felt boots.

"Good morning. I'm Sergeant Hartmann. You must be our new officer. This is our reserve line – the front is up there". He pointed to the North. "It's about half a kilometre. Half the men are up there at the moment, the other half back here. They are rotating in eight-hour spells in the front line. They're HIWIs, mostly Ukrainians. They're pretty good fighters, but they're shit scared of what will happen to them if the Russians catch them" He looked hard at Kuhlmann. "Not too good for us, either, being with them. Still, the fighting has been on and off recently, but our officer died yesterday. But come down into the dug-out while the driver unloads the ammunition supplies."

Kuhlmann looked at him. "That won't take him long; there's not much of it."

He followed the Sergeant down into the gloom of the dug-out. The fug stung his eyes but he could just about make out the shapes of some of the other soldiers. There had been no deference in the way the sergeant had addressed him; as far as he had been able to tell from the brief look at the cadaverous face, the man couldn't have been any older than he was himself. But we all seem old before our time in here, he thought. Most people's adult lives last for years; for us, these few months in this charnel-house are all there is. And nobody outside, in the end, will ever know the full horror of what's going on here.

A radio crackled and one of the soldiers picked up the mike. After grunting something in a language Kuhlmann didn't understand, although he recognised it as Ukrainian, the man handed the mike to Hartmann, who had a short, testy conversation about the lack of ammunition supply. Hartmann clicked off, and turned to Kuhlmann. "Hardly any ammo, and they don't even talk about food. Still, that pony on your cart looked on its last legs. Shall we take it?"

Kuhlmann nodded, and Hartmann, gesturing to one of the men to follow him, slipped out of the dug-out. Moments later, Kuhlmann heard a muffled shot.

The next few days followed a dull pattern. They could still hear the fighting off to their left and the roar of the Katyushas flying overhead was a constant strain on the nerves, but there was little movement or firing from the Russian trenches 200 metres ahead of the German front line. The discomfort was extreme and the trenches, just barely scraped out of the frozen ground, hardly merited the name. But the Russians bided their time.

They had no new rations brought up to them and the pony had had pitifully little meat on it. Still, they'd made the most of it while it lasted.

On 15th January they heard that Pitomnik had fallen, leaving Gumrak as the only usable airstrip in the Kessel. Goering was still swearing black was white that his Luftwaffe transports could supply the beleaguered army from the air; but then, Goering was back at the Air Ministry in Berlin, not sitting in a frozen hole in the ground or the ruins of a city watching the parachute-drop supplies drifting across the sky to fall unerringly into the arms of the Russian soldiers. When he heard that Pitomnik had gone, Kuhlmann feared for his friend Klaus Müller. They'd been together since university. There were rumours of a massacre as the enraged Russians discovered the fate of those of their men who had been captured and held prisoner there. The Germans had left them outside, with no shelter and no food. The story was that the Russian prisoners had resorted to cannibalism in their suffering, and that their comrades, coming upon this, had set about the Germans they had captured with a ferocious savagery. Kuhlmann could only hope Müller had made it through.

That same night, the Russian loudspeakers positioned behind their lines started again, with the same refrain they had used at Christmas, blaring out: "Hello Fritzis! Did you know that every seven seconds, a German soldier dies in Russia? One...two...three...four...five...six... bang! One... two... three... four... five... six...bang!" So it went on all night, echoing around and shredding the already tattered nerves of the defenders. The Germans all knew the end-game was approaching; they wouldn't be able to hold out for long in their weakened condition and with such limited ammunition.

In the artificial calm of those few days, though, Kuhlmann spent his time sketching the men in his company. The grey, cadaverous faces stared out of the paper at him, devoid of expression apart from the hollow despair in their eyes. The men couldn't believe what they saw when he showed them their own faces; they all saw the deterioration in their comrades, but somehow were shocked to see it in themselves. But even in that short time, the HIWIs came to respect their new officer. He sat with them in the front-line trenches, with the constant blaring Russian broadcasts and he went as hungry as they did.

That brief hiatus of calm was shattered a few days later by the Russian guns opening up on their positions in the north of the Kessel. The guns thundered and the Katyushas roared creating a nightmare cacophony. When it stopped, although their ears were still ringing from the assault of noise, the defenders could hear the dull rumble of the diesel engines as the tanks began to roll forward. They burst through the smoke of the artillery and advanced. The German anti-tank guns on either side of Kuhlmann where he lay with Hartmann ready to use their one heavy machine-gun began a rapid fire. The German gunners were accurate; three tanks in the first line immediately burst into flame and then the others drove into the minefield in front of the German line. They were held there, the infantry behind them unable to advance while the tanks were held up.

The anti-tank gunners kept firing and Hartmann kept his fingers on the triggers of the HMG. For the moment, they held the advance. But Kuhlmann knew it couldn't last, not with their dire lack of ammunition and the overwhelming numerical superiority of the Russians. "Hartmann," he yelled above the noise of the gunfire, "while they're regrouping we need to withdraw. This is the end for us. Tell the HIWIs to fall back while we have the chance. This front can't hold. We need to retreat back into the city and link up with what's left in there." The sergeant moved off to the next firing point, to give the order to retire.

Kuhlmann grabbed the radio mike to let HQ know his intentions, but he got no reply. All he could hear was a stream of panic-stricken calls from other outlying posts radio-ing in. He shrugged his shoulders; HQ must have been taken, leaving the defenders out here on the perimeter to fend for themselves. He tugged his pistol from its holster and put two

Beyond Stalingrad

bullets through the radio set; no way was he going to lug that with him, but he couldn't let it fall into the enemy's hands. Crouching low, he ran across to the shelter of a wrecked tank where Hartmann had gathered the remains of the company.

"OK," he said to the HIWIs. "Sergeant Hartmann and I will be attempting to fall back into the suburbs of the city to link up with the German forces there. But this is the beginning of the end; the last stand. You men may have a different problem with the Russians; I won't think any the worse of any of you who want to ditch those uniforms and see if you can get out without being taken. It's your choice; if you want to slip away, this is your opportunity." The remaining HIWIs spoke briefly amongst themselves, and then the corporal said in halting German, "No, Sir, the men would rather stay with you. You've been fair to them; they don't want to desert you here."

So they set off, one group amongst a steady stream of starving, frozen, terrified German soldiers falling back into the ruins of the city. Once among the shattered rubble the survivors set up their final defensive positions. Kuhlmann, Hartmann and their HIWIs were sent back to the Tractor Factory as part of the defensive ring around Strecker's command bunker.

In front of them, as they waited, the Russians took back their city, building by building, street by street. The defence mounted by the exhausted Germans was savage in its intensity, fuelled by their sheer terror of captivity. Metre by metre, though, the Russian infantry bludgeoned its way towards the river, squeezing the Germans into an ever-shrinking pocket. Conditions – bad as they were already – got yet worse. The wounded were put in ill-lit, cold cellars, where the remaining medical staff tried to do their best for them without drugs or facilities. There was no food left and ammunition was rapidly running out. The half-hearted attempts the Luftwaffe was still persisting with to re-supply the pocket from the air still saw most of the parachute-borne supplies drift down amongst the Russian positions.

Then, on 30th January, sitting in comfort in the Air Ministry in Berlin, Goering delivered what was effectively the funeral rites of the 6th Army. Crouching, cowering in their bunkers and cellars under the incessant Russian bombardment, the remains of that army listened to that speech over their radios with increasing bitterness. Goering compared them to the Spartans at Thermopylae as he effectively condemned them to death. Because death before surrender was the subtext of his words, and while for the rational amongst them it was a confirmation of what they had known ever since the trap was sprung and the Kessel was closed, for the diehard Nazi fanatics it was the bitterest of pills that their beloved Führer and his closest circle had abandoned them; there would be no miraculous rescue. The next day, Paulus was promoted by the Führer to the rank of Field Marshall, and as Colonel Groscurth pointed out to Kuhlmann while they sat in the bunker "That that may be a hint to Paulus– no German Field Marshall has ever surrendered an army."

And then, despite that, later the same day, Paulus did surrender. The resistance in the southern sector of the pocket was over. Strecker, with the remains of his XI Army Corps, augmented by the odds and sods like Kuhlmann and his group, fought on for another two days, believing that the longer they kept the Russians engaged, the better for the German armies trying to escape from the Caucasus. The shellfire rained in for those couple of days, but time finally ran out, and on the 2nd February the survivors crawled out of their bunkers to give themselves up. Rags wrapped round their heads, unshaven, cadaverous, lice-ridden and diseased, what was left of the mighty 6th Army was marched off to the camps. As they left the ruined city of Stalingrad, the crock of shit at the end of Hitler's rainbow, an NKVD officer screamed at them to take a good look at what they had done, because that was how Berlin would look by the time the Russians had finished with it.

But only a tiny number of them would ever get back from Russia to see the truth of his words. Their long march was a march to oblivion.

1978 Sussex, England

Chapter Three

I was visiting my parents at the beautiful Arts-and-Crafts house deep in the Sussex countryside where I had grown up when my mother called me into the dining room. She was sitting at the table, a large metal box open in front of her.

"Here, you might be interested in this." Her English was fluent and idiomatic, but she still had a marked German accent. "This came from Grandfather's, when he died. It's been up in the roof for ages; I came across it last week when I went up there looking for something else. There are all sorts of old documents and things, going right back to before the First World War." She riffled through the box. "Look, here's a passport." She held in her hand a greeny-grey soft-covered booklet with 'Deutsches Reich Reisepass' and the German eagle on its cover. "1926." She flicked through the pages of stamps. "Look, UK visas, Czechoslovakia, France, what's this one?" She showed me a smudged page dated April 1927. I took the passport and tried to read it. "This bit says Srba, Hrvata, and then the rest is illegible. That must be Serbia and Croatia, itemised as part of Yugoslavia, I guess. Those stamps are the name of the border town, I think, but I can't read them. But look, it's stamped three times, in 1927, 1928 and 1929. You were 10 or 11 then. Any idea why he was going to Yugoslavia?" My mother shook her head. "No, he travelled a lot. I guess it was selling the factory's products."

I carried on flicking through the passport, and found three banknotes stuck between the pages. "Hey, look at these. Two one hundred mark notes, both dated 1922, one issued in Munich and one in Köln. Wow! Look, this little one is a 25-pfennig note, Landkreis Aachen, dated October 1918. That's First World War currency."

She took it from me and examined it. "No, it's not regular currency. Look here" - she pointed at the tiny Gothic script on the face of the note -"it says it loses its value one month after issue. It must be some sort of warrant for something, rather than an actual banknote."

"I suppose by then the writing was already on the wall and they knew they were going to be defeated and that the value of their money would be uncertain, to say the least."

My mother nodded, but she was already opening a tattered grey file that she had pulled out of the box. She started leafing through the contents – a stack of old letters, some handwritten, some typed. She skimmed the first few, then started reading more closely. After a short while, she passed some of them across to me.

"Some of these are quite interesting. They are the letters written by friends to be read at the Tribunal that decided whether Grandfather should be interned or not in 1939." She shook her head, then said "I don't know half these people, but they seem to speak well of him. Here, this man I do remember; his father was a baronet with an estate near where my Granny and Grandfather lived. This is the son writing – he was a barrister. We used to see him sometimes when we came to visit England on holiday. Listen to this – it's written to my mother." She read from the letter: 'The very fact that you showed your opposition to the present regime in Germany as much as 5 1/2 years ago, by refusing to let your children be put into Brown Shirts and listen to Nazi teaching is strong evidence of where your sympathy lies; for you took that step without any thought that it would be useful evidence as to your British sympathies. Any facts as to your experiences in Germany, simply and briefly told, will, I am sure, carry weight with the examiner. When you appear before the tribunal, please show the Examiner this letter. He will be a Barrister-at-Law, and I am quite certain he will be fair. If necessary, I will endeavour to come myself, or write anything further, so let me know. Signed, Sir Blah-di-Blah, Barrister-at-Law and formerly MP.'"

"But it didn't work, did it?" I said. "He was interned, wasn't he?"

"Yes, he and Franz, on the Isle of Man, where they put all the Germans and Italians. But they weren't actually there long, so I think it had some effect. It was all very confused then. Suddenly, Papa and Franz were gone, and there was just Mama, me and Elisabeth, and the housekeeper, in that big house in London. We just wanted to do something to help. That's when I started working at the BBC." She stood up. "I'll make us a cup of tea. Pa will be back soon. He only went into Horsham to see the people about the garden machines."

While she was out of the room, I picked up one of the other letters, and started reading it. This one was handwritten, signed by a man called Rupert and then I couldn't decipher the surname. It started with the same sort of stuff as the others, about producing it to the tribunal and about general good character. Then I became transfixed by the reality of what had happened to my family over forty years earlier.

The correspondent wrote: 'Let me recall a few incidents. I first realised there was such a person as Hitler when I visited you in Aue, the December

Beyond Stalingrad

before he came to power. I remember how you gave me a history of him and his party, and how concerned you expressed yourself about his rising power. I still remember how strongly you expressed yourself, which was so rare in you, with your liberal ideals. The next time I was reminded of Hitler, was when you one day appeared at my office in the City of London and told me you had left Germany for good. I had not realised conditions under Hitler were so grim, but you enlightened me, and told me how your sons and daughters had been persecuted for not joining the Nazi youth movements, by their schoolmates. How Nazi hooligans had set fire to your house on account of your known anti-Nazi views. Finally how you had decided to throw up your position in your factory in Germany and start again in England. It was a great blow to you, but you have often told me since how glad you were that you had done it, if only for your children's sakes. I repeat therefore that I can certainly vouch for you to the authorities and am prepared to do all I can to help you in these difficult times, for I know you wish for the total destruction of the Nazis, as much as I do myself.'

I sat holding the letter in my hand. Persecuted by schoolmates? My mother and her siblings? House set on fire by hooligans? This was a new twist to me.

She put her head through the door. "Bring the box into the drawing room. We'll have tea in there."

I smiled to myself. She'd been in England most of her life, married here, brought up her children here, but there was still an element of pre-war German formality to my mother. On a winter afternoon, tea happened in the drawing room. On a summer's day, it happened outside on the terrace, or, if it was raining, in the summer-house overlooking the rose garden. She'd put the tray with its three cups and saucers, and plates for the rich fruit cake that she always made when she expected visitors, down on a coffee table. She sat on the settee, poised with a tea-strainer to pour.

"I've made Earl Grey, since that's all you'll drink. Pa will just have to accept it, when he gets back. Now, bring the box over here. I want to see what other forgotten things are in there."

"No, before we look at anything else, I want to know more about what this guy says." I held up the letter I had been reading. "What is all this about persecution at school and the house being set on fire?" She took the letter and skimmed through it.

"Yes, I remember him. He was a good friend of Grandfather's. They were immigrants too, but from earlier – I think they were Hungarian Jews, who came here before 1914. He and Grandfather were very close."

She sat back on the settee, still holding the letter in her hand. She was a grey-haired woman in late middle age, sitting in her big comfortable house in the peaceful Sussex countryside. She looked into the middle distance, and started to tell me the story of a different time, a different place.

1934 Saxony, Germany

Chapter Four

"Armin and I were born in Berlin, during the First World War. Franz was born there just after it finished, and then we moved shortly after that to Vienna for a few years and Elisabeth was born. In the late 20s, Papa took over the factory in Aue and we moved there. It was beautiful there; it's on the edge of the mountains that lead to the Czech border. We lived in a big house with a great park-like garden, and we had house-servants and gardeners to maintain it all. Papa's factory was the main employer in the town, so he was an important man locally. We had a wonderful childhood there. The three of us – Elisabeth was still too young, to start with – went to school in the town, we had lots of friends. Franz and I weren't very good at our lessons, but Armin was the school's star pupil. He was specially good at maths and science, but what he really enjoyed was drawing. He was really very talented and he always wanted to go to university to study art.

"The biggest city nearby was Chemnitz, with Dresden a bit further away; Armin used to go there to sketch the great baroque and rococo buildings. They're all gone now, destroyed in the bombing. Sometimes Mama would let me and Franz go with him, to see the big cities. " She laughed at the happy memory. "He used to be so serious about the responsibility he had to look after the two of us. We'd play up and pretend we were going to run away from him as soon as we got off the train. We never did, of course, but it was our trick to bribe him into buying us ice-creams and lemonade to make us behave." The smile on her face faded into something that looked more like wistfulness. "We had such a happy childhood." She looked severely at me. "I hope you and your sisters say the same when you get to my age."

Before I could make any answer, the drawing room door opened, and my father came in. He was slightly shorter than me, grey hair turning to white. He greeted me with a smile and then cocked a questioning eye at the deed-box open on the floor. "Ma's just telling me some of her family history," I explained.

"Ah, OK. I won't disturb you then. You are staying tonight, aren't you?" I nodded. "OK, well you carry on, Gaby, I'll take my tea through into the study. I've got a couple of things to finish." He picked up his cup of tea, helped himself to a piece of cake, and left the room.

My mother continued. "In retrospect, we were living in a bubble. The country as a whole was suffering big problems, with the inflation of the money, and such terrible unemployment. But we were kids in a comfortable home; we didn't know anything about all that."

"Was it difficult being half English?" I asked, curiously.

"No, not at all, not then. It just seemed perfectly normal. We went on holiday most years to England, to see our grandparents, and that was just how it was. We knew our English cousins, we saw people like that barrister whose letter we found earlier, and never thought ourselves in any way unusual. It was like Papa's business friends who used to come to the house. Lots of them were Jewish, but we never thought of that as an issue. But then slowly all that started to change and we began to see the Brown Shirts on the streets and around the town.

"With the benefit of hindsight, of course, it all seems so terribly obvious, now. The social and economic problems that we weren't aware of in the 1920s all started to bubble over as we went into the 30s and the Nazis took advantage of the country's problems. That's when we started having our own problems at school. Most of our friends were joining one of the Hitler youth organisations, but Papa wouldn't hear of that for us. I think the angriest I ever saw him was one day when Franz talked about joining the junior wing of the Hitler Youth – I can't remember what they called it; he went absolutely crazy and forbad Franz to ever talk about it again." She smiled in reminiscence. "It was so stupid, really. All Franz knew was that it was a bit like the boy scouts, and he was the sort of boy who always wanted to be outside, doing things, so he thought he would like to be with his school friends in their camping and hiking and stuff. He had no idea of the political or ideological implications. For the adults though, well, they were already beginning to sense that it was deadly serious. Papa was so utterly opposed to everything the Nazis said and did. And he was such a broad-minded and generous man, that when he was so opposed to something, you had to take note. So Franz obeyed him. That must have been in 1932, and then when they won the election in 1933 it got worse as more and more people, even people we knew well, became Party members. Most of our friends stopped coming to our house, and we didn't get invited to many places any more. Other children wouldn't sit next to us in class, or play with us at break time. It was worst for Franz and me. Elisabeth was still very young, she'd only just begun school, and they hadn't really started with the propaganda with the very small ones yet, and Armin was such a charismatic boy that people followed him regardless of their parents or teachers telling them

Beyond Stalingrad

to avoid him. But Franz and I were just ordinary, and we were picked on, day after day. Some of the teachers didn't help, by always commenting on us being half English, and blaming us as foreigners for the problems. We didn't understand what was going on; Papa had been such an important man in the town, but now we heard people criticising him as a friend of foreigners, a friend of Jews." She paused for a moment or two, as if getting her thoughts back in order.

"And then, it all sort of came to a head. It must have been in the summer of 1934." She looked sharply at me. "You know your history and you have to remember where we were. The Erzgebirge formed the frontier with Czechoslovakia and on the other side of that frontier was the Sudetenland. I know that name didn't really hit the international headlines until 1938, by which time we were already long gone to England, but the Nazis had started cranking up the nationalist German feeling virtually as soon as they came to power. There were lots of ethnic Germans on the Czech side of the border and the Nazis were determined to make mischief about it. It was all part of the mess the politicians made after the First World War, when they carved up the Austro-Hungarian Empire without really thinking through the consequences." She paused for a moment, and it suddenly hit me that this stuff that I had learned about as dry, historical fact was part of my mother's direct experience; the family had been caught up in those events which had seemed no more than pages in a history text book to me.

She carried on. "Well, I say they didn't think through the consequences; the reality, of course, is that like all politicians, they frankly had no idea of what they were doing." I grinned at that; my father was quite involved in local politics, and my mother, although she dutifully attended fund-raisers, barbecues and such like, had never been shy of broadcasting her contempt for politicians. Perhaps I was now finding out why.

"Anyway, that summer there was to be a visit to the whole region by some Party bigwigs, banging the Aryan drum. The town council of Aue decided that there should be a parade of townspeople to show their support for the Party, and Papa's factory was the biggest employer. So naturally, they needed him to be involved, and so they told him to instruct all his workforce - including himself and the rest of the management staff - to turn out for the parade. Well, that was like a red rag to a bull for him. First of all, he just told them outright he wouldn't do it. But they kept on, and in the end they ordered him to tell his workers that they had to march, with him leading them, behind the local SA unit. They were to parade through the town and then stand in the square to listen to the Party members giving all their speeches of welcome to the bigwigs and praise for the Führer. So then he called all the workers together at the factory, and told them all about this. Then he told them that he'd die before he took part in any of what the called this tomfoolery and he had no intention of ordering any of them to turn out. He left them under no illusion as to what he thought of the Party and said that they should make up their own minds about what they wanted to do. We children only heard all this at second hand, of course; our old governess, who still lived with us, even though we were all at school and she didn't really have a job any longer, she went down to the factory and heard Papa. She'd always virtually hero-worshipped him anyway, and she was so proud of him when she told us all this later."

I interrupted. "Was that the governess you used to send Christmas presents to in East Germany?"

"Yes, Beate; when we left, she moved to Chemnitz, and was still there after the country was split. It used to make me spit when I had to address the parcels to Karl Marx Stadt instead of Chemnitz. You can't change names hundreds and hundreds of years old to suit your stupid ideologies."

She paused for a moment, then continued with the story; "Anyway, that really set tongues wagging. Now, Papa was not only the rich man in the big house who consorted with foreigners and Jews, he was also an enemy of the Party. It was all a bit futile, though, as Mama told me much later, because, although the workers had a lot of loyalty to and respect for Papa, the truth was that lots of them were seduced by the Nazi promises so they turned out for the parade anyway. The only difference was that Papa was not there with them.

"Well, things rumbled on through the summer, but Mama took us to visit her parents in England, so we didn't really see how unpleasant it was becoming." She paused again for a moment, to gather her thoughts and I stood up and switched the lights on in the room as the winter evening descended.

"When we got back at the end of that summer holiday, we could see how things had changed. We had to walk past the factory gate on our way to school every day, and now most days there were SA troopers outside with placards denouncing Papa and the factory. They shouted really horrible things at us as we walked past with our schoolbags, and after a few days of that, Papa sent us in the car instead. That just made us stand out even more, particularly at the end of school each day, because while all the others just walked off home, chatting and playing together, we were swept off in the big black car, just showing we were different. And, of course, the car was a British Daimler, not a German Mercedes, so that was another reason for abuse.

"So by that autumn, it was all very unpleasant. We got abused in the streets, and so did the servants – a couple of them left, because they either sided with the abusers or they just couldn't stand it any longer. Papa was away travelling a lot; I think, with the benefit of hindsight, the factory was probably also having problems, because I assume the Nazis were putting pressure on customers to stop them buying from him. So I think the travelling was to try and find more customers to keep things going. And of course I don't know what the other shareholders thought." I looked quizzically at her.

"Papa didn't own it all; he had taken a small shareholding when he took over the management, and he'd made a great success of it, which had been good for the other investors as well as him. Now, since they owned most of the shares, they were the ones whose wealth was most at risk if things went downhill. I remember they all came to the house quite a few times that autumn. There were four of them. Three came from Chemnitz, and the other one was from across the border in Czechoslovakia. I'm not sure, but I think he was Jewish.

"Anyway, Christmas came round that year with all this going on. Mama was determined that it shouldn't be spoilt, that it should be like every other Christmas. So just like every other year, we had a great big tree in the central hall of the house, lots of decorations and cards and everything to make the house sparkle. You know the little wooden angels we have over there" – she pointed towards the hearth – "every Christmas? They were there; they came with us from Germany. Then on Christmas Eve, there we all were, round the tree lit with its candles and the house lights dimmed. Mama compromised to an extent on the German Christmas; in Germany, they treat Christmas Eve as the main family celebration and they traditionally eat carp, but we always had goose. Mama said it was a kind of Anglo-German agreement. She always said she wasn't eating that boring, muddy-tasting fish; she said she would uphold her right to the last as a freeborn Englishwoman to eat meat on Christmas Eve! We used to have dinner quite early, so that we children could stay up and open our presents and sing carols afterwards." She smiled, and I could see she was lost in her memories. "I know you don't think much of me and Auntie Elisabeth as singers these days – and you're probably right – but then, as children, we were quite good. We always sang 'Stille Nacht' together, just us two as the first carol. It was so pretty, in the flickering candle-light from the tree, Papa and Armin - terribly grown-up in his formal suit - holding their wine-glasses and Franz just waiting to open his Christmas presents. Mama would be smiling so proudly at Elisabeth and me." She blinked her eyes, as though tears were forming, and then blew her nose. "Anyway, that's how I want to remember it, not think of what happened later on. But if I'm telling you the story, I have to tell you all of it."

It was by now fully dark outside, and I stood up to draw the curtains. She seemed to have retreated into her memories again for a moment. Then she spoke again, her voice a little more brittle. "It was the last Christmas we had in Germany, in that lovely house. By the next year we were in England and Christmas never seemed the same – until your sisters and you were born, and your cousins, and the whole family cycle started again.

"Anyway, it was the night of Stephanstag – Boxing Day – and we had all gone to bed. Papa was always very careful about putting out the candles on the Christmas tree, but because he blew them out rather than using a snuffer, they made more smoke and the smell drifted through the house. So when Elisabeth came into my room and shook me awake, saying she could smell burning, I just assumed it was the candles that had disturbed her. But she insisted it wasn't the candle smell, it was something else, and refused to go back to her room until I had gone downstairs with her to make sure everything was all right. Well, by the time we got to the door through to the servants' part of the house, the smell was really strong and clearly nothing to do with Christmas tree candles. So I sent Elisabeth back upstairs to wake Mama and Papa, and I went on myself. When I got to the kitchen and opened the door, I can tell you I shut it again pretty quickly! There was a blazing fire in there and with all the wooden cupboards and furniture it looked like it had really taken hold. I ran back and found Papa coming downstairs in his dressing-gown. He took one look through the door, and then phoned for the fire brigade straight away. It took a while for them to come (I suppose we were lucky that the SA hadn't yet infiltrated them, otherwise they probably wouldn't have come at all). Papa got everybody out of the house, then he and Armin and Franz and the gardeners started filling buckets from the garden taps and throwing water in through the kitchen door and windows. Elisabeth and I just clung on to Mama – we could see the flames burning all the wooden cupboards and furniture in there and we could hear the glass of the windows cracking and breaking from the heat – it was terrifying standing out there in the dark and cold, seeing our house on fire. Anyway, eventually the fire brigade came with their fire engine and put it all out pretty quickly. Really the only damage was to the kitchen and the scullery, but all that was badly damaged. Everything in there was burnt and blackened and it was pretty much unusable."

She paused and I saw a picture in my mind of the family standing outside their burning house, Grandfather and the two boys hurling buckets of water at the fire and the girls clinging in fear to their mother.

"What caused the fire?" I asked.

"Well, they never actually proved it, but the general belief amongst us was that it was some of the Nazi sympathisers who'd levered open the windows and thrown burning rags onto the wooden cupboards. There was some graffiti on the garden wall about 'death to the foreign Jew-lovers' and it seemed logical to assume it was all related. For me and Elisabeth it was terrifying, that anybody could want to harm us like that. Franz marched around swearing he was going to find out who did it and get even with them. And Armin, well, he was near enough to being an adult.

Beyond Stalingrad

He was seventeen and just about to leave school that Easter. I know he and Papa had a lot of serious conversations about what we should all do. The police, of course, were not remotely interested in discovering what had happened. I think most of them thought we deserved it. Anyway, the upshot was that Mama and Papa decided the time had come to move to England, at least while the Nazi phase played out. You see, at that time, even Papa didn't really believe it would last. Well, you can understand it. He didn't want to believe that his country had en masse taken leave of its senses. He still thought it was an aberration that would pass."

She looked at her watch. "I'm going to have to go and make some dinner in a minute. Anyway, that's the story of the house on fire. We came to England that Easter, when Armin had finished school. Now, go and tell your father we're having beef, if he wants to get the wine." She bustled out, carrying the tea tray.

1978 Sussex, England

Chapter Five

Later that evening, sitting at the dining table, I brought her back to the subject.

"I can't believe you never told me all this stuff about 1930s Germany before – it would have been really useful when I was doing my history A-level. You wait till I'm 23 before you tell me all this."

She glanced at my father. "Well, you have to remember that Maggie" – she was the elder of my two sisters – "was born only just after the end of the war. Being half-German then wasn't something you wanted to advertise. So we played it down, and having done that with the first child, we just carried on the same with the other two of you. For the same reason we didn't teach you to speak German, although that would have been easy. In retrospect, that was probably a mistake, but you can't see into the future. You make your choices at the time. So many horrible things had happened that I just wanted to forget about it and get on with my life. We were all here – well, until Franz and his family went to Canada, anyway, and I just wanted us to be an ordinary English family."

My father interrupted. "All here, except for Armin."

"Yes," she agreed, "except for Armin, my wonderful big brother. He wasn't here." She looked down the length of the table, over my father's head. I followed her gaze to the painting hanging on the panelled wall; four children sitting on a settee together. The two boys were wearing suits, the girls matching purple dresses. Despite the old-fashioned formality, they were all smiling happily and a large Alsatian dog lay on the floor in front of them. She nodded at the picture. "That was painted when I was ten. Armin was twelve then. We'd just moved to Aue. The dog was younger than he looks in the picture; he was only a puppy really, but the artist was a portrait painter – I don't think he was very good at animals, so he just made him a generic dog. That was my mother's favourite picture of us."

"Why did Armin go back to Germany, just when you had all escaped?" I asked. "It seems like a bit of an odd thing to do, quite frankly."

Beyond Stalingrad

"With hindsight, yes, but we can all be wise after the event. You have to remember that, horrible though the fire and everything was, at that stage many people, including my parents, still thought it was a passing phase, and that after a while, the German populace would reject the Nazis and all would be back to normal. There was a lot of discussion between him and my parents about what he should do. But he'd always wanted to be an artist – he was really talented; well, you've seem some of his pictures." I thought of the two pretty watercolours hanging in my parents' bedroom and the drawings in the study and the hall, all with the distinctive 'AK' signature on them.

"He had got himself accepted for a place at the university in Hamburg just before we left. That was a really prestigious course – the one he really wanted. My mother was very much against him going; she was English, after all, and was back home. But Armin was insistent, and Papa, despite all his opposition to the regime, in the end sided with Armin and agreed that as a student, with his home in England, after all, which he could always come back to, he would probably not be so affected. Papa came from Hamburg, as well, and I have a suspicion he thought that the sanity of the north Germans would prevail over the Bavarians and Swabians, which was after all where the Nazis came from. Looking back, it seems a crazy decision, but at the time I suppose it was rational. Nobody could really have foreseen the consequences."

My father spoke up again. "But eventually, they put on travel restrictions, and Armin still had a German passport, didn't he?"

"Yes, we all did; no-one had thought about naturalisation then. That only became relevant later. It was when he came back for Christmas in 1938 that it began to hit home; I know Papa tried very hard to persuade him to stay. By then, Papa understood that there could very likely be a war, things had got so bad. But Armin only had two terms left, and he really wanted to finish it. The three of us other children tried to persuade him as well, but he was adamant that he had to go back to Germany to finish his studies. So off he went, back to Hamburg. Then the really strict travel restrictions started, and because he was of military age he wasn't allowed to leave the country again. And so in June 1939 we got a letter from him saying he was to be conscripted for military service." She sighed. "Christmas and New Year 1938/39……..that was the last time I saw my big brother." She blinked her eyes again. "He'd be in his sixties, now; he'd have had a full life, a family, like the rest of us. We'd always been together.

"Anyway, after he was conscripted, to start with he wrote lots of letters and made a bit of a joke about the army. Then, when war started, the letters got fewer - they had to come via Switzerland, and of course the army would have censored what he was sending. We got letters from France, when they really weren't involved in any fighting, then the

Balkans, which also seemed fairly quiet for them, and then he was sent to Russia. The last we knew was that he was in the Stalingrad pocket, when the Germans surrendered. They'd made him an officer by then. Papa tried hard after the war to find out what had happened, but lots of German records were destroyed as Germany imploded and the Russians didn't really seem to care about the fate of German soldiers, so he didn't ever find anything out. Mama never really got over it. He was her first child, after all, and they'd had such high hopes of him. He was really exceptional, and that's not just hero-worship of my big brother. He was so special." She shook her head. "Anyway, that's all in the past. But now at least you know the whole story."

"Well, not really."

She looked quizzically at me.

"We don't know how it finished; was Armin killed, did he survive the battle? Was he a prisoner in Russia?"

"It was those thoughts constantly going round in her mind that was the problem for Mama. She could never reconcile herself to not knowing. When she was bedridden, in the last year, she had those paintings of his that are now in our bedroom on the wall of her bedroom. They were like a constant reminder. She couldn't get away from the pain of it. The truth is we'll never know; the best thing is to believe he was killed, that he didn't have to suffer the dreadful Russian captivity."

My father broke in again. "That's certainly the best way. I've met a few Germans over the years who were prisoners in Russia and they had a terrible time, they were effectively just used as slave labour in the factories and the mines. And it was a long time before they were released. The last ones were not repatriated until about 1955. If they'd been captured at Stalingrad that would have been twelve years. But I don't think many of those survived. You know," he continued, "whatever the privations we suffered here during the war - and your mother knows more about that than I do, I was away in the Far East - they were absolutely nothing compared with what happened on the Russian Front. That was something like medieval barbarity with modern automatic weapons. The stories are horrendous. The Russians putting NKVD troops behind their front line, with orders to shoot any of their own men who didn't advance as ordered into the German guns; they were shot from both sides. The Germans were freezing to death, with disease rampant, no food and no ammunition in the end. They just kept going as long as they did out of fear of how they would be treated if they were captured. And in the middle of it all, there was the civilian population of Stalingrad. I don't know how many crawled out of the cellars when it was finally over, but it was multiple thousands who had been hiding through all the fighting." He shook his head. "Incredible."

Beyond Stalingrad

I looked across at my mother. "Yes," she said, "it gave us no comfort when the fighting was over. And we heard it first, Elisabeth and I. By that time we were both at the BBC and the news of the German surrender at Stalingrad was buzzing through the building before the official details and news broadcasts."

London January 1943

Chapter Six

January 31st was a cold day when Gaby and Elisabeth Kuhlmann left their father's big house in St John's Wood to cycle their normal route into central London to their work at the BBC. The bombing of London was no longer anything like as intense or as frequent as during the blitz a couple of years earlier, but nevertheless they saw a smoking new crater just off the Edgware Road as they cycled past. They reached Bush House and left their bicycles chained up at the side of the building. The commissionaire on duty at the door gave them a cheerful smile and a word of greeting. The Kuhlmann sisters were popular at the BBC. Pretty, vivacious and with an infectious laughing good humour, they were translators for the network's German service. Their German accents passed almost unnoticed amongst the eclectic group, most of them refugees of one sort or another from the Nazi takeover of Central Europe, who staffed the BBC's various foreign language services by that stage of the war. Many of them went on to become household media names in post-war Britain. The purpose of the German Service was broadly propaganda, be it in the emphasis given to news bulletins or the daily radio dramas broadcast to Germany. Gaby and Elisabeth worked on ensuring that whatever went out was idiomatic and sounded real to Germans. The clunky broadcasts of 1939 and early 1940, with their obviously 'English' German became smarter and more credible through the efforts of the two girls and their colleagues.

They worked in a big room, with all the other European translators. As well as the positive message beamed out by the BBC's own transmitters, there was a darker side in the output of Sefton Delmer's Buckinghamshire-based Political Warfare Executive through its 'Gustav Siegfried Eins' broadcasts. Although technically the PWE was a totally different entity from the BBC, in fact there were considerable staff crossovers, and the two Kuhlmann girls spent almost as much time working on the black propaganda as they did on its more palatable sibling.

By mid-morning, they were sitting in the translators' room with five or six others, all working hard with a typewriter in front of them. Some were wearing headphones, translating direct from tapes, some had sheaves of paper in front of them. The telephone on Gaby Kuhlmann's desk rang. She picked it up, and immediately recognised the voice on the other end as one of the PWE producers.

"Good morning, Gaby. I've got a little job for you. Urgent. A motorbike is just bringing you some things we need as soon as possible. One is a broadcast we picked up from Stalingrad by a German communist called Walter Ulbricht, who is there with the Russians. It seems to be claiming that the German Sixth Army has finally surrendered and the Russians are in full control of the City. Read it through and see if it sounds authentic and convincingly German to you. We need to be sure whether or not it's genuine. And then, more important, is a piece we've just written to broadcast to break the news to the Germans on the home front. We've got to judge it to get just the right level of gloating. So that needs putting into German. They should be with you within the hour. Should take precedence over anything else." Without waiting for her reply, he hung up. The man had had a triumphant note in his voice; it was news the country had all been waiting for, hardly daring to hope that 'Uncle Joe's' men could really pull it off.

For Gaby, it wasn't such clear good news. Getting to her feet, she gestured over to her sister, sitting at the next desk, to follow her. She led them out of the translators' room and along the corridor to the canteen. At ten thirty in the morning, it was deserted. The two girls sat down at one of the tables near the door.

"Whatever's the matter?" asked Elisabeth. "You look as though you've seen a ghost."

Gaby shook her head. "No," she said. "No ghost. But I just had a call from Peter, the producer at PWE" – Elisabeth nodded to indicate she knew whom her sister meant – "they've got a report that the Russians have taken Stalingrad back. The Germans have surrendered." She looked hard at her sister. "So Armin's either dead or a Russian prisoner."

The canteen was bare, furnished simply with plain tables and chairs. It wasn't a welcoming room, and in the midst of total war, with the need to conserve fuel, it was poorly heated. But it wasn't just the cold that made Elisabeth shiver as her sister went on, "We can't pretend it will be all right any more and that they will somehow be rescued and retreat back to Germany, which would be a lot safer. They've been surrounded since November so there's no chance they could have escaped. Anyway, it's thousands of miles back to Germany, so there's no way they would have been able to cross all that Russian territory even if they'd managed to break through the Russian encirclement. There's no hope that Armin can have got out of it."

"Mama will be shattered. She's been convincing herself he would be OK."

"Yes. It's going to be very difficult. And people will be celebrating." She sighed. "Why does it all have to be like this? We want England to win the war, and the Russians are our allies. Why do we have to be torn in half like this? If only Armin had stayed in England, we could be out there cheering with everybody else. Look, we've got to try and protect Mama; probably best to try and make her believe he was killed. The idea of being a German prisoner of the Russians doesn't bear thinking about."

Elisabeth started sobbing. "We'll probably never see him again. Even if he is alive, with the war going on, he'll just be in a camp, and the Russians won't treat prisoners of war like we do. They won't survive. They'll take revenge on them for the destruction of Stalingrad."

Gaby looked sternly at her. "Elisabeth, listen to me. That's exactly what we mustn't say to Mama. We mustn't let her think of him slowly dying in a prison camp." Her voice softened. "I know it's horrible, Lizzie, but we have to protect Mama. That's the most important thing."

"I know." She dried her eyes with a handkerchief. "It's just the thought of him being there all alone, on the wrong side. It's all so crazy."

Gaby stood up. "Come on, we'd better go back, or someone will come looking for us. You'd better help me with the PWE Stalingrad piece when it comes. If we do it together, perhaps we won't keep bursting into tears thinking about it."

As the news of the Russian victory spread round the building, people bumping in to each other in the corridors and the canteen shared the good news. The two girls finished the piece for the PWE, with its references to the number of German soldiers lost in the futile campaign and its recognition by the western powers of the heroic struggle of their Soviet Allies. By the end of the day, when Gaby and Elisabeth left to cycle home, the official news broadcasts were also carrying the story.

Leaving Bush House, they cycled one behind the other, each alone with her thoughts; the dark streets of black-out London were never pleasant, for although there was little traffic, what there was was badly lit and difficult to see. Added to that, a cold rain had started to fall, soaking the roads and meaning that each time a car or a bus passed them they were spattered by the spray. They got home wet, cold and miserable. They parked their bicycles at the side of the house and went in through the back door. Having hung up their wet coats they went through to the front of the house and found their mother alone in the drawing room. One look at her tear-stained face told them she had already heard the news from Russia. Silently, she hugged them both.

Then, "It's what I've been dreading hearing," she said. "This awful war. How can we survive it? How can any mother see one of her sons in one army and the other in the other? It's four years since we saw Armin and now we have to get used to the idea that we will probably never see him again. And then the British army will take Franz off somewhere where he'll be fighting as well." She buried her face in her hands. Just then, the telephone rang; Gaby stepped out into the hall to answer it.

Beyond Stalingrad

"Hallo, Juniper 3840." There was silence from the other end. "Hallo? This is Juniper 3840. Who's there, please?"

"Is that the German house? Filthy German scum. You heard the news about Stalingrad? Your lot are all dying."

She slammed the receiver down before the voice could say any more, her face rigid with shock. The calls had come on and off since September 1939 – with a name like Kuhlmann and the German accents, it was hardly surprising. Her father had had the telephone number taken ex-directory, but that had made virtually no difference. But today, on top of everything else, it was too much. She sat down in the telephone chair and wept.

Wept for her brother, wept for her family, wept for the whole world's craziness.

The drawing room door opened and Elisabeth came out. "Gaby! What's wrong? Quick, come into the kitchen with me. I'm making Mama a cup of tea." She put her arm round her sister's shoulder and led her through to the kitchen. Sitting her down at the table, she asked "What's the matter?"

Gaby wiped her eyes. "One of the spite calls. It's too much, Lizzie. What do they want from us? Franz's in the British army, I'm engaged to an RAF officer, you and I go up on the roof fire-watching every evening, Mama is English, Papa hates the Nazis as much as anybody. Yes we're German. But we still want the British to win the war. And now my brother's dead and they still have to make their hate calls. What if Mama had picked up that call? Why should she have to suffer their stupidity?" She twisted her fingers together and looked blankly at the curtained window. "It's like we're living in a nightmare we can't wake up from. And you can't talk to anybody about it – they just look at you as if there is something wrong with you, to have a brother on the other side." She sighed deeply. "Come on, let's take the tea through to Mama. Papa will be home soon." As she spoke, they heard the front door opening. "That must be him. We'll see what he says about Stalingrad."

But Sepp Kuhlmann was just as confused as the rest of the family. He desperately wanted to see the end of the Nazis and the pernicious influence they had had on his country, but he was a father as well and he couldn't bear the thought of his son in that dreadful place. He'd suffered as an internee on the Isle of Man in the early months of the war, but he knew internment under British rule was in no way comparable to what a prisoner of the Soviets would experience. And so, in a series of conversations with his daughters over the next few days, they decided to adopt the course of assuming Armin was dead, as a comfort for his mother, clearly, but also for themselves.

But Sepp couldn't make sense of it. He sat long into the night in his study, way after Margaret had gone up to bed, often with a bottle of wine and a glass in front of him. He remembered that last, unsatisfactory argument with Armin. His children, his family, meant everything to him; would he have to remember for ever that harsh words had been the last ones between him and his eldest son?

Chapter Seven

War didn't let you forget the pain; the reminders were everywhere, especially working at the hub of the news services. Elisabeth couldn't just accept that those few precious letters she kept in a drawer of her dressing-table were all she had left of her adored brother.

One of the other translators was a Czech, ten years older than Elisabeth, whose husband Jan had been killed flying with the RAF in the Battle of Britain. Mathilde wore black and seemed surrounded by sorrow. At first, Gaby and Elisabeth avoided her; she was older and somehow so different and gloomy. But gradually, Elisabeth started talking to her - their desks were next to each other - and she began to learn her story. Her husband had been an officer in the Czech air force, and as Nazi control of the country had tightened, he'd told his wife they had to leave. They went first to France, where Jan had established Mathilde in Paris. He volunteered for the Armée de l'Air and flew a Dewoitine against the German Messerschmitts in the spring of 1940. In late March, he sent his wife to London, where he joined her later after the chaotic fall of France. The RAF was crying out for experienced pilots, and Jan was one of the many Czechs and Poles without whom they could never have held off the Luftwaffe in the summer of 1940. In late September, his Hurricane had been blown out of the sky in a dog-fight over the Channel coast. He'd been trapped in the blazing aeroplane as it plunged into the sea. His body was never recovered.

Bit by bit, she told Elisabeth her story. A comfortable life as the wife of a member of the Czech officer corps, country houses, dancing, fun. All brought crashing down by the German invasion and the war that helped to spark. Now, here she was, alone in a foreign city, her husband at the bottom of the English Channel.

One day, Elisabeth found herself telling Mathilde her own family's story of how they had lost a son and brother and how desolate she felt. Mathilde listened and invited Elisabeth to lunch with her. They went out to a café just along the road from Bush House, and sat in front of the inevitable gristly brown meat that was all that was generally available.

"My dear, it must be awful for you, not knowing of your brother's fate. At least I can have no false hope; Jan is dead, and nothing can change that. But you and your sister, and your parents, it's just open-ended. There's no certainty."

Elisabeth nodded. "Yes, that's exactly it. We pretend for Mama's sake that he's clearly dead, because the alternative of a Russian prison camp is just too awful to bear, but really we just don't know. He could be suffering dreadfully, be starving, or have some horrible illness. The stories you hear about Stalingrad are just too hideous. And Gaby and I keep seeing it here, in the news we translate and the propaganda stuff. You can't get away from it."

Mathilde smiled sadly at her. "My dear, I wish I could say something to make it better. But maybe there is something I could do. After Jan's death, when I was so distraught I didn't know what to do, I met a lady who lives in the same apartment block as me. She is much older than me, and she lost her husband in the Battle of the Somme, in 1916. She had only been married for a few months when he was killed. But she can still speak to him. She goes regularly to visit a lady in Maida Vale who has the ability to communicate with people who have died. She has taken me there and I have heard Jan speaking." Her eyes took on a distant look. "It's a great comfort. Perhaps I could ask if you too could come."

Elisabeth stared at her. "Spiritualism, do you mean?"

Mathilde nodded. "Yes, I suppose that's the word. But that has echoes of such silliness, and of desperate, deluded people. But it's not like that. The lady, the medium, is just very ordinary. We don't all join hands, or anything like that. We just sit around her dining room table, with the lights dimmed, and we can hear the dead, talking through her."

"But Mathilde, how do you know it's real? She may just be making it up? And I suppose you pay her, don't you?"

Mathilde smiled sadly again. "That's what I thought, at first. How can this be real? She must just be a charlatan. But I've been there about six or seven times now, and all I can say is that I feel a great sense of peace when I am there, listening to Jan talking to me. Maybe I am deluded, but it helps me. And I think for you, the peace you may find could be welcome. I don't know how it works; I'm not particularly religious. We were nominally catholic, but this isn't a religious experience for me. It's just feeling that I am still able to have Jan in my life. Think about it, my dear. I will introduce you if you wish." She looked at her watch. "Come, we must go back and make some more news stories."

Elisabeth did think about it, and that evening, sitting with Gaby after their parents had gone to bed, she mentioned the conversation to her sister.

"Spiritualism, Lizzie? Are you mad? That stuff's not real. They're just frauds who try to make money out of unhappy people."

"Well, I don't know. Mathilde is a sensible woman, and she says she gets something out of it. She's not stupid or gullible. She seems to believe that there is something to it. I thought I would take her up on her offer of going along. I'm sure she'll introduce you as well, if you want."

Beyond Stalingrad

"Lizzie, you can't. It's stupid. Armin is either dead or a prisoner. Whichever it is, he can't speak to us through some woman none of us have ever heard of before in Maida Vale. You're just deluding yourself. You'll only feel worse if you do go. It's a stupid idea; I can't believe you're actually thinking of it."

There was a frostiness between the two of them the next day; one thing guaranteed to make Elisabeth do something was if her big sister told her it was a stupid idea. At lunch time, she made a point of sitting down next to Mathilde in the canteen. Gaby saw them sitting together and went over to join some of the other translators at a different table.

Two days later, after eating dinner with her family, Elisabeth picked up a torch and slipped out through the front door before anyone could ask where she was going. She walked down the darkened streets, the feeble beam from her taped-over, blackout-compliant torch barely illuminating the pavement in front of her. A nagging drizzle was falling as she crossed the Edgware Road towards Maida Vale. She knew the area well; she'd finished her schooling just a quarter of a mile or so from where she was heading. As she turned into Randolph Avenue that led down towards the Regent's Park canal, Mathilde was waiting for her. Together, they walked on down the road, and then up the steps to the front door of a stuccoed house. There was a line of doorbells, marking it out as having been converted into flats. Mathilde pressed one of the bells. "She lives on the second floor", she said. After a pause, there was the click of the latch and an old woman opened the door to them.

"Welcome, Mathilde," she said, "and you must be Elisabeth. Please, follow me."

The hall was dimly lit, but even by the single bulb, Elisabeth could see the stair-carpet was worn and threadbare and the walls in need of another coat of paint. At the top of the second flight of steps, the old woman stood aside and ushered them in through her front door. Mathilde knew the way and took the second door off the corridor, leading them into a large room. Although it was still not very bright, with subdued lighting, Elisabeth could see straightaway that the décor in here was of a much better standard than the common parts of the building. Two other women were already sitting at a round table; they smiled at the newcomers.

"Let me introduce everyone. I'm Enid and I will be helping you to find your relatives this evening. Mathilde, you already know Margaret" – she gestured to the older-looking of the other two (she must be the Somme woman, thought Elisabeth) – "and this is Jane, who is joining us for the first time this evening, like Elisabeth, here, who has been brought into our group by Mathilde." She put her hand on the back of a chair. "Elisabeth, perhaps you could sit here, that will be next to me, and Mathilde, if you can sit between Margaret and Jane, so that our two new friends are one on each side of me." They sat as she had requested.

Elisabeth was beginning to feel somewhat nervous; perhaps Gaby had been right, and this was all nonsense. They'd both been to see 'Blithe Spirit' when it had appeared the previous autumn, and Elisabeth found herself thinking of Madame Arcati; she giggled, and got a stern look from Mathilde.

Enid seemed not to have noticed, as she went on: "Mathilde and Margaret, you know how this will work, but I should just explain a bit for the sake of our new members. So, I'm sure you've all read things about spiritualism and speaking in tongues and ectoplasm and trances and all sorts of things like that. Well, I don't know if all that is real but it's certainly not how I work. I don't have any of those sort of outward signs. We shall sit here quietly, and if the souls of your lost ones want to communicate with you, you will hear them in your own head. I'm just the medium to enable them to speak to each of you individually. I can't promise anything; sometimes they will communicate, sometimes they won't. I have no control over that, and I really don't know how it works; I just know that it can work, through me, and many people find it helpful. But before we start, I must know some more about you and your lost ones, to help me. Mathilde and Margaret, I already know your stories, so perhaps I could ask Jane and Elisabeth to tell us a bit about themselves and who they have lost. Perhaps you could start, Jane?"

Shyly, quietly, in a London East End accent, the woman began. "My husband, Jimmy, was a sailor. We got married in June '39 and he'd just agreed to leave the Merchant Navy and get a job ashore 'cos I was pregnant, when war was declared. He wasn't allowed to leave, then, you see, because the Merchant Navy was a reserved occupation. Well, to start with, he still worked on the coasters, mostly bringing coal down from Newcastle to the power stations in London. That's the run he'd been on before the war – it wasn't too bad, really, not like he was away for months at a time on the deep-water ships. But then at the end of 1939, the company moved him onto the transatlantic route. To start with, I went up to Liverpool and we had a little flat there, but then when the baby was nearly due, what with him being away at sea almost all the time anyway, I came back down to London to be with my mum. The baby came, and Jimmy got down here whenever he could. He was a good man, and a good father, even though he didn't see much of little Henry. Anyway, the convoys got worse, and more ships got sunk. I begged him to try and get shifted back to the coasters, but he just said he had to do what he could; it was his job, and if he didn't do it, somebody else would have to. He was a good man," she repeated.

"Anyway, he survived the Atlantic, and in February 1942, his ship was sent north, on a convoy to Russia. He couldn't believe it, nor none of his mates. Going to the Arctic in February!" She stopped. Then, "Well, they were right. It wasn't sensible. One of the sailors from one of the other ships came and told me. 'Vagabond' - that was Jimmy's ship - got slower and slower as the ice slowed them all down, and then in the middle of the night, with a gale blowing, ice everywhere, a U-boat got them. The other sailor said one minute it was pitch black, the next like bright daylight as 'Vagabond' went up. They guessed she was carrying ammunition for the Russians, what they needed to stop the Germans. There were no survivors from 'Vagabond'. That was the end of my Jimmy, and little Henry will never really know his dad. He left us in London when he set out for Liverpool to rejoin the ship before they went north, and that was the last we saw of him. Now he's at the bottom of the arctic sea." She stopped, and dabbed a handkerchief to her eyes.

Enid reached towards her and took her hand. "My dear," she said, "how awful. And a little boy without a father. I hope he'll come and speak to you this evening, just to give you some comfort that he's still thinking of you and little Henry."

She turned to Elisabeth. "And now you, dear, tell us who you are missing, then perhaps they will come to us."

Elisabeth paused for a moment. Did she really want to do this? To tell her story to a group of strangers? Then she caught Mathilde's eye, and the latter nodded at her almost imperceptibly. She would do it, for her mother's sake.

"Well, it's my brother. I haven't seen him since Christmas 1938. We all came over from Germany in 1935 but he went back to finish his studies there."

There was a sharp intake of breath from Jane as she said that. She continued.

"After that Christmas, he went back for the last part of his university course but then he was caught by the German conscription and forced to join the army; at first, we had letters from him, from France and then from the Balkans. But then he got sent to Russia, and finally to Stalingrad. We hadn't heard anything of him, and then there came the surrender and we don't know if he's dead or alive. He might be in some dreadful Russian prison camp, starving or diseased; or he might have been killed in the fighting. We just don't know." She paused and looked at Enid. "I don't know if you can help, but I just can't see what else to do."

Jane interrupted her. "I'll tell you what else you can do. You can get out, with your worries about your German soldier brother. My Jimmy died taking weapons to the Russians to fight your lot. You come in here with the idea that he can speak at the same time as my Jimmy who was a brave man struggling to stop you lot taking over Europe. Get out! Get out, you filthy German."

Elisabeth raised her hand to her mouth, her eyes wide with shock at the outburst. "But I don't want the Germans to win. My brother shouldn't be there; we all came to England because of the Nazis. He shouldn't be there," she repeated. "It's just bad luck."

"Don't talk to me about bad luck. I can hear from your voice that you're German. Just get out and leave us here to grieve with decent people."

Stunned by the woman's words, Elisabeth jumped up, the chair falling over behind her. She fought back the tears in her eyes. Grabbing her coat, she stumbled through the door into the corridor. Mathilde caught her up, just as she was halfway down the stairs.

"Elisabeth, my dear, take no notice of her. She wasn't thinking of what she was saying. She's overwrought. Come back, and I'm sure we can calm things down."

Elisabeth couldn't hold the tears back any longer. "No. I'm going home. You can't understand, Mathilde, what it is to be torn in two like this. I just want to go home." She stumbled down the rest of the staircase and out into the street. She ran home through the drizzle.

Chapter Eight

Armin was never forgotten, but he remained frozen in time as the rest of the family moved on. Both girls left the BBC in early 1944, Gaby to get married to her pilot and Elisabeth because she wanted to move to the country to grow food. Her father bought her a smallholding, which she ran, by a quirk of fate using German prisoners-of-war as her labourers. She also married, a year after her sister, a lieutenant in the Canadian army, whom she met while he was convalescing from losing an arm as he hurled himself ashore onto Juno Beach in the D-Day landings. They bought more land after the war was over and expanded from smallholders into full-fledged farmers. Margaret Kuhlmann was frail, the shock of the loss of her elder son permanently etched on her psyche. Sepp never seriously contemplated returning to the ruins of Germany - particularly since Aue was now deep in the Soviet Zone - and instead turned his energies to rebuilding his trading businesses in London. Gaby's husband, when he was eventually sent back from the Far East in late 1946, joined him. Franz had fought in the British army up through Italy and was demobilised and sent home from the Austrian border in the middle of 1945. He married, and, like his little sister, went off to work on the land, first buying a farm in the Scottish border country, and then in the early fifties taking his family off to farm in Canada.

1978 Sussex, England

Chapter Nine

Later that evening, after my mother had gone up to bed, my father and I sat in the great hall of the house over another bottle of claret. A log fire burned brightly in the big fireplace, the wall lights reflected back off the highly-polished oak panelling.

"You know," my father said, "I don't really say too much about your mother's family background. I never met Armin - the war had started by the time I got to know Ma and the rest of the family. What they went through was awful - I had it easy. I flew my aeroplanes, and then for the last three years I was sitting out in the Far East in the tropic sunshine. Yes, it was war, but we had a good time; our Mosquitoes were faster than any plane the Japanese had and our base was on an island way out of the range of their bombers. Our biggest threat was getting lost flying over millions of square miles of ocean. I never had to face the split loyalties that the Kuhlmanns did. Don't get me wrong; all of them were implacably anti-Nazi, but they were nevertheless Germans, and one of their family was fighting on the other side. It's difficult to imagine how that must have felt, and then on top of that there was the internment and all the abusive phone calls. Your mother doesn't say much about that, but Elisabeth once told me a bit. It was constant, almost daily abuse from strangers, who knew nothing except the name and the German accents. The two girls tried as much as they could to shield their mother, and with all that going on they must have been worried sick about Armin, especially as the situation in Stalingrad got worse – or better, if you were British." He smiled. "That sums it up, really; was it better or worse? They wanted the Allies to win, but what did that mean personally?"

"Elisabeth went to a séance once, you know." He must have seen my surprise, because he smiled. Sensible old Auntie Elisabeth at a séance? He continued. "Yes, it does seem slightly surprising, but remember, she was not even the age you are now, trying to cope with her mother's distress. She and your mother had to develop very broad shoulders. She told me about the séance; your mother was horrified at her, and it

Beyond Stalingrad

turned out badly. They chased her out for being German and wanting to communicate with a German soldier.

"It must have been dreadful, always having to watch what you said. Then by the time I was back permanently – we were married by then and your mother was expecting Maggie – it had sort of faded into the background. We always had the pictures, though, as a sort of reminder." He pointed to the wall above the fireplace. The drawing up there had been there as long as I could remember. It was a line drawing of the Hamburg town hall, dated June 1939, and signed with the distinctive 'AK'. Its twin, depicting the Binnenalster, with the Jungfernstieg in the foreground and the Vier Jahreszeiten hotel in the middle distance, was opposite, on the wall behind us.

"He really was a talented artist. Those must have been done either when he was still a student or when he had just been conscripted. He must have sent them pretty much as soon as he had done them. And the two water colours upstairs were done while he was still at school.

"Is that bottle empty? I'll fetch another one. And there's something else I've got to show you." He got up and left the room, leaving me looking at the drawings, and pondering. What they all said was true - they really were very good. Anybody would happily give them house room, regardless of the family connection. I got up and looked more closely. I'd never examined them before - they were just a constant feature of the house, a part of my life. I looked at the signature; the A and the K were flamboyantly intertwined, with the date of June 1939 neatly written vertically, in the opening of the K. I'd been to Hamburg many times, but of course Armin had drawn it before the bombing that had ripped the heart out of the city. A lot had been rebuilt or repaired as a copy, including the town hall itself, but there were obvious differences. Next time I went, I would photograph the scenes from where he had painted to compare how the vista had changed. I was still standing in front of the fireplace when my father came back, a bottle in one hand and a small white envelope in the other. As we sat down again, he poured the wine and put the envelope on the coffee table next to him.

"When I came back from the war, I didn't really know what to do. I hadn't finished my degree, but I didn't want to go back to university - I had a wife and then a child to think of, so I had to earn some money, but apart from flying aeroplanes, I wasn't really qualified for anything. And there were far too many of us pilots sloshing around to staff the civilian airlines. So when your grandfather suggested I might join him in his business, it seemed the obvious solution. Of course, I knew nothing about the business, and in fact, I didn't really know that much about him - or the rest of the family, for that matter. But I learned a few things very quickly. First, that he was a rich man - far wealthier than I had realised. He was also very, very well respected, and genuinely popular with his business contacts. He was truly a charismatic man - they always talked about Armin in that way, and I guess he was the one who inherited it. That gave us a great head start in re-establishing the company he had first built up when they came over from Germany in the thirties. So taking those two things together, it didn't take long to get the business back up and running".

He grinned at me. "There's a lesson for you there: money and popularity - that's what you need to succeed in business. Anyway, by 1948, it was all going well. So then he told me I would have to run things pretty much alone for a bit, because having got things back on an even keel, he needed to try and find out what had happened to his son. He spent a lot of time and money chasing information that really got him nowhere. The records were chaotic, both German and Russian. He went back and forth to Germany, trying to find people who could help him, who knew something about what had happened at Stalingrad. But he was caught a bit in the middle. Those who were back in Germany were by and large unable to help because they hadn't been there at the end - otherwise they wouldn't have been back in Germany - and those who had been there at the end were still in Russia, either dead or in a prison camp. He tried numerous times to get permission to go to Stalingrad to see for himself, but that was a complete no-go. The place was completely closed, I assume while they were clearing up and starting to rebuild it. I don't know when private individuals got the right to go there again, but it was much later.

"He was going round and round in circles, getting nowhere. I think I was the only one who really knew how much time and effort he spent on this, because he wanted to shield his wife and kids from it all - I think in fact he wanted to find the answer and then present it to them as a sort of closure. Anyway, finally he met a man who had been with Armin at the beginning of the war, and this man then put him in contact with another one who had been with Armin right through to Stalingrad. He was very excited, and thought he was finally getting somewhere. This" - he picked up the envelope from the table - "is the letter he received from that guy in late 1950. I'll leave it with you; your German is good enough to read it. But, you must understand, he asked me all those years ago to keep it. I was not to show it to your mother, or Elisabeth or Franz; when you read it, you'll see that it's not conclusive, and he didn't want them to read this with other histories of the battle and its aftermath and just torture themselves again with doubts. He thought it was better to leave it lie, since he couldn't find a definitive answer. And I haven't shown it to any of them. But you're the next generation, and you're my son, but you're also part of the Kuhlmann family. He would have been your uncle; I've just been like the banker, looking after it. Now, it's for you, your sisters and cousins to know what happened in the past. I was going to give it to you at some point; this seems like an appropriate time." He paused for a moment, lost in thought. "There was something else as well. He told me that the last time he saw Armin, at Christmas in 1938, before he went back to Hamburg, they had had some sort of row about it. He couldn't bear to think his last words to his son had been angry. That was eating him up. But, you know, that's how life is. You never know what will happen."

He drained his wine glass and stood up. "I'm off to bed. I'll see you in the morning."

I bad him goodnight, and opened the letter he had left me.

It was headed "Dusseldorf, 19th November 1950."

"Dear Herr Kuhlmann,

I recently met Herr Karl-Heinz Lutz, who was a war-time comrade. He asked me to take the time to write you something about Armin. I was with Armin for some time and I am of course happy to do that. To begin with, I must sadly tell you that I cannot clarify the final outcome, but can only say that on 2nd February 1943 (when the fighting in the Stalingrad Kessel finally came to an end) Armin was still alive. But now I'll treat everything in order.

I first got to know Armin in 1939, when we were conscripted in Hamburg. Karl-Heinz has already told you about our time as recruits, in the Eiffel and the French campaign, so I will take up the story at the point where Karl-Heinz left our company.

After the French campaign, we returned to our old garrison in Münster and there we were retrained as tank troops and got our black Panzer uniforms. We spent a few months in Thüringen and then in November 1940 we were amongst the first troops who marched into Romania, where we were greeted with friendliness by the population. Here I became the radio-operator in Armin's tank. Armin was then a senior NCO and I was a corporal. From then on, I worked with him all the time and I got to know him as a person. In service, I saw him as a superior and he was an example. Personally, we became close. He told me a lot about you, his mother and his sisters and brother, whom he had not seen for so long. Though Armin always had a happy nature, I saw, especially later, how his thoughts were so much of home. As we were not involved in any fighting in the Balkans, Armin busied himself getting to know the country and the people and their customs and manners. The Balkans were full of interest for study. We visited towns like Budapest, Bucharest, Timeschburg, Herrmanstadt, Philipopel and Sofia and criss-crossed the whole Carpathians. Armin was taken with the beauty of the region and the life of the civil population was fascinating to him. We were received in the greatest houses as guests and also did not miss the opportunity to visit the primitive parts of Romania where the people effectively lived underground in caves. He also studied the history of the whole population. In the quiet evenings Armin happily kept himself occupied. He wrote short stories and a number of poems, mostly lyric ones, but of course being Armin he was always sketching and drawing. He never thought of showing his poetry to the Company. Only his closest circle of friends could from time to time get a glimpse of his work. We were surprised that such an otherwise tough, robust, yet thoroughly good-natured man could be capable of such delicate verses. It was at this time that Armin began work on a major project. He wanted to rework the Song of the Nibelungen after his own style. At that time he shared with me the scope of his thoughts in such a way that even now, so much later, I could still put them on paper. His drawings, though, he let everybody see. He did portraits of some of our comrades and some of the officers; I know some of them sent them home to their families. He also had a portfolio of landscapes from all over the Balkans, wherever we went. Sadly, I believe all those pictures were destroyed in the fighting in Russia.

After what was this happy time in the Balkans, the Russian campaign began for us. We were from the outset directly involved, and had many tough weeks to get through. We were always in the southern sector. Our first big operation was the battle of the Kiev pocket. Then we were part of the battle to break through to the Black Sea at Nikolayev, and in the autumn to Rostov, where the ferocity of the Russian winter first hit us. We were by then such close friends that we shared everything. Every parcel that came from home was split between the crew (4 men). How many times Armin and I smoked together the last cigarette or shared the last piece of bread (getting supplies was always a problem for us that first winter). Our toughest fight was during the winter, when we were in Nikiforowka, near Artemowsk, and had to resist a Russian breakthrough. We were part of the battle group. In temperatures down to -50C it was a hard fight. But Armin never lost his good humour and at that time didn't believe we would lose the war.

I enclose four photos with this letter; they are the only ones I have left of Armin and you are welcome to keep them.

Although as I said before, Armin never tried to appear the 'biggest' in the company, his abilities became more and more known and he became more and more popular. A small circle formed around him, where interesting discussions took place. It included a nice man, in civil life a public prosecutor, another who subsequently became a clergyman and an art historian from the Landesmuseum in Münster. They all gathered round Armin as he was not only knowledgeable about all things but also had his own opinions. Then there was also his best friend, Klaus Müller. They had been at University

Beyond Stalingrad

together in Hamburg and had been conscripted together. I still have fond memories of those discussions, always good-natured. His superiors also valued Armin. Our officers frequently sought him out in a friendly way.

At the end of the winter campaign we were attached to another battle group in another powerful breakthrough attempt in the Donets Basin near Izyum. Finally, there were a couple of happy weeks at Artemowsk where we were out of the battle. The biggest battle up to that point was the tank battle at Kalach, which was the biggest tank battle of the whole Russian campaign. In the spring we found ourselves at Stalingrad. Our division had alone achieved something. Overnight we had created a bridgehead over the Don and by the following evening we were already through the 75 km wide defensive band into the northern part of the industrial city of Stalingrad which is strung out for 35 km along the Volga. For three days we were alone until the other divisions caught up and made contact with us. The fight for Stalingrad was hard. The taking of the city was left to the infantry divisions and we took up a defensive position to the north of the city to hold off the strengthening enemy. The steppe around Stalingrad is broken by big gorges. We took our tanks into these and built bunkers. Armin had by now been promoted to lieutenant and had been decorated with the EKII and EKI, tank battle stripe and Eastern Front winter battle medal. I was also promoted to senior NCO and had my own tank and crew. My bunker was right next to Armin's though, and although he was now an officer and I remained an NCO, we were still as friendly as ever.

As I had been 27 months without leave, in the first days of November I was sent on leave. We spent the last few hours before my departure sitting together in the twilight of his bunker; when we said goodbye, neither of us could have thought that we would never see each other again. Shortly after that, the Russians succeeded in breaking through and enclosing our Stalingrad divisions in an iron ring. When I came back from leave, I found the door to all my comrades was shut. I know only too well that the position for us in the Kessel was not good. Resupply in the winter was always very difficult for us and in the Kessel there was a severe lack of everything, especially fuel and ammunition. In the middle of December a mechanized force was prepared to supply the necessities to the Kessel to give the divisions trapped there the chance to withdraw to the west. That attempt failed and marked the beginning of our retreat.

I subsequently met a former lieutenant. He is until now the only survivor of the Stalingrad Kessel that I have seen. He reported the following:
'Our Company had had to retreat further and further into the city and finally reached the tractor factory. On 2nd February the fighting in the northern part ceased (the southern part had already surrendered). In the early

morning, Armin was seen still alive in Groscurth's bunker. He had therefore survived the Battle of Stalingrad. What happened beyond that remains unclear.'

Right here, where your questions will undoubtedly begin, my knowledge finishes. I would like to satisfy your uncertainty about Armin's fate. I would not like to give you false hope, so it will perhaps be hard for you when I write that little hope remains of hearing any more of all those brave men who lost their lives so far from home in that dreadful place. You may be sure that I share your grief for Armin.

I myself survived the war and then finished my studies as an electrical engineer. You know yourself how difficult it is in the bleak state of our industry to find an appropriate job. So for the last two years I have been working in the mining industry in order to feed my family.

I believe, Herr Kuhlmann, that we all wish as soon as possible to live without the threat of another war and to rebuild our civil existence in true peace.

With this hope, I greet you and your noble family and I hope that this short report has given you a glimpse of Armin's life amongst our company.

Lothar Krumm
Dusseldorf

I sat back in my chair. I had a reasonable knowledge of the Second World War, gleaned from history books, films and my own father's stories about his flying. But somehow this was different. There was a raw, visceral edge to this story of the little cogs in the machine rolling across Eastern Europe into Russia that was far more immediate than any measured historical view. I didn't recognise all the place names, but those I did gave an idea of the sheer size of the area they'd covered. And it was all so matter-of-fact, how they'd seen Bulgaria and Rumania and Ukraine, before reaching Russia itself. The arbitrariness of it struck me, as well, the way in which the relatively routine fact of taking his leave had effectively saved Krumm's life, in contrast to the bleak fate of his comrades. Although there was no real description of the horrors of the fighting, I was not surprised my grandfather had not wanted his other children to read the letter. By 1950, they all had their own family lives to lead and I could see that being faced again with the unknown fate of their brother would just have reopened wounds. It must have been heartbreaking for him, as well, to reach so far and yet still not have the final answer he was seeking.

Beyond Stalingrad

I tucked the letter into my pocket and went to bed.

The next day, I had to leave before lunch, as I had a meeting to attend in London. We didn't talk more about Armin that morning.

In fact, as our lives rolled on, we didn't really talk much about him at all. My focus was on my career, then my marriage and my children, and it was just an awareness in the back of my mind that I had unfinished business to attend to at some point. I kept the letter my father had passed me in the back of a drawer, although at that stage I didn't mention it to my sisters or my cousins. It was just on a future 'to do' list.

1995 Sussex, England

Chapter Ten

In the summer of 1995, I was sitting at my work when I got a phone call from my sister Isobel. "You better come down," she said. "Ma's had a stroke; they've taken her to hospital in Brighton." Her voice cracked. "It doesn't look good, Alex. Can you get down here quickly? Maggie's on her way, as well."

The quickest way to get to Brighton from London was by train, so I jumped in a cab to London Bridge and was lucky enough to catch a train almost immediately. Less than an hour later, I was fighting my way through the labyrinth of the Royal Sussex Hospital to the emergency unit where they had taken my mother. I eventually found the right corridor where Isobel was pacing, outside the closed door of the room.

"The doctor is with her at the moment," she said. "They said they wouldn't be long, but they've been in there half an hour. The room is full of screens and electronics and stuff." She sounded on the edge of tears.

"Why don't you take a break for a couple of minutes," I said. "Go and see if you can find us a coffee or something. I'll be here if they want to tell us anything."

She nodded. "OK, I'll be as quick as I can."

I sat on one of the chairs outside the room as she walked off in the direction of the nurses' station. No sooner had she turned the corner and passed out of sight than the door opened, and a doctor and two nurses came out. They looked questioningly at me.

"I'm Alex Butterfield," I said. "That's my mother you're treating. My sister has just gone to get us a coffee."

The doctor nodded. "OK; well, Mr Butterfield, I'm afraid the situation is not good. We have stabilised your mother's heart, but I fear we may have been too late and irreparable damage may have been done to her brain. Is your mother German?"

I looked at him, amazed at the question. "Yes, but why?"

"In these cases there can often be a regression to childhood; the only recognisable words she is saying are German, so I wondered if that were the case. You may go in now, as I say we have stabilised her, but please don't expect too much. All we can do is monitor the situation; if you can speak to her also in German it may help to bring the brain back, but I'm afraid I don't hold out too much hope." He looked directly at me. "I'm sorry, I'm not being unfeeling, but it is best you know the truth of the situation. That way any surprises will be positive, at least."

One of the nurses opened the door and gestured me to go inside. My mother was lying in the bed, tubes and electrodes attached to various points on her arms; she looked diminished, lying there. Her normally neat and tidy hair was a mess, her face showed barely any more colour than the pillow her head rested on and her breathing looked shallow. Her eyes were closed, so I quietly sat on the chair next to the bed. Then I leaned back in it, and it creaked loudly. The sound roused her and she opened her eyes. She turned and I could sense the effort she was having to make to focus on my face. Then she spoke, hesitantly, almost a whisper.

"Armin? Bist du es? Es tut mir weh. Geh mal Mama suchen. Ich bin durstig."

I could help with the last bit and picked up the glass of water on her bedside cabinet. Carefully, I put it to her lips so she could drink. A little of the water trickled down her chin and when she had finished, I gently wiped it away.

She looked around, her face fearful. "Armin, wo bin ich? Hier ist nicht zu Hause. Wo ist Mama?" She stretched out her arm and took my hand, her grip feeble and her skin dry.

Isobel came into the room and my mother looked up. "Elisabeth? Du bist auch hier? Es fehlt nur Franz, dann sind wir alle zusammen, wie immer." Her eyes closed, and she seemed to drift off to sleep. Her hand slipped out of mine.

Isobel sat next to me and handed me a cardboard mug of coffee. I sipped it and grimaced. "I know," she said, "I took one mouthful of mine and chucked it. So she's still speaking German?"

"You knew?"

"Yes, the doctor told me earlier. He doesn't think there's much hope, you know."

"Mmm. Where's Pa?"

"He was in France this week, so I was looking in on her every day." Isobel lived close to our parents; a lot of the routine of checking of the old people fell on her. "I spoke to him earlier and he's on his way back, but he's got to drive to the ferry and then cross. He reckons that way will still be quicker than getting to an airport and then having to come down from Heathrow." She shrugged her shoulders. "I don't know, but he seemed sure. Maggie's on her way as well." Our sister lived in Edinburgh with her Scottish dentist husband. "She should be here by late evening."

It seemed unreal; although she had been getting old, reconciling the frail figure in the bed with the mother we knew was difficult. We chatted quietly, about everything and nothing, all the while skirting round the reality that our mother was probably dying in front of us.

Eventually, Isobel asked me: "When she was speaking German, when I came back into the room, did it make any sense?"

"Yes. She mistook me for Armin, and told me she was in pain. Could I fetch her mother and she was thirsty. I gave her a drink, and then when she saw you at the door she thought you were Elisabeth and she said all they needed was Franz and they would all be together, as always." I shook my head. "Bizarre. Why does the brain do that? Go back to childhood?"

My sister fancied herself as a bit of a psychologist. "Well, it's just reverting to a happy time. Going back to somewhere comfortable."

"Mmm. But you know as well as I do that it's not only in her childhood that she was happy. Why go back to there?"

"Maybe the brain is going back to a state where she felt protected – when parents were responsible and everything was well ordered and safe."

"I guess, maybe. But it's quite strange that she mistook me for Armin and you for Elisabeth."

"Not really. She hasn't got her glasses on and if her mind has gone back to those days then it's logical that that's who she should think she was seeing. Come on, Alex, her mind's wandering in the past – whatever she sees must be just a blur to her and she's simply interpreting things as if it were the 1920s."

We sat there for a long while. Later in the evening Maggie arrived from Edinburgh. Around eleven, the nurse came back and suggested that we leave for the moment – well, in fact she basically told us to go and come back again in the morning. My sisters went back to Isobel's house and I went home, so I could come back with my car the next morning.

When I got back at eight o'clock in the morning, it was all over; she'd died peacefully during the night. The two girls were with our father, who had arrived just before she'd died; he at least had had a chance to say goodbye to her, after so many years together. With them was Elisabeth, tears in her eyes as she hugged Isobel.

Chapter Eleven

Three years later, they were all gone. First, Elisabeth's farmer husband Walter died unexpectedly one day of a heart attack as he wandered through his orchard. Then Franz, far away in Canada, followed within weeks by Elisabeth, the aunt who had been like an extra mother to me and my sisters. Finally, almost three years to the day after his beloved Gaby, my father succumbed to a massive stroke. I, my sisters and cousins were now the older generation, the ones who held the knowledge of the family together, to pass on to our own children.

In the weeks after our father's funeral, my sisters and I set about the task of rationalising the contents of the house in which we had all grown up. When I clambered up into the loft, one of the first things I saw was the deed box that had been our grandfather's. I took it down into the study where the other two were surrounded by books as they tried to separate what should be sold and what kept. When I told them what the box contained, they sat down and immediately started delving into it, finding the same fascination as I had years before in the clues it gave to the lives of the previous generations. We spent the rest of the afternoon immersed in it, leaving the sorting of things for another day. That reminded me of the letter my father had given me, and when I told my sisters about it, they begged me to give them a translation. When I got home that evening, therefore, I dug it out from the back of the drawer where I'd shoved it all those years earlier, and sat down in my study to work on it. It didn't take long, but seeing it again made me think once more about the story my mother had told me. I reached an atlas down from the bookcase and started trying to find the places Lothar Krumm had mentioned. Most were pretty easy but the old German names of one or two of the cities had me stumped. I was just tracing what I thought was their route on the map when Emily, my wife, came in with a bottle of wine and two glasses. She'd been bathing the children when I got in and had just greeted me perfunctorily. Now she was more relaxed. "The girls want you to read them their story this evening, since you're home early," she said.

"OK, I'll just take a glass of that up with me. Oh, and here, you may be interested in this. It's a letter I've just translated, sent to my grandfather about my mother's brother and the Stalingrad battle. Maggie and Isobel wanted me to put it into English for them; we found loads of stuff about the family today, and this seems to belong to that." I handed her the letter, picked up the wineglass and went up to read to my daughters.

When I came back downstairs again, having persuaded two excited young girls it was time to go to sleep, I found Emily sitting at my desk, pouring over the atlas, just as I had been doing earlier.

"This is fascinating," she said, glancing up at me. "I can recognise some of the names and work out some of the others, but there are a couple I just can't get. Where is Philipopel, and Herrmanstadt?"

"I'm pretty sure Philipopel is now Plovdiv, which I think is in Bulgaria, and for some reason I think I know that Herrmanstadt is Sibiu, in Romania. But there are a couple of others I just don't know. The only Artemowsk, or anything like that, I could find was much farther east than where they could have been, in the Urals, and I just couldn't see anything like Nikiforowka. I guess they are in Ukraine, and they went through there as they were advancing eastwards."

She looked up again from the atlas. "Mmm, yes, and then they went on into Russia proper. And that was really the last your grandparents and your mother and aunt and uncle knew of him?"

"Yup; my mother told me the story once, about how he just disappeared. She last saw him at Christmas 1938 and then he went back to Germany, got trapped and then conscripted. But she never saw this letter. That was sent to my grandfather, when he was trying to find out what had happened to his son. He gave the letter to my father to keep, and made him promise not to show it to my mother's generation; he thought it better for them to believe he had been killed than to think of him being captive in Russia."

"D'you think that's what happened? That he was held in a camp and eventually just died?"

"I guess so. I think that's what my father thought Grandfather thought. And he just didn't want the others to think of their brother being some sort of slave labour. Apparently he tried quite hard to find things out, but this letter was the only actual fact he got. I suppose the records would have been pretty sketchy, anyway, and, let's face it, the Russians weren't going to go out of their way to give out any information. I suppose things there would be a little easier now, but, to be honest, it's all about fifty years ago, so I doubt one could find out anything."

"Mmm. It just seems wrong, simply to leave him in limbo. I mean, from the tone of that letter, he was obviously quite a character."

"Yes, whenever my mother or Auntie Elisabeth talked about him, they always described him as really clever and talented, and charismatic. I agree it seems wrong for him just to disappear off the face of the earth; even just to know where he is buried would be something, but I honestly don't think it's going to happen."

Beyond Stalingrad

I gave the translated letter to my sisters and to all the cousins, and for a couple of months there was a lot of chat in the family about Armin. Nothing came of it, though, because nothing could. Armin was one man; I looked into it a bit, and the best estimates of German dead and missing on the Eastern Front came in at between two and three million. That put it into a harsh perspective. Mind you, even those numbers were dwarfed by the toll of the Russian dead. After a while, I stopped reading about it; it was just too depressing, and I began to understand my grandfather not wanting to re-awaken the memories in the minds of his wife or children. I hung on to the deed box, though, as my sisters and I slowly emptied the house before we sold it.

1999 Russia

Chapter Twelve

My career had developed well, and since the early 1990s I had been a senior metal trader at one of the most influential players in the business. As the Soviet Union imploded under the pressure of Reagan's defence spending, what had previously been a bureaucratic monopoly dealing with Russia's enormous mineral wealth fragmented into separate entities, auctioned off by the state to a variety of different entrepreneurs, as we were encouraged to describe them (or gangsters, as we called them amongst ourselves). Developing my company's relationships with these new entities, getting access to their production, was one of my main activities at that time.

And so in early 1999, I found myself flying into Moscow with a group of other brokers and traders from London on a trip organised by the Arctic Mining Company, which operated nickel mines at Norilsk, with the aim of broadening their customer base in the west. We were to meet the top management in Moscow, and then, a day later, to fly to Norilsk, up above the Arctic Circle, to see the mines and treatment plants. Along the way, the company would take the chance to lavish entertainment on us. I'd been to Moscow a fair few times before, and this trip followed the usual pattern. A couple of dinners, lots of vodka toasting and a meeting with the head of sales whose task was to impress on us how the new management were commercially-minded, unlike their Soviet predecessors, and keen to meet our demands as important future customers. It was fun being with the whole group; we all knew each other well, as competitors and rivals in the business, and some were good friends. The dinners were entertaining, the meeting less so, but then, the main purpose of the trip was the visit to Norilsk itself. It was – and indeed still is – a closed city, meaning that we all had to be vetted by the authorities before they could issue our travel documentation. Arranging that took most of the afternoon ahead of the flight, and then after an early dinner we were driven to the airport as dusk fell

Then, after all the bureaucracy was through, we were herded to the departure gate by the three Russians who were accompanying us. It wasn't a private flight and we boarded the Tupolev along with a gaggle of Russian passengers. I found myself sitting in a row of three, between a London Metal Exchange broker who had been a friend for years and a younger guy, a Serb, who worked at a major physical trading house. As we sat watching the other passengers file past to their seats, the LME broker said, "Why are all these people going to Norilsk? All there is there are the mines. They don't look like miners going back after a break in Moscow." He was right; the majority of them looked like old age pensioners on an outing.

Goran, on my other side, spoke up. "They used to be. What happened is that when the people who had previously been forced labour up at Norilsk were released, many of them had nowhere to go back to; their families had been broken up or died, and so they just stayed on in Norilsk. It was the place, in the end, that they knew. So now as well as the current generation of miners and other workers, there is quite a big number of pensioners. It's also much cheaper for them to live there than in the big cities further south." He grinned. "In my country, in Yugoslavia, we learnt a lot of modern Russian history, even if it wasn't what the Soviets wanted us to know."

"Have you been to Norilsk before?"

"Yeah, sure. Before the whole system collapsed, we were already buying nickel from them. It was kind of different visiting with the Soviets, though. Less relaxed." He grinned again. "Asking them about slave labour was not on the agenda, but I believe now there's even a museum devoted to the development of the mining complex. They started work in the early thirties, and the slave labour went right through even beyond the end of the Stalin era."

"Who was sent there?" I asked, curious.

"Mostly political prisoners, I think. But some petty criminals as well. I think it was sometimes just the luck of the draw how the judge felt the day he pronounced sentence. It was tough in the thirties; that was the time of the purges, when Stalin and his cohorts were determined to stamp out any form of resistance. So you could be classed as a subversive for simple things – making a joke about the party, for example, or just getting on the wrong side of a commissar in some way."

The flight attendant walked past, checking seat belts and then the aircraft started to roll. It was already dark as we lifted off from the runway.

It's not a particularly long flight from Moscow to Norilsk, but there is also a four hour time-zone change, so we were scheduled to land early morning the next day. There was nothing like in-flight service on Russian internal flights at that time - most of the operators were still trying to work out how to make money out of the break-up of the former monopoly that had got them into the business in the first place - and shortly after take-off, the cabin lights were dimmed to allow the passengers to sleep. I did no more than doze fitfully and chat quietly to the broker sitting next to me.

In the early morning light, I heard the aircraft's engine noise change, and the nose dipped as we began our run-in to land. We passed through a thick layer of cloud and came out in semi-darkness above a flat snow-covered landscape. It wasn't long before we touched - quite hard, actually - onto the runway, and the engines screamed in reverse thrust. The pilot came on the PA system, in Russian and frankly badly muffled as well. Next to me, Goran came out of his deep sleep and, looking around him, said, "Ah, we've arrived, have we?" The aircraft taxied over until we could see through the windows on our side what must be the terminal building. It was a rough breeze-block construction, single story and with the name in Cyrillic letters on a board over the shabbily-painted door. As the rest of our party began getting out of their seats, although the Russian passengers didn't move, Goran looked again at the building. "Mmm. I wouldn't bother getting up if I were you," he said, "we haven't arrived. This isn't Norilsk." He gestured towards the sign on the building. "That says Igarka, not Norilsk. I didn't know we had to land anywhere else first." As he spoke, the captain came on again, and this time Goran listened attentively. "OK, he says that due to high winds at Norilsk, that airport is closed and we have to wait here until it clears. For the moment we are going to stay on the aircraft."

By now our three Russian guides had passed the message on to the rest of the group as well, and they all sat down again. So we sat while the scene outside slowly emerged more clearly into the growing daylight. After forty-five minutes or so, our contingent started to get restive; they hadn't spent the night in uncomfortable aircraft seats in order just to sit on the ground at some god-forsaken airstrip in the Russian arctic while waiting for the weather to change. They were bombarding our Russian guides with demands to be allowed at least to get off until the plane could resume its journey. Meanwhile, the other passengers, those returning to Norilsk, just sat, seemingly immune to the delay. Eventually, the captain came back on the PA to announce that as the airport in Norilsk was not expected to reopen for at least another couple of hours, we were to be allowed to disembark from the plane and wait in the terminal. We all filed down the stairs and hurried across through the biting cold to the building. Its shabby outside was mirrored by the condition of the interior; ranks of tired plastic seats were set in one half, with a single check-in desk in front of a hole in the wall, through which presumably baggage could be pushed to be taken from the other side to load on to departing aircraft, although in fact it all looked so run-down that I wondered if really it was completely disused.

Beyond Stalingrad

The passengers all sat down, and our Russian guides were still besieged with questions, this time demanding to know how long we would be stuck here. One or two of my companions pulled out their mobile phones but pretty soon realised there was no coverage at all. Goran laughed. "This is quite funny. You guys have all been to Moscow, but I bet this is the first time any of you have been stuck out in the sticks like this." That wasn't entirely true; I'd been to Siberia before, but further south, to the aluminium towns of Irkutsk and Krasnoyarsk. But none of us had been to a place like this before.

It was pretty much as boring sitting there in the terminal as it had been on the aeroplane. After a bit, I got up, and wandered around, finding a small side-room where there was a counter with some tired looking packets of biscuits and cakes and a stack of tea bags. Looking closely, I saw what I assumed to be the sell-by dates; they were all at least a year old. I sauntered on. Goran joined me. "Let's take a look outside," he suggested. So we pushed open the door and stepped out into the cold. One of the guides followed us.

"What is this place?" I asked him. "Is there a town here, or is it a military airfield or what?"

"This place, Igarka, is a small town. It's here for the logging. They cut the trees and then send the logs down the river to Dudinka, which is the same port where our nickel is shipped from. The river is the Yenisei." He looked at me with a questioning eye. "I don't know if that means anything to you, but it's the biggest river in Siberia, with its source right down in Mongolia. The various hydro power stations along it generate most of the region's electricity. And it was actually the agreed dividing line in Asia between the Germans and the Japanese: where they thought their two empires would meet after they had defeated the Soviet Union in World War Two." He grinned. "That didn't go quite according to plan. So, it's the ice melt in this river that causes the flooding at Dudinka which creates the so-called flood season, when the whole port has to be closed for a month or so because the flow of water is too fast and too strong to allow safe operations. I'm actually not really sure in which direction the town lies from here, but it should not be far away. But for sure, the river is why the settlement was started here. At the moment, of course, it's still frozen and they won't be able to float the logs downstream until after the flooding. With the logging here, where they actually float the logs themselves rather than use barges or anything like that, they really only have about two months of the year when they can use it, between flooding and freezing. For us it's a bit better – of course we have to suspend shipments during the flood, but when it's frozen we have icebreakers to keep the shipments going. But we'll visit Dudinka while we're here so you can see it for yourselves." He grinned at us. "This place is shit, isn't it? I hope we can get out soon; I don't want to spend all day here. But sometimes the wind storms can last a while up at Norilsk, so I hope we're lucky this time. I have no idea how we are going to keep you guys occupied if we're here for any length of time."

His name was Andrey and he'd visited London several times, as one of the sales team; through those visits, he'd become quite a good friend. He was good company and had a relaxed sense of humour. "The idea of a bunch of London metal traders cooped up in a dump like this doesn't bode well. I haven't been able to find any food, either. I saw you looking at that stuff in there, but it's all about a year out of date. The last thing I need is to give you all food poisoning as well." He laughed this time. "Still, no doubt Mother Russia will provide, as ever."

"Let's go back in," said Goran. "It's getting bloody cold out here."

Back inside, we were greeted by one of the other Arctic Mining staff; he and Andrey started a rapid conversation in Russian, while Goran and I watched our fellows. Some of them were reading, a few were playing spoof with the Russian coins they had in their pockets and a few were just staring into space. Andrey finished his conversation and clapped his hands to attract the attention of the group.

"OK," he said, "just over there" - he pointed out through the window - "about half a kilometre, there is a hotel. They have agreed to let us use the rooms to get some rest, since we've been on a flight and we've lost some time zones. They will also have some food there. Not sure if I'd eat it," he said, laughing, "But it may be better than nothing. At the moment, the crew say the aeroplane will not leave for at least three hours, so anyone who wants to should go over there now. I will show you the way." Anything seemed better than sitting in that drab airport hall so most of us followed him out through the door. It was still grey and there was a light dusting of snow in the air as we made our way across the airfield. The building we were heading for was a two-storey construction, built of concrete blocks. There were evenly spaced metal-frame windows down the side, giving it the air of something like a barrack block. I found myself next to one of the Russians, and I said that to him. He shrugged. "It probably was. The timber industry here is quite important, so I guess there would have been a detachment of troops here, to protect it. I can't believe it does much business as a hotel, though. This is hardly a place you would come to on holiday. By the time we've paid them, they probably will have doubled the year's takings."

The building didn't look any more attractive up close than it had from across the airfield. We went in through a double door at the end into a hallway with a reception desk. A conversation followed in Russian, then we were told, "You can use any of the rooms, either on this floor or the one above. Most of them have two beds, some have three. They will try to have some food in about half an hour, in that room there." He pointed across the hall. "OK, and the flight crew will come and tell us as soon as they know more about our schedule."

I followed the general movement up the bare concrete stairs. A cursory glance into three or four of the rooms opening off the corridor running the length of the first floor convinced me that I didn't want anything to do with them; bleak, undecorated cells with two or three iron-frame cots as the only furniture in them. The uncovered mattresses and grey blankets looked ominously grubby. Dead flies littered the window ledges and the floor below them. I turned back down the stairs and went into the room off the reception, where I found Andrey sitting there on his own, a beer bottle on an otherwise bare table in front of him.

He turned as I walked in. "Hi Alex. Not tempted by a doze?"

"Frankly, no. It all looks pretty unappealing up there."

"In that case, would you fancy one of these?" He held up the beer. "You can get one from behind the reception counter outside there. They're just in the cupboard below the desk."

I followed his pointing finger and then came back and dropped down in a chair opposite him. "Do the flights up here often get diverted like this?"

"Well, it's not often, but it's also not that rare. The weather at Norilsk can be very difficult - not only ice and snow, but, like today, sometimes very strong winds. I know you've been to various places in Siberia, but I'm not sure about all the others. I think they may not appreciate just where it is we are going. Norilsk is a mining town, and it's inside the Arctic Circle. It's a hard, tough place. There isn't a civilised developed-world airport, for example, with all the modern technology. I know we're on a scheduled jet flight, but it's not like landing at London or Paris. It's an airstrip out in the middle of nowhere - very primitive. It's going to be an eye-opener for some of your colleagues."

"I guess so. How often do you come up here?"

"Not that much. Maybe a couple of times a year. Actually, I do have some relatives up here, but I don't really know them. One of my grandfather's brothers was sent up here in the late 1930s for some suspected political crime. His descendants - I guess they are my cousins of some degree - still live here."

"So was he a political prisoner?" I asked, curiously.

"Sure, and he was sent up here for a long sentence."

"We were talking about that on the aeroplane. Did he stay when his sentence was over, and carry on living here?"

"Yes. He was married and had a child and they joined him in Norilsk when he was let out. I think it was not uncommon, because in the end it was the only place they had to live."

He paused and stared out of the stained and dusty widow. "It's a strange part of our history," he began again. "This place, Igarka, had a forced labour camp. The logging was done by prisoners from the thirties right up beyond the end of the Stalin period. I think here they were more petty criminals than politicals, but nevertheless they were dumped here to do the work as slaves. I'm sure this building was some kind of barracks for the guards. The actual prison huts would have been single storey and made of wood. It must have been hellish. Right now is not mid-winter, but you felt how cold it is outside. In winter, they get serious minus temperatures up here. I think the record low in Norilsk is somewhere down below minus fifty. There's snow on the ground for getting on for eight months of the year. So the prisoners were just dumped here and put to work. Many of them were intellectuals from European Russia, suddenly shifted to this extreme climate and put to hard, physical labour. Some of them didn't even know what they had done; maybe they'd done nothing, they'd just been accused for who knows what reason, and their lives were completely ruined." He paused again. "There's not much to see here - I was stuck here once for a couple of days, so I had a chance to have a look round and there are just a couple of ruined watchtowers, but at Norilsk, there is a museum which shows many aspects of the development of the town and the mines. It's very interesting, if you want to know about the past. There's not a lot about the labour camps, but enough to give an idea. They're beginning now to acknowledge the reality of what went on in those times and I think now they have a mock-up of the interior of one of the barrack huts, so you can really see what it was like. Of course, many people do not want to see that; they would rather not know how it was - just keep it all under wraps, a kind of secret history. I've scheduled a visit to the museum because I think it's interesting, but I don't know whether it will be well subscribed by your colleagues. What do you think?"

"Well, to be honest, quite a few of the people in our group would not be natural museum visitors, but for this actually I guess most of them will be interested, just because it is so far outside our normal range of understanding. But there's one thing I've always been curious about. Mining is actually a skilled operation – did they employ foremen or something to make sure it was all done correctly and efficiently? Or did they just leave the prisoners to get on with it?"

"As far as I know, and I'm not an expert, it was a bit of both. If you were a miner prosecuted for something, you could be pretty sure this is where you would end up, just so they had some skilled men. But also, they just sent them down the mines with the digging tools and set them to get on with it. They were always given targets, so many tonnes per day and so on, and that's what they had to achieve. I don't believe you could ever have called it an efficient operation; but then, if you have a seemingly limitless supply of free labour, your criteria are different. Frankly, many of the prisoners were just worked to death. They were just an economic input and they had to keep up to the required standard, otherwise they were simply disposable. It was a grim system, but, you know, it went on for a long time. It was a strange period in the middle of the twentieth century. Such sophistication and civilisation in some places, like the US or your country, and yet in both Germany and Russia - two of the traditional great powers - there was the use of slave labour. By the time I was at school, such things were taught, up to a point. The generation before mine was almost totally in the dark about how our infrastructure had been built in the thirties and fifties. And it was, you know; not only the mines, but the dams and power stations, roads, canals – so much of everything was built by forced labour."

"Did they use prisoners of war, as well?" I asked. "Germans who had been captured?"

"Sure, Germans, Rumanians, Hungarians – any who were taken. And then of course the Poles and Ukrainians who'd fallen foul of the Red Army. But I don't think the PoWs were sent up here. They were mostly kept rebuilding Stalingrad after the battle, and doing construction around Moscow, and then some I know were sent to the Far East. Technically, there were two systems; one handled prisoners of war, and the other handled what you might call the domestic crop." He glanced at his watch. "We're not going anywhere for some time, frankly. If you're interested, we can take a stroll into the woods over there and I'll show you the remains of a watchtower."

"Yeah, OK. It gets a bit dull just sitting around."

Chapter Thirteen

We pulled on our coats and went out again into the cold air. The sky was still grey, but there was no more snow falling; just an icy-cold breeze, presumably the tail-end of what was causing the problem up at Norilsk. Andrey led the way between a couple of other tatty buildings and out through a gate to the woodland. The going was not too difficult – although the ground was covered in snow, it was hard-packed and I managed to keep my footing even in my leather-soled city shoes. About a couple of hundred metres into the wood, we came upon the remains of the watchtower. Four rusting metal piles sunk into the ground and sticking up a couple of feet.

"So," said Andrey, "I think this must have been the far side of the camp from the hotel building – the barrack room: it's about the right distance. There would have been one of these towers at each corner, and a barbed-wire fence all the way round, with just one gate. By those other buildings" – he pointed back in the direction we had come – "where there is a hard surface, that must have been the open ground, where they would have made the prisoners parade each day before and after work, to count them and make sure they were all accounted for. Try and imagine it; that open space there as a kind of parade ground, prisoners all standing there in ranks and the guards with rifles surrounding them, then marching them off to work at the logging camp. This is within living memory, Alex, in one of the world's major powers. Think about that; it's almost incredible. And this was probably a very small camp and I guess also seasonal. Like I said before, the logging is dependant on the time of year. But elsewhere, like in Norilsk, the numbers were big and the work every day of the year."

I looked around, trying to picture the scene. The woodland stretched off into the distance and was visible also behind us, across the other side of the airfield. The buildings were ugly, but the forest had a sort of peace and tranquillity to it. It had been there long before the camp and would still be there in a thousand years. It struck me that it played its part as well: "Presumably they didn't really need too many guards. I mean, it's not like there is anywhere to go, even if you got out through the fence."

"That's true. The arctic Siberian winter would be a better gatekeeper than any number of military guards. But there are some stories of escapes. I guess when people are desperate, they will try anything."

Beyond Stalingrad

I shivered in my London city overcoat. "Come on, let's go back. It's cold. You would need a bearskin to stay outside here for long."

He grinned at me. "Pah, you westerners are so weak." Nevertheless, he led the way back to the hotel building. Inside, we found a number of our party had discovered the beer store and were sitting around the table.

Eventually, the flight crew got word that the weather had improved, and we were shepherded back across to the aircraft to board. After the relatively short hop to Norilsk, we finally landed in the late afternoon, about eight hours behind schedule. The terminal facilities were marginally better than at Igarka, but not by much, and once the baggage had been sorted, we boarded the bus to take us in to town. The terrain was different from Igarka – bleaker, and completely treeless. On the horizon, as we drove along, we could see the beginning of a range of mountains to the east and the dead flat plain stretching away to the west. The road was in a dreadful state – rutted, potholed and at times reduced to a single file. Still, I mused, you couldn't really blame them. With the range of temperatures they experienced, it would be virtually impossible to maintain it in any better shape. We trundled on, the only other traffic being the odd van or light truck, all belching out streams of black diesel smoke. As the sky darkened with the dusk, we passed the unmistakeable buildings marking a pit-head, and Andrey came onto the bus's PA system to start describing things to us as we approached the town. The inevitable blocks of apartments were the first sign we were hitting the built-up area. They were identical to those I'd seen elsewhere in Russia and Eastern Europe, the hurriedly erected constructions to accommodate the rapidly-growing post world war two urban population. Finally, with darkness fallen, we drew into an open square, at the centre of the town. Andrey stood up at the front of the bus and spoke briefly.

"Over there, in that courtyard, is our hotel. The bus will not drive in because the ground is too icy for him to be able to turn around in the tight space, so we will have to carry our own baggage over there. It is really slippery, so be careful.

"Obviously, our schedule today has gone wrong, with the delay at Igarka. We were intending to take you over to the port at Dudinka, but clearly that is not going to work, so we will have to see how we can rearrange things. This evening, we will just be having dinner here, at around seven thirty. Tomorrow is the visit to the mine, so we will need to leave quite early. I'll give the exact timing at dinner, when I've spoken again to the mine management. It will take a while to check in here, because they have to check all of your papers and visas, so I would ask you to bear with them. I know it's been an uncomfortable day, so let's get the formalities done, then we can relax over dinner and a few drinks. As I said, be careful on the slippery ground! We don't want lawsuits from traders with broken legs!" Everyone laughed, then piled off the bus to pick up bags and get into the hotel.

The next morning saw us back on the bus after breakfast heading for one of the pit heads to start our mine tour. The wind had dropped completely, the cloud had lifted and there was a clear blue sky above us. The road was as potholed and damaged as the one the previous day, and we ran out of the town past the glowering sheds of the smelter plant. Andrey was acting as tour guide again, pointing out the different bits of the plant, the newly-developed sites and the abandoned workings as we headed eastwards, the mountains clear in the distance. The journey took about half an hour, then we pulled into the mine complex. The winding tower stood stark against the blue sky, surrounded by a jumble of buildings. The bus pulled up outside the main block; it was fronted by an impressive stone staircase leading up to a set of glass doors, through which we passed into a large two-storey high atrium. We were ushered up the staircase and into a conference room, where we took our places on two rows of chairs facing a small raised dais. We chatted for a few minutes and then a stocky middle-aged man came in and took up his place on the dais.

"Gentlemen, good morning and welcome to the Kilometre Seven mine of The Arctic Mining Company. I am Anton Shumsky, the General Manager of the mine, and I am going to give you some details of our property before we take you underground to see for yourselves, first-hand, how we extract the treasures of the earth up here in the Arctic." His English was excellent, but heavily accented. He switched on the projector on the desk in front of him, and led us through a series of slides describing the rock formation of the area, and the way the company had exploited it over the previous sixty or seventy years. There was no denying it was an impressive story; I'm not an engineer, but I'd visited enough mines in my time to understand that operating over a kilometre below the frozen tundra created some of the most difficult mining conditions anywhere in the world. As the speaker himself said, nobody would choose to have to put their mine here; but then, neither could they choose where they would find the deposits. His presentation took about half an hour and he finished by reminding us that mining is a dangerous occupation and that we should pay heed to the safety briefings we were going to hear in a few minutes from those who would accompany us underground. Telling us he would be available for a question and answer session later, he handed us over to the underground staff who led us downstairs and out through the back of the building. From there, they took us into what was effectively the miners' changing block. Here we were each issued with coveralls, steel-toed boots, light and respirator. After we had changed, we were assembled for the safety briefing. I'm not massively nervous, but whenever I go to a mine, when the safety talk reaches the part about fire,

Beyond Stalingrad

how to deal with it and how to use the respirator, I begin to wish I was somewhere else. This time was no exception. Indeed, I have to confess that I found myself wishing that the respirator I had slung across my shoulder said 'Made in England', or 'Product of the United States', or something like that; unfair thoughts, I know, but I bet I wasn't the only one.

Finally, equipped, briefed and ready to go, we went across the small courtyard that led to the lift. The cage was a double-decker affair, solid up to waist height on each level and then finished with a wire cage enclosing the passengers totally. It was big enough to take our whole party at once. In fact, I reckoned that at the beginning and end of a shift, it could probably take about fifty men at a time. We had been told that the working level we were going to be taken to was at 1500 metres and that the seam currently being attacked was around one kilometre from the base of the lift. Descending the dark shaft wasn't a pleasant experience. It was difficult to judge the speed at which we were dropping in the pitch black but I could feel my ears popping and the temperature rising as we went down. It seemed to take a long while – but then, I guess fifteen hundred metres is actually quite a way to drop. Eventually, the cage braked and then settled the last few metres very slowly. As we came down into the light, Andrey, standing next to me, said "That was for our benefit. For the miners, they don't have that nice slow finish; they just come down and stop dead. They're being gentle with us."

From the lower level of the cage we stepped straight out into the gallery. Opposite us was a small train. We crammed ourselves four by four into the low steel carts, ducking our heads down to fit. A miner checked that the bars across the doorways were all securely fastened then got into the engine at the front and started us moving off. We were going down a big passageway, both broad and high and gently descending. It was lit by a string of bulbs along both sides and every so often we passed side galleries, some open and some blocked with wooden stakes. The ride was noisy and uncomfortable. The seats were metal shelves welded to the framework of the carriage and, with either no or very limited suspension, every jolt and lurch was painfully transmitted directly to our spines. The rattling and clattering of the wheels over the rails made conversation impossible and I guess everyone was as pleased as I was when we reached our destination. We piled out of the train wagons and gathered around a miner who explained – through Andrey as interpreter – that where we were now was one of the active mining galleries, operating twenty-four hours a day, seven days a week. We would not, for safety reasons, be able to approach where the machinery was currently in use, but we would see in some of the side-galleries where the ore had been extracted. It was all pretty extensive down there, with numerous galleries and passageways, almost an underground grid of streets and squares. The noise of the drilling machines was a constant backdrop, a rumbling sound rolling round and round through the tunnels. At one point we passed the conveyor taking the rock back to the elevator system that lifted it to the surface. There were small vehicles constantly moving around, some with fork-lifts, some with shovels, others of indeterminate purpose. It struck me that they all seemed quite new, of modern design, and I commented on that to one of the Russians, who agreed proudly that the new management had put in a great deal of investment in equipment in the mid-nineties; in fact, he told me, the only piece of kit which really harked back to the forties was the train system that we had used from the bottom of the cage. That was the sole relic of the old days. That made me think for a moment; the slave labour Andrey and I had been talking about in the forest at Igarka must have travelled on those same rail wagons we had used. Somehow, that brought it home a bit; they had sat on those wagons day after day, shift after shift, all those years ago. What had it been like to be down here then, with no hope of escape? For us, it was an interesting morning outing; for them, this had been their entire lives. It sent a shiver down my spine, despite the warm clammy air at that depth.

Back on the surface, they lunched us in the executive dining room, where Shumsky answered questions about the mine, almost managing to send some members of the party to sleep as he ploughed through various statistical analyses.

Chapter Fourteen

After lunch, as we clambered back on to the bus to take us to our next destination, the smelter, Andrey swung into the seat next to me.

"Enjoy the mine?" he asked.

"Yeah, it was interesting. The actual mine equipment was more modern than I'd expected. But I kept thinking that that train we were on was the exact same one the slave labourers had been on. It was a strange feeling."

"Yes, I got the impression from Igarka that you're quite interested in that part of the history. So I thought I'd tell you that I've had to rearrange the schedule, because of yesterday's delays. As you know, we should have gone to the port at Dudinka yesterday and then we were going to look at the museum and the historical stuff tomorrow morning. Well, I've had to reschedule Dudinka for tomorrow, which means cancelling the museum. Now, although you are all supposed to be kept together, if you want to dip out of Dudinka and go on your own to the museum, since that's what interests you, that would be OK. I've checked that they would let you in without the party, and they will be co-operative." He looked at me. "So it's up to you. Ice-bound port, with a lunch that is almost certainly going to be a massive vodka-toasting session – there's nothing else to do there – or the history lesson?"

I grinned. "This may seem odd, but I'm going to go for the history. I don't know why, but it's begun to fascinate me."

"OK, I'll tell you how to get there this evening. Now, the smelter; you know you said you were impressed by the modern kit down the mine? Well, don't expect the same at the smelter. It's still the original and looks like it's held together with bits of string. You know the pollution from this place is huge? Well, most of that comes out of the smelters. Norilsk has the highest level of sulphur pollution anywhere on the planet. I work for the place, and I'm prepared to admit it is horrendous. But" – he made an open gesture with his hands – "it does the job and brings in the profits. To be honest, if it were left to me, I wouldn't show this to visitors. All it does is reinforce their view that we Russians don't care about pollution, when the real truth is that it will be improved, but we can't do everything at once. At the moment, we still cannot do anything with the sulphur. Every other smelter in the world converts it to sulphuric acid and sells it – mostly at a loss, to be truthful – but we can't do that. There is no way to ship it out of here. The management have plans to do things, but they won't happen for another ten years. So, the sulphur just goes up the chimneys and the life expectancy is the lowest in the country, something just over forty years. It's not the mining that is the real danger, the real killer, it's the smelting and the effluent it produces. They're doing their best up here, but they inherited a nightmare from the old system." He shook his head, sadly. "It's the same thing we were talking about before – if the people don't matter because they're just a replaceable economic input, then you just don't care."

As the bus rolled in through the gates and we got off to stand waiting outside the smelter buildings, I began to see what he meant. The mine environment had been basic but workmanlike and looked active and efficient. Here, the sheds were tired-looking, the ground where the snow had been trodden away was formed of cinders, and pipes and electric cables criss-crossed the spaces between the buildings seemingly at random. The smell of the polluted air caught in my throat and made my eyes sting. They took us quickly through the plant, embarrassed, I think, to be showing it to visitors from the west. My over-riding memory is of the difficulty we all had in breathing, so noxious was the air. It was not difficult to believe Andrey's life-expectancy statistic. For all of us from London, more used to sitting round boardroom tables discussing prices, it was a day to remind us of the reality of the product in which we dealt.

It was still daylight as we drove back into the town, giving us the first real chance to see it. It was a strange mixture – mostly brutalist architecture from the Stalin era, with the odd elegant, almost St Petersburg-like arched building dropped in amongst it. We passed the first house built, in 1921, a simple wooden cabin, preserved near the centre of the town as a memorial to the founders. It made me think a bit about the nature of the place; such brutal conditions, so many hundreds of miles from anywhere else, it was an impressive feat to have managed to build a town, let alone develop a world-size mining operation. I said as much to Andrey.

"Yes," he replied. "I know you have been thinking a lot about the forced labour issue, but just put that aside for a moment. The founders had remarkable foresight in believing that they would ever be able to mine and produce in these conditions. We're judging it from the point of view of our own time, but that's not entirely fair. The world of the thirties, forties and fifties was very different here, and they lived according to the ways of those times. We cannot condone that, but neither should we simply condemn. They made one of the world's major mining facilities. I have no stomach for the old system, but we shouldn't ignore the developments they made. They were no more than a stepping stone in Russia's history, leading to where we are now."

In some ways, it was a fair point, I mused. All societies have some guilty secrets in their past, so why should this be looked at any differently?

Chapter Fifteen

The next morning, I watched the rest of the group board the bus taking them to visit the port of Dudinka, and then wandered off along the broad boulevards of the centre of Norilsk. The bright sky of the previous day had surrendered again to the cloudy grey snow-flecked weather of a couple of days ago. After a few hundred metres, I realised I would have to walk a bit quicker to keep warm. No time for leisurely tourism in Arctic Siberia. Andrey had marked my route on a tourist map, which had some facts about the town in English as well as Russian, and I looked at the town as I walked. The map informed me that Norilsk and Murmansk shared the title of the most northerly city on Earth, with the latter being slightly the larger. The first house in Norilsk, which we had seen from the bus the previous afternoon, dated from the early 1920s, but it was not really until the establishment of the Norillag camp system in the early-mid 30s to service the development of the mine that the population really started to grow. I found it impossible even to imagine how it would have been, arriving in such an unwelcoming environment, tasked with building both a city and a major mine. Before that, I supposed the only human activity would have been seasonal visits from fur-trappers. And for the prisoners arriving in the camps, it must have been unbelievably grim. As Andrey had suggested when we were looking around at Igarka, many of them would have been European Russian intellectuals, dumped in such a totally alien place. I'd travelled a lot and seen many different environments to which humans had successfully adapted themselves, but this was without doubt the toughest. And yet, looking around me, I saw, not in truth a city to rival the elegance or attractiveness of many others, but nevertheless a functioning environment in which people were carrying on their daily lives.

Musing on the development of Norilsk I may have been, but I found myself walking faster and faster in an attempt to keep warm. Soon I arrived at the doors of the city museum. It was a red-brick building with imposing white pillars framing the entry. On the desk were two people, a formidable, very well-built middle-aged woman and a thin youngish man with gold-rimmed glasses and a balding head. True to his word, Andrey had phoned them to let them know that a lone, non-Russian-speaking visitor would be arriving, and once they had checked my passport to ascertain that I was indeed that person, they were charm itself in their welcome. Well, it's not exactly on the tourist circuit, so I guess they didn't get too many visitors, especially on a weekday morning.

The woman was obviously the cashier, but she waved away my attempts to pay the entry fee with a beaming smile; the man seemed to be a curator and very proudly welcomed me in excellent English. He clearly saw it as his job to escort me around the exhibits to make sure I got the full experience. There was a lot of geological stuff, background as to how the mineral deposits were formed and so on, and I soon learned that my thoughts about the lack of indigenous population was completely wrong, because we passed a large display of cultural exhibits of the Taymyr aborigines. I metaphorically took my hat off to them – surviving in this habitat without modern heating was something I wouldn't have enjoyed.

As we wandered past the showcases, my companion explained a little about the history of the museum itself; most of it was largely forgettable, but one thing stuck in my mind. In the early days, indeed until 1948, the museum itself was a closed display – under the control of the NKVD. So the museum telling the story of the closed city was itself a closed exhibit, all held under the control of the secret police. I had difficulty getting my mind around that one. Anyway, we got to the modern period, with photographs of the original explorers who started the construction of the city, a model of the original mine surface workings and diagrams of how it operated underground. Then we reached the items about the camps and their inmates. There were a few photographs of camp buildings, there was a display board with a summary of the Stalinist system of labour, and some background information about the purges and how their victims had contributed to the development of the mines. This was the stuff I had come to see, and my companion, sensing that I would like to spend a little more time here, left me to my own devices. The photographs were fascinating; I'd seen the remains of a bit of watchtower at Igarka, but now I could understand better how it all fitted together. The huts were in rows and there seemed to be an open space in the centre, between them. There looked to be a pair of wire fences surrounding the whole camp area, but there were no close-ups so it was impossible to make out any detail of the people who could be seen. You couldn't really see which were guards and which were prisoners, although it was just possible to perceive the forms of the guards in the watchtowers. I spent some time here, looking at the pictures and reading the captions and display boards, which – somewhat surprisingly – were in English as well as Russian.

I walked into the next section and found myself in a mock-up of the interior of a prison hut. Bare bunk-beds, bare floorboards and bare walls; and on the walls, some drawings, grey charcoal on off-white paper, unframed.

Beyond Stalingrad

I crossed to look at the first of the drawings. It was a portrait of a man – a prisoner, I guessed – with a cadaverous face, shaven head and eyes staring blankly into nothing. It was a portrait of despair. And then my eye caught the signature at the bottom.

It was like a kick in the stomach; the intertwined A and K, with a date vertically between them. This was one of my uncle's. I looked at the others, not taking in the works themselves, but just the signature. It was the same on all of them. I stepped back, and tried to get my mind around what I was seeing. I was dumfounded. If he was last seen at Stalingrad, did this mean he had subsequently been here? Or were the pictures brought in from somewhere else? I looked at them, more closely now. There were four other simple portraits, all with the same hopelessness of spirit oozing out of them, the blank eyes and emaciated, deathly faces; then, across the other side of the section, there were three drawings of men at work. The first two, to an Englishman, looked like something out of the early days of the industrial revolution. Men, on their hands and knees, were hauling wagons full of rock up an incline through a narrow tunnel. Next to it, a group stood, caught in the act of emptying much bigger trucks into a giant furnace. There was no colour, but the ferocious heat of the flames was clear in the sweat poring down their bare torsos. Their chests were almost concave and their arms skeletal. The last picture showed a group formed up in almost military ranks, standing on a parade ground with snow falling around them. Behind them was a row of – presumably – guards, armed with rifles which they held at the ready.

Chapter Sixteen

I walked back and found the curator. I beckoned him to follow me, and then, pointing at the drawings, asked "Do you know who drew these? Where did they come from?"

He looked curiously at me, shrugged, and replied "They came from a prison camp, I suppose. I don't know who drew them, I would suppose it was a prisoner, or maybe a guard. They have been in the archive for a long time, but we only put them on display when we expanded this part of the museum concerning the prison camp. That was two or three years ago."

"So you don't know the name of the artist, or what happened to him?"

He shook his head. "No, I was just told to fetch some of the pictures out of the archive and put them on display."

"Some? Do you mean there are others here as well?"

"Yes, there are some others downstairs. They are all very good. They capture the hopelessness of the prisoners really well, don't you agree? Whoever the artist was, he was clearly very talented." He pointed. "You can see his signature here, at the bottom, 'AK'. When I first saw the drawings, I tried to research if there was any record of this signature anywhere in the art world, but nobody knew anything of it. I suppose he probably didn't make it out of the camp, in the end." He sighed. "Clearly, a great talent, but I guess we'll never know his name."

I paused for a moment, trying to organise my thoughts. I knew from the letter my father had given me all those years ago that Armin had last been reported seen as the battle of Stalingrad finished, on the day of the surrender. If - as one had to assume - he had been taken prisoner, it was possible that he had ended up here. I knew there had been a prison camp, although it seemed that had been mostly filled with Russian political prisoners. But if I made my interest clear straight away, I risked that the man may be evasive, and not tell me whatever he knew. There may still be some sensitivities about the whole gulag system.

"Yes," I said, "they're very expressive. As you say, the artist was clearly very talented. But that signature, 'AK', is in roman lettering; surely it must be a prisoner, and not a Russian? A guard or a Russian prisoner would have used Cyrillic, wouldn't they?"

"Yes, that's true," he replied, a little shortly.

"You say there are other pictures; could I look at those, do you think?"

Beyond Stalingrad

He looked at me. "Not immediately. I would have to get permission to let anybody in to see the archive. We select items to put on display and retain others to rotate with them from time to time. But I could ask, if you particularly want to see them. Probably it should not be too much of a problem. If you wait here, I could call the director now."

I nodded. "Thank you, I would be most interested to see the others." He walked off, leaving me alone. I sat on the edge of one of the bunks and stared at the pictures. What I really needed was to see the records of the prison camp. Somewhere, there must be a tally kept of the names of those incarcerated. It was unlikely that that information would come from the museum, but perhaps Andrey could help me. It was just about possible that there could be some survivors from that time still living here in Norilsk. I stood up and looked more closely at the signatures on the drawings. As ever, Armin had written the date in small characters between the open arms of the 'K'. The dates ranged from 1949 to 1951. That meant he had lived for at least eight years after the surrender. It also meant that any survivors – even if they had been sent to the camp at a very young age – would have to be in their seventies, at least. That seemed a tall order, requiring them not only to have lived through the camp regime but also to have survived the poisonous atmosphere of Norilsk for many, many years. On the other hand, some of the passengers on the flight had looked pretty old, so it was not a complete impossibility.

I wondered also about the Russian records of prisoners of war. I knew from what my father had told me about my grandfather's searches that the German records were largely non-existent, but the Russians may have kept track. But in the chaos of the ruins of the city? Would they actually have cared who their prisoners were? Looking at the drawings, I could see each prisoner had a number stencilled on his clothing – would the Russians, in the aftermath of Stalingrad, have bothered to record anything other than those numbers about their captives? If they had been swept into the forced labour system, then they would have been as disposable as Andrey had described earlier. Why would they care about any more than that? But I could at least try and find out.

The curator came back. "I have spoken to the director about your wish to see the other pictures by this unknown artist in the archive. Unfortunately, he is not prepared to allow visitors into the archive collection; that is our standard policy, I'm afraid." He must have seen the look of disappointment on my face as he continued, "However, in the circumstances of a visitor from Britain, he is prepared to have some more of the pictures brought up into the museum so that you may see them. We could have this done tomorrow morning." He smiled. "I hope that is acceptable to you. The director was most anxious that we should do our best to satisfy a visitor who has come so far and shown such interest in our museum."

I thought quickly. Our flight back to Moscow was scheduled to leave tomorrow morning, so it would probably mean missing it. That would no doubt create visa issues, as my permission to be in Norilsk was directly linked to being part of the group. On the other hand, I could not ignore the opportunity to discover more about my uncle's fate. I would have to give Andrey the problem of extending my permission.

I nodded to him. "OK, I'll be here tomorrow morning. And thank you, I appreciate your help."

He smiled. "It's not often we get foreign visitors. We're rather away from traditional tourist country. But, if I may say, you obviously have some particular interest in these pictures. May I ask what it is?"

I hesitated. But he seemed genuine, so why not? "I think I recognise the signature on them. I have seen it before, and I'm curious to know what became of the man. Are there any records still in existence of the fate of the prisoners?"

"Yes, in fact we have some of this kind of information in the archive. But again, it's not normally publicly available." He paused, clearly debating whether or not to say something. Then, deciding, he continued, "You understand that there is still a concern that the excesses of the Stalin era are not something that we are proud of today. It's a part of our history that we really do not like the rest of the world to put under scrutiny. So I cannot myself give you access to that information, but I can request it from the director. In order to help me persuade him, perhaps you could give me a bit more background, more detail about yourself?"

I didn't want to tell him that the artist was a relative of mine; a direct relationship might cause them to clam up, reluctant to acknowledge what their predecessors had done, just as he had hinted. Time for a little prevarication. "I've seen a couple of pictures with that same signature in a house in England. I believe the artist was German. But were there any Germans here?"

"Well, I believe there were a few. You know, there were in the end many Germans taken prisoner-of-war, especially in the advance by the Red Army to Berlin. Numbers are difficult to be totally sure of, but the best estimates I am aware of suggest a bit more than two million. Of those, many were put to forced labour, although in most cases they were kept separately from the Russian political prisoners. But there were some cases, particularly where the prisoners were from the SS, where they were sent to the non-military camps, that is, into the Gulag system. There were some of these prisoners, taken after the surrender of Stalingrad, who were sent to the Norillag, which was the camp system here in Norilsk, during the second half of 1943. Maybe this man was one of them. Do you know any details at all? His name, his SS rank? Anything like that?"

"I believe his name was Armin Kuhlmann, hence the 'AK' signature. But was it only SS people who came here?"

"Well, obviously it's difficult so many years later to be absolutely certain, but that is what I have been told. Or at least, SS and the military Feldgendarmerie. They were sent to these tougher camps as a kind of revenge for what they had done as they advanced through Ukraine and Russia. The massacres, the burning and looting."

That sounded wrong. The letter my father had shown me made it clear that Armin had been amongst the front-line Wehrmacht troops, not behind the lines where the odious SS killings had taken place. So why would he have been caught up in that kind of retribution?

"How long were they here?"

"Again, difficult for me to say with certainty. Although there were Germans who were not released until maybe 1954, 1955, most were sent back by around 1951. But that was from the regular military POW camps. What the NKVD did here was not necessarily in line with that. I'm sure many of those who came here died here – that was true of all prisoners here. It was a very tough place." He gestured with his hands. "They were not treated well. They worked at very physical tasks, down the mine or in the smelter, in extremely harsh conditions. The weather and the pollution alone make this a difficult environment, let alone the work and the inadequate food they had. It's part of history now, we can't change it; but it is not a part to be proud about. Anyway, I would guess that any survivors here of the Germans would certainly have been repatriated by the end of 1955. The camp continued, though, until the middle of 1956. By then, the prisoners were not only working on the mine combine, but effectively were involved in all the economic activity of the region. Some were even made into fishermen! When the camp finally closed, many remained here; they had by then really nowhere else to go, especially the long-term prisoners, those who had been here for twenty or twenty-five years." He must have seen the look of shock on my face, for he continued, "Oh yes, twenty-five years was the standard sentence for certain political crimes. I suspect, though, that very few indeed managed to live through the full sentence."

"So if there are still any survivors, maybe they will know about this man?"

He grimaced. "I think that's a big if. There may be some who are still alive, but personally I doubt it. Look, I would like to help you. Come into my office; we can have a cup of coffee and think about how we should proceed. My name is Mikhail, by the way, Mikhail Khorsky."

"Thank you. I'm Alex Butterfield." Gravely, we shook hands, and he led me into a cubby-hole with a desk, a chair for a visitor and papers littering every surface. He cleared the visitor chair, gestured for me to sit and took his place behind his desk.

"So, it's nice to find somebody who is interested in the events of that time. Most people here are still reluctant to talk about it; I had to struggle hard to establish this part of the museum. Most of the people in positions of authority in the town are still from the Soviet era, and it is almost second nature to them to avoid talking about these matters.

"But first, we must sort out your stay. When the man from the mining company called to check that we could admit you today, he mentioned that you were part of a party which will leave tomorrow. That's why today was the only possibility. So, I suppose your group will take the morning flight to Moscow, which means your permit would expire after tomorrow. I will call the director and explain, and as long as he agrees then I can arrange for you to be allowed to stay longer, as we can sponsor you as an academic visitor to the museum. It will need a bit of persuasion, but I should be able to arrange it. Excuse me while I make the phone calls."

He spent the next ten or fifteen minutes on the phone, while I wandered back out into the museum. I stood in front of the pictures Armin had drawn. The portraits were particularly unsettling, the vacant zombie-like faces staring out. I tried to imagine the horror of being cut off from everything he had known, dumped in this alien landscape amongst people who probably hated him. And then the labour; I'd read books about the Gulag, but he had actually been in it. Then my mind flipped back to the SS issue. It was quite clear from the letter I had seen that he had been captured – presumably – as a regular Wehrmacht panzer soldier. How and why had he got swept into the camp with the SS? The chances of survival in any of the camps must have been low, but from what Mikhail had intimated, it was even lower here than elsewhere. I thought of all the effort and money my grandfather had expended to try and discover the fate of his son, and then I had seemingly just blundered into it just by pure chance.

I heard Mikhail put the phone down and strolled back into his office. He smiled at me.

"OK, that is all arranged. We have extended your stay as a guest of the museum. The hotel will be able to make the changes to your documents this evening. The director has agreed that tomorrow as well as seeing the other pictures, we may search the archive to see if we can find any reference to the man you seek." He rubbed his hands together. "This is quite exciting. It would be great for the museum if we could really find an attribution for the work. Who knows, if they could then be exhibited elsewhere, that would be real kudos for us." His face fell for a moment. "But actually, they may well not be allowed out of here – those sensitivities I spoke of before are not restricted to Norilsk. There are many people who do not want to see the events of that era revisited.

"First things first, though. Let us prepare what we already know." He pulled a pad towards him and picked up a pen.

"So, first, you say his name was?"

"Armin Kuhlmann."

Beyond Stalingrad

He noted it. "OK, and any other information you have about him? Any details may make our search easier."

"He was a junior officer in a Panzer regiment at Stalingrad. He was last seen alive the day they surrendered, I think in the centre of the city. After that, there is no trace. He was twenty-five years old and had been through the whole Russian campaign. He had the first and second class iron cross."

"Where did he come from? Do we know anything of his background?"

I hesitated. I didn't want to get into a discussion of his family background for the moment. "Well, he was conscripted in Hamburg in early 1939, as far as I know. I believe he was a student at the university there. But I'm puzzled by your reference to the SS. As far as I know, he was regular army, not SS, so I don't understand why he would have been with SS prisoners."

"Well, we should not forget that things then were quite chaotic. It was in the middle of a war. It's quite possible that he was wrongly categorised in the confusion. After all, we know that many people were quite erroneously imprisoned in the camps without having done anything wrong at all. I would guess they were more likely to err on the side of taking more people than to risk letting SS men escape what they felt was due to them. I know that initially the Germans at Stalingrad were all held in transit camps before being sent to their final destinations, so that again would have given potential for confusion. But the records are quite sparse, anyway. Mostly, they just list a name against a camp number; those guarding them had no interest in knowing any more than that. But where there are records of release, those are much more detailed. I don't really know how the process operated, but presumably they were obliged to give the German authorities some means of identifying who was being repatriated. So for those who died here, the information is very scanty, whereas for those few – and it really was very few – who left alive, we have more knowledge."

I nodded. "I think it unlikely that he would have been one of the ones who survived – I think something would have been heard of him if that were the case. So probably we must assume that he died at some point. Is there a cemetery, or burial ground or something?"

He gave me a strange look. "No. You must remember, the authorities had no interest in these people, except insofar as they could be used as a workforce. When they died, they were just buried in mass grave pits, with no markings. To be honest, we don't know where. It's amazing how quickly knowledge dies from one generation to the next. There is a memorial in the town." He looked at his watch. "Perhaps we could go now and look at it, if you would like?"

"Yeah, OK, that sounds good."

Chapter Seventeen

As we got into his car – a rather dilapidated old Volvo – he explained: "The memorial is a little outside the city, at the bottom of Mount Schmidt. It's not really a mountain, of course, but as you may have seen, it's quite a noticeable feature. The memorial is to all the prisoners who passed through the camps. You know, I suppose, that the so-called Norillag camp system comprised a number of different camps, mostly clustered around Norilsk, but also including Dudinka and, I believe, even some as far away as Krasnoyarsk. There were also some agricultural camps spread out from here. In total, probably around 400000 prisoners passed through the system. We will be able to check more accurately tomorrow, but I think the majority were Russians and Ukrainians, and about three quarters were political prisoners." He glanced across at me. "Although I suppose you could probably make a case for saying that all were actually political prisoners, in reality; that's the truth of that time. There were few Germans, but I guess the ones there were would pretty much have been SS." As he spoke, we were bowling along a wide road towards the edge of town. Traffic jams were certainly not a problem in Norilsk and soon he drew up next to the memorial.

I don't really know what I had expected, but I've seen the Memorial to the Missing at Thiepval on the Somme, with Lutyens' soaring arches over the lovingly-engraved names of the missing; I sort of thought in those terms. I was wrong. This was a small, triple-arch construction in wood, with a sloping roof and a little onion tower topped with a cross. There was a bell hanging in each of the arches. Snow lay around it, with just the odd patch of the ubiquitous cinder ground sticking through here and there. It was on a small rise, with Mount Schmidt a little way behind it and in front, as the ground dipped away, one had a panorama of the combine. Filthy coloured smoke was pouring from a clutch of chimneys and trucks and fork-lifts were scurrying about their business between the buildings. I thought again of Thiepval and its beautifully tended, peaceful avenues of green grass and trees, and wondered. Were those commemorated here not also the victims of war? The undeclared war of totalitarianism on its people? I looked at Khorsky. "Is there no list of names somewhere? The dead it is commemorating?"

"No, there's nothing like that. This is actually on the site of one of the burial pits. It's not clear how many people were buried in the various different places; indeed, we don't really know for sure how many pits there were, and I think the monument was put here just because it is slightly elevated and maybe a bit quieter than the other places. There was a camp behind here; so for the prisoners, that view down to the factory was what they would see each day as they were marched down to work. You can see the pollution coming out of those chimneys now; although they have still much work to do, this is after some years of clean-up. So you can imagine how bad it must have been in the forties and fifties, when the camps were at their most active."

"Yes." Looking down over the factories, I pondered that for a bit. How could it have been, seeing that sight every day, knowing you would be here for years and years, at best, and at worst that you would die here? It again brought home what Andrey and then Khorsky had both said – the men weren't seen as individuals, they were just like one of those trucks or forklifts down there: consumable equipment, to be used until they were worn out and then discarded.

We stood in silence, looking at the scene for a few minutes and then the nagging cold got through my overcoat and I shivered. "Let's go," said Khorsky. "Perhaps we could have some lunch?"

"That would be nice. It's getting a bit cold here."

He grinned at me as we got back into the Volvo. "It took me my whole first winter here to get used to that. For that year, I was cold the whole time and I wished I'd never taken this job when I could have been on the Black Sea or somewhere where I could be warm. But then, once you do acclimatise to it, you can live with it." He started the engine and we drove off, to a restaurant he chose about ten minutes away.

Over lunch, he told me a bit more about himself and what had drawn him to Norilsk. He'd studied history at Moscow University and had become fascinated by the twentieth-century story of his own country. The job in Norilsk had included a specific brief to broaden the museum to include exhibits from and information about the Gulag system and how it had helped to create the modern-day mining complex and city. They were still in the process, under his direction, of developing that part of the museum and what I had seen was just the first part of the job. He was younger than me, and part of the last generation to have completed their studies entirely under the Soviet system, before it imploded. He talked a lot and was obviously very proud of the fact that his museum was facing up to the past head-on, and not shying away from the unpleasant aspects of how the city had grown and developed. Eventually, after a long lunch, he drove me back to the hotel and left me, urging me to be at the museum early the next morning so we had a full day to spend on the records.

Late in the afternoon, the rest of the party got back from their trip to Dudinka. They were fairly raucous, bearing out Andrey's indication that it had been a vodka-drinking exercise. We had dinner in the hotel, and then the Russians dragged the whole party off to Norilsk's trendiest bar, where drinking was interspersed with ten-pin bowling. Strange, but curiously enjoyable. I left at about one, leaving some of the guys still partying, and fell gratefully into bed. I had explained my change of plans to Andrey, who had duly made the necessary adjustments to his travel party documentation, so I was ready to go in the morning. I slept like a log, this time.

Chapter Eighteen

Promptly at nine the next morning – having left the rest of the group groggily eating a pre-flight breakfast – I arrived at the museum. Khorsky was waiting and led me through the back of the display area to a narrow staircase leading down into the basement. At the bottom, there was a central corridor with a number of doors leading off it to either side. We stood for a moment at the bottom of the stairs. "OK," he said, "I must make certain things clear to you before we go any further. Strictly speaking, the part of the archive we are going to look at is confidential and the property of the security services. They originally set this museum up, as a closed archive, in the late nineteen-forties, and we still technically come under their authority. Over the last few years, my director and I have slowly put some of the material from the Gulag era on show, as you have seen upstairs; like me, he believes the story of that time should be told. You know from my conversations with him yesterday that we have agreement for you to look at some of the contents of the archive, but you must agree that you will not attempt to photograph anything, nor will you publish any details of what you may see. There may also be some files which are sealed as confidential and we cannot look at those. Is all that OK with you?"

I nodded. "Yes, I have no interest in publishing anything and my concern is to see what happened to this one man, the artist. So I can agree with all that."

"Good. Let's go and look first at the other drawings down here. With those, we are not sure whether to continue showing only some, as we do at present, and rotating those with the ones currently stored down here, or to exhibit them all, all the time. They're just in here. Follow me." He led the way into the first room on the right-hand side. It was dusty, concrete-floored, with a single light-bulb dangling from the ceiling. There were pictures stacked against the walls, and he went straight to the ones opposite the door and began looking through them. "Here we are. The light's not very good, but you can see they are very similar to the ones upstairs." I stepped across as he lifted the drawings one by one out of the stack and propped them up for me to see. They were indeed clearly in the same vein as the others, again the dead eyes in cadaverous faces staring out hopelessly. It was impossible not to be moved by the power of these seemingly simple grey/black drawings with their message of despair and desolation.

"There's no denying that these are very potent works," said Khorsky. "Personally, I think we would be better to show only some at a time, as we do at present, but the director feels that we should have one wall of that end of the museum devoted to them and display all at once. I think that would be too much for most visitors; as I said, we are still discussing it."

"Mmm. I think I agree with you. After all, you're trying to interest people in the story, not frighten them." I squatted down in front of the pictures to see the dates on the signature. They were all 1949 and 1950. I got up and stood back, looking at them. I pointed. "Look, that one. That shows where we were yesterday, with the mountain in the background. There's the camp, and that must be the track they followed down to the factory each day. You can see watchtowers in the background."

"Yes, I remember seeing that one before. Upstairs, there is a photograph in the display taken from almost the same place. But come, we can come back to these. Let's go and see what we can find in the records." He led the way out and down the corridor to another door, on the opposite side. He opened it, revealing rows and rows of filing cabinets.

"OK," he said. "Again, I must explain some things to you. The first records we will look for are the details of those German prisoners who were repatriated. We do that because those are the best records. Although the Soviets did not particularly care about details of their captives, when they sent them back, they had to supply that detail to the Germans, where they were sending them. So at that point, they did record names, military rank and, very often but not always, the military number, together with details of where they were going to be sent. So, if we don't find his name there, it probably means he was not repatriated. That means then that we have two possibilities. We can look for his name coming in to the camp, and we can look at the lists of those who died. Those records, I would say, unfortunately may not be complete. Some of the arrivals are well-documented, others are not. We will need to guess at the time of arrival, as closely as we can, and then start looking either side of that time, to try and cover it. The death records are frankly the least reliable. I suppose it is inevitable, given the way they used these prisoners, that the authorities were not too concerned about the detail of their deaths; once they were dead, they were of no more use, so why bother keeping details of them? The other reason for starting with the list of repatriations is that it is the shortest. There were few Germans here, and even fewer sent back."

He led the way into the room. "So once we have checked the repatriations, then what we want next will be in that bank of files there." He pointed to one set of shelves towards the back of the room. "So, you think he was taken at Stalingrad." I nodded. "OK, so that was February 1943. Now, we know that initially the prisoners from there were held in the Stalingrad area for some weeks, even months, before they were moved

Beyond Stalingrad

to their final destination. So if we guess that he would not have come here before, say, April of that year, and that the last of the Stalingrad survivors to come here had arrived by September/October of that year, we need to look for records from that six-month period, to start with. Of course, it could be complicated if he had been somewhere else, and was then transferred to the Norillag later, but let's work on the easiest assumptions first. Unfortunately, as I have not yet told you" – he grinned across at me – "to make our task more difficult, this archive here also has details from two or three other camps – don't ask me why, but it does. And there is no central list of names, we have to look at each discharge document individually. And they are in Russian, so you may have difficulty. I think what I might do is write the name in Cyrillic, so you can see what you are looking for. Anything that looks vaguely similar, you must tell me and I can check. But we will need two of us working in order to finish today. So, if you start from April 1943 and work forwards, I will start from October that same year and work backwards. Let me show you first of all what the documents look like, then let's start with the repatriations and go on from there."

It wasn't long before I realised why I was a trader and not an archivist or museum curator. We sat at a small table in the dusty room and ploughed through the files. It was tedious and difficult, because although Khorsky had written out for me the key words in Cyrillic letters that I should be looking for, a lot of the papers were handwritten and I had to go over them very slowly to be sure I didn't miss what I was seeking. A number of times I excitedly thought I had found something, only for him to point out on checking that I had mistaken the writing. It was hot down in the basement; I guess we were not too far from the boiler that heated the building. After a couple of hours I had to take a break, and sat back in my chair rubbing my eyes. We were about three quarters of the way through – Khorsky was able to work far faster than me, as he could skim the documents since he understood them, rather than painstakingly seeking patterns as I was. I got up to stretch my legs, then thought of something.

"Even if we don't find him here, these are the people I could contact to ask if any of them knew him."

He looked up at me, half way through reading a document. "Yes, but in reality, how many of them do you think are still alive? And finding them may be difficult. We know from these papers where they were sent to, but there's no reason to suppose they stayed there. They could be anywhere in Germany. Or indeed, they could have left the country."

"Mmm. I s'pose so." I sat down again and resumed my tedious task.

Half an hour later, we reached the end of that batch of files. We had drawn a blank, although we had the names of all German prisoners who had been repatriated from the Norillag camp system, together with the names of the towns to which they had been sent, either by train to the border or by ship to a seaport."

"OK, so he wasn't repatriated. That means that the likelihood is that he died here, although it's also possible he was sent to another camp. We should now start to sift through the records of arrivals."

"It's all a bit haphazard, isn't it? We know the records are very unlikely to be completely accurate, so even when we find nothing, we can't be sure enough to rule out that possibility. Was there really no definitive listing of who was imprisoned?"

Khorsky paused for a moment, before answering. "Umm, for the Russian prisoners, I believe there would be. The problem is that the Germans were caught in such a confused way, in the middle of a war, sometimes even with a battle still going on around them, that they were just sent en masse back to holding camps, and from there simply despatched as a total number to the labour camps." He pondered for a moment. "Actually, there may be one other thing worth trying. The bulk of the German prisoners were actually taken after the Stalingrad time, as the Red Army advanced westwards. They were simply caught unable to retreat as fast as the Russians were moving forward; that's when the logistics became most difficult. The numbers at Stalingrad perhaps did not swamp the system immediately. Normally, when prisoners arrived at a camp, they were numbered. That number was then their camp identity and was worn on their uniform, and was then the way they were known to the system. It's possible that when the Germans arrived here they were treated in this way, just as the Russian prisoners had always been. I do know that later on in the war, when the huge numbers were taken, this formality was generally overlooked. However, we could see if the arrival record here was correctly kept." He sat back in his chair for a moment, his face eager. This was, of course, his world, and if he had found a new angle to speed up research, well, that's what he enjoyed. Me, I just wanted to find the record of one man. Khorsky continued: "The only problem is, that record is actually classified. Because it's the one that links prisoner names and numbers, it's regarded as more sensitive."

State secrets or lies, I didn't care about that. "Is it stored in here as well?"

"Yes, the classified files are all kept down here, but in a different room."

"So nobody apart from you and me would know if we looked at it?"

"That's true. But as I told you, we here do report to the security service, so I would be seriously exceeding my powers if I were to let you see those files. On the other hand, it would be a coup for the museum to be able to attribute the drawings. I don't know. Anyway, let's take a break and go upstairs for a coffee. I need to think about this, because I do believe it may be the solution for us."

Beyond Stalingrad

It was a relief to get out of the dusty, stuffy basement room and back up into the museum. I understood that Khorsky was in a bit of a dilemma; He wanted to achieve the same end as me, but he needed to do so in a way such that his methods would not be subject to too much scrutiny. I sensed that pressing him may be counterproductive, so I sat quietly opposite him in his office while he looked through some of the paperwork on his desk. The silence wore on. Then, finally, he sat back in his chair and looked at me with a smile.

"OK, my friend. I think I can see how we do this. If you can wait up here, then I can go and investigate those particular files, which I have the authority to do. If my hopes prove valid and I find a reconciliation between names and numbers, then that will help, because then we will also have a possible list of prisoners who arrived at Norillag at the same time as Kuhlmann. We can then check those names against the list we already have of those who were repatriated. If any appear there, then you will know who to search for in Germany. Of course, that still doesn't cover the case if they are all dead, but it's a starting point. What do you think?"

"I think that sounds good. Thank you. You're being very helpful."

"Well, I'm also intrigued by the problem. We can't just keep shying away from what happened, pretending it never took place. If we keep hiding things, the world will continue to distrust us. So really, it's in everybody's interest. Although I don't think they would all realise it. So, if you can wait here, then I will go and see what I can find. I warn you, it may still take a while." With that, he walked off towards the stairway.

I had a long wait. To begin with, I sat finishing my coffee in his office. Then I took another tour of the museum, this time spending a bit more time on the Taymyr region aboriginal stuff. It was interesting, in the sense that I hadn't known any of this before, but frankly I could see why Khorsky was so keen to develop the twentieth century part of the displays. That would be what he could use to try to attract more visitors, although stuck up above the Arctic Circle, it was never going to be massive in the tourist business. Eventually, I got round to Armin Kuhlmann's drawings again. I stood for a long while looking at them; no matter what I did, I couldn't get my mind round the idea of the desperation they showed. What must it have been like to face the fact that your life was as a slave up here, thousands of miles from home and with only a slim prospect of ever getting back there? However much German aggression had brought their fate upon them, surely it couldn't have been right to have exacted such an inhumane punishment? These places were evil, whether they were in Germany, Poland, Russia or anywhere else, and regardless of which side ran them. I was glad my mother and her siblings had been spared the pain of seeing or learning about this place. But now, a generation further on, I felt certain that I had to do everything I could to find out the details of what had happened. I couldn't believe Armin had been sent back to Germany – if he had, the first thing he would have done would be to have contacted his family. And if he hadn't, then the inescapable conclusion was that he had died. That my mother's brother had been worked to death as a slave. It was a grotesque thought, at the end of the twentieth century. And he'd been like me - born and brought up in the supposed cradle of civilisation in Western Europe. Abruptly, I turned away from the pictures and went outside into the cold arctic air. Snow was again drifting in the breeze and the fumes belching out of the chimneys had settled over the city, giving the air a strange yellowish tinge. I shivered.

Chapter Nineteen

It was a long day. Khorsky appeared about half an hour after I went back inside and suggested that I might like to go and have some lunch while he ploughed on through the records, which I did. It was frustrating not to know whether or not we were really making progress or whether this would all turn out to be a complete waste of time. I would have explored the town a bit in the afternoon, but frankly it was too cold to be wondering around. Also, it's not a particularly prepossessing town, so I lingered over a couple of coffees after lunch, before making my way back to the museum. By late afternoon, I was bored with looking at the exhibits and beginning to get a bit twitchy. Since I hadn't seen any other visitors all day, I was also getting an idea of task Khorsky had in trying to grow the museum.

Eventually, he reappeared up the stairs and came over to the office, where I was sitting with a three-day old English newspaper I had brought with me from Moscow and re-discovered at the bottom of my briefcase. In his hand, he held a sheaf of papers.

"OK," he began, dropping into his chair, "I think we are making some good progress. First, as I had hoped, the arrivals at that stage of the war were still being recorded in the same way as internal prisoners, so I have found Kuhlmann's name and the camp number he was allotted. That's helpful. Here, look," he said, handing a sheet of paper to me, "this is a copy of the list." He pointed about halfway down. "There. That's him. There's his name and next to it his number."

I looked at it. It was in Cyrillic, so I couldn't actually read it, but it gave me a funny feeling; definite proof that my uncle had been one of the unfortunates imprisoned in this place. Khorsky went on. "So the other names on that list are fellow-prisoners who arrived at the same time as Kuhlmann." He took the list back from me. "That's the information you're not supposed to see, of course, because it links names with numbers. But if we can find any of these names on the list of the repatriated, that gives you the names of potential survivors who may have known him. It will still take me a while to match this list with that of the repatriated; perhaps you would prefer to return to the hotel, rather than wait here any longer? Then I can join you later with my findings."

Frankly, anything was better than another couple of hours waiting in the museum; I gratefully accepted his suggestion and took myself off.

I dozed in my room for a bit, then went down and sat in the bar with a beer or two. The place was pretty much deserted now that the rest of the party from London had left and when my mobile rang it sounded like the clappers of doom in the silence. It was Andrey, calling from Moscow.

"Hi, I've just got back from the airport. Guess what? Our flight was delayed, but not as long as on the way. Have you had a good day? Seen the stuff you wanted to see?"

"Yes, it's been interesting, thanks. I've seen a lot of stuff about the building of Norilsk, including the exhibition about the camps."

"Did you find out anything about the artist guy you were looking for?"

"I've spent a lot of time sitting looking at records with the museum guy, Khorsky. He's being very helpful. He's still going through some things trying to put together different bits of information to find the answer we want, hopefully."

"OK, well, look, just so you know, I got a bit of earache from one of the D-Gs about leaving you up there. I don't know how he knew, maybe the museum people told him, or somehow he found out that the hotel was extending your permit, but he was seriously not pleased. Reminded me that all that sort of stuff is still 'sensitive', even though we are supposedly becoming more transparent. It's not a problem, but just be aware that there are those who would rather you - or westerners in general - didn't have access to the sort of information you're looking for. You might warn the museum man - what's his name? Khorsky? - that people are aware." He laughed. "Don't worry, I'm sure nobody will come hammering on your door in the dead of night. That's not how it is any more!"

"Thanks Andrey, I'll sleep sounder for knowing that," I said sarcastically. "I'll be on planes all day tomorrow, so I'll speak to you when I'm back in London."

"Bye."

Maybe things were no longer how they had been, but I still found it slightly disturbing that people were not only interested in what I was doing, but also able to keep tracks on me so easily.

When Khorsky eventually came over to the hotel, I mentioned the call to him, before he started telling me how he had got on.

"Don't worry," he said. "I know my director mentioned your interest to a couple of people. He has to do that, for the sake of his own position. In the hierarchy of this town there are still quite a number who cannot get used to the new ways in the country since the system was changed. They still think in terms of trying to keep everybody in the dark as much as possible. And, to be fair, they were educated in that way, so the idea that all those dark things that happened during that time could be brought out into the light is unbelievable to them. But now you will maybe see why I wasn't going to let you see the confidential records. This way, nobody has done anything wrong, and it's just some old-style politicos who will be a bit upset.

"Now, I've got some names. There appear to be six people who were brought to the camp with Kuhlmann and who then were subsequently repatriated in 1954 and 1955."

"Six? Is that all? Out of all those who went there?"

"No, no, no. This is more precise than that. This is out of those who actually arrived in the same draft as him. Obviously over the whole summer and autumn of 1943, there were several drafts, but we can't precise them in the same way. No, this is the people who were brought with him, presumably from the same holding camp, and survived right through the whole time in the camp. We have to hope at least one of them is still alive and remembers him."

"Does the list give any idea of their ages? So we can guess whether there is any chance of them being alive?"

"No, there is no personal information. Just the name and the prison system number. It's not perfect, but it is the best we can get. So, here you can see the names and the points where they were handed over to the Germans; four were sent through Poland to the German border at Frankfurt-an-der-Oder, presumably they went by train. The other two were sent by sea to Hamburg." He grinned across at me. "Now it's going to be your turn to do the research in Germany, to see what happened to them and where they are now, if they are still alive. But it's already a big step for me here at the museum, because I can now attribute those pictures to an individual, known prisoner. We can show that information, and if you could give me any background you may know of this man, then we can really strengthen the display."

"Yes, I can see that. I'm still only half way; I've tracked him this far, but I still need to know what actually happened to him. I've no idea how you trace people in Germany, but I guess I'm going to find out. The easiest ones will probably be the ones in Hamburg. That's got to be a better bet than what used to be the DDR."

1999 London

Chapter Twenty

Sitting in Norilsk with Khorsky over dinner and a few glasses of wine, it had seemed pretty straightforward: ring up someone in the right position and ask them for details of six German citizens, then go and talk to any of them still alive about their time in the Russian prison camps. Back in London, three days later, sitting in my office in the City, it looked a lot more daunting. The major question to address first of all, was obviously, 'who is the someone?' I knew, in a vague sort of way, that the requirements to keep the authorities informed of your whereabouts were more exacting in Germany than in the UK, but beyond that it was all a bit of a mystery. Fortunately, my business brought me into contact with a lot of Germans, and indeed at that time we had a young trainee over in the office with us from one of our customers to teach him what we did. I called him in and gave him the task of ascertaining if any of the six names on my list could be traced, while I got on with my normal work.

That evening was the first real chance I had had to talk to my wife about what I had discovered in Norilsk and what I intended to do about it. She was interested from the point of view of history, but had reservations otherwise. "I can understand you think you want to know all the details, but are you sure? For your mother and your aunt and uncle, it would have been some sort of closure, I see that, but it's all so long in the past. It won't be a pretty story. I'm no expert in modern Russian history, but even I know enough to know that. At the moment, you know he was captured and imprisoned, and you assume he died. If you go chasing the details, you'll find out that maybe he starved to death, maybe he was worked to death or maybe he died of some ghastly disease. Are you – and your sisters and cousins – going to be better for knowing that? Don't you think it would be less painful for you all to leave things be? You could tell them you saw some of his pictures at Norilsk, so he must have been a prisoner there and then just let it go."

"Yeah, but I can't just do that, can I? If I hadn't seen the pictures, then I'd agree with you. After all, we've all known he disappeared all our lives; I've had that letter my father gave me for years without doing anything about it. You know, it's interesting history, but although when he first gave it to me I was all fired up to investigate, I never did, and probably never would have done. But now, now that I know a bit more and I've seen some of his work, I just think I have to find out as much as I can. I know it won't be a pretty story, but somehow it all seems so much closer now. I mean, look, he died up there, as you say, probably horribly; he was alone, well, not exactly alone, in a prison camp, but you know what I mean. Apart from all of his family – alone in that sense. Thousands of miles from home, caught by a war on the wrong side – and then just disappearing into oblivion. Don't you think I owe it to him to find out what I can, so that at least this generation can acknowledge what happened to him, so he doesn't just stay in limbo?"

"Mmm. I s'pose that sounds right. But I'm still concerned that what you find out may be really unpleasant."

"But doesn't that make it even more important that he's not just forgotten? In a way, I'm thinking that it's precisely because his death may have been so awful that we ought to know about it. Just so that we show there's somebody still thinking about him. It's a bit like the First World War memorials to the missing – people want to know there is a record of the passing of their relatives. The name engraved on the stone somehow proves they were real, even though that's all there is left. That's what this is - I just don't think we should forget about it, and ignore him. You'd feel the same if it were your uncle, I'm sure."

"Yes I would, I'm sure, and I'd want to do something, just like you. But I'm standing back and looking at this, and it's not quite the same as the missing from a battle. He wasn't killed on a battlefield, and his body just not found. He was - we have to assume - in some way worked to death, as a slave. Surely his memorial should be the pictures, if they're as good as you say. I'm just worried that you replace a degree of uncertainty with a reality that's too awful to contemplate - and I don't know that that will be good for all of you." She smiled. "But I don't think I'm going to change your mind, so I guess I'd better ask if there's anything I can do to help."

I did understand her point; but it was one of those awful positions where even though you know you won't like what you find, you have to keep on looking. I couldn't just let my uncle disappear again, back into the oblivion of the destruction of war.

"Thank you," I said. "I'm not sure if there is anything you can do for the moment. I've got to wait for now until Dieter comes back with something - if he does. I may of course get no further, if we can't trace any of those men, or if they are all dead by now."

"They'd be quite old, wouldn't they? And they've obviously had a tough life, at least for part of it. If we can't find them now, this is probably the last chance."

"I know. If we don't solve the issue now, it will just drift into history. But Dieter seemed to think that tracing them in Germany would probably not be too difficult. Their records are pretty exhaustive about their own citizens."

Chapter Twenty-One

It was in fact a week before Dieter came back to me and reported that he had some news. He walked in to my office with a smile on his face and announced that whatever jokes we British might like to make about it, he could demonstrate that the German fetish for order and regulation had its positive side. He had traced the two prisoners who had been repatriated to Hamburg. He hadn't considered the others, the ones sent back to the DDR, until we'd seen what we could get out of the easier ones.

"So," he said, settling down in the chair opposite my desk, "we have two names, Rolf Dietzer and Max Hartmann. They are both recorded as being admitted to West Germany at the port of Hamburg in June 1954. The paperwork has them as being repatriated from the Russian prisoner-of-war camp system, but actually doesn't specify where they had been imprisoned." He looked up at me. "The guy I was speaking to in the record office knew something about that. He said that where the camp was not specified, it normally meant they had been in Gulag forced-labour camps, rather than regular POW ones. Apparently that was some sort of breach of the Geneva Convention, so it was kept quiet. Anyway, it doesn't make any difference to us. So, Dietzer then appears as registering his address and residence details a week or so later in Bremen, which is where he originally came from." He looked up again. "So he basically went straight home. He occurs quite a few times in police records over the next few years, as a suspect in various minor crimes, although there seems to be no evidence of any convictions, and then we have his death certificate dated September 1968. He was beaten up and died of his injuries. Reading between the lines, he was a petty criminal who fell out with his accomplices once too often and paid the price." He must have seen the look of disappointment on my face; if the guy was dead, he was of no use to me. "So that was a dead-end. The other one, though, Max Hartmann, is more interesting. His arrival record in Hamburg is dated the same day, but he obviously stayed in the city, because his registration, also about a week later, is at an address in Altona – that's part of Hamburg." I nodded; I knew Hamburg well enough for that, anyway. "So, his record is quite clear. He lists himself as a transport operator, and then in 1959, he turned himself into a GmbH – a limited company. You will have heard of it, I'm sure, or at least seen their trucks on the roads – HartmannLogistik."

I stared at him. "Really? That's a big outfit. Bit different from his mate being beaten to death by the underworld. Being in the camp doesn't seem to have held him back too much – he must have made a fortune out of that business." A thought struck me. "He is alive still, isn't he?"

"Yes, he's alive and living in retirement in a suburb of Hamburg. If I remember correctly, he sold the company out some years ago, so effectively he took the money and ran. Do you want to contact him?"

"I do. Most certainly. Do you have an address?"

"Better than that – here's his phone number." He passed a sheet of paper across the desk to me. I stared at it. Was this really going to happen? And really, so easily? Had I stumbled and bumbled my way to what my grandfather had spent months and months and loads of money trying to find out fifty years earlier?

Dieter continued. "But there's one strange thing, though. The other name you told me, Armin Kuhlmann, the one you are actually looking for, I found his name somewhere else."

I looked quizzically at him.

"Yes. I made an enquiry at the Office of German War Graves – they're the people who keep the records of war dead and where they're buried or commemorated, if there is no grave. They have a record of an Armin Kuhlmann, commemorated as missing in January 1943 at Stalingrad. His name is on one of the memorials at a place called Rossoschka, which is near the city of Volgograd – that's what used to be Stalingrad."

"Why is that strange? Missing – that means there's no body been found, so that fits with the story I think we are uncovering."

"Well, yes, I suppose so; I just thought it was odd to find him there when you believe he died much later thousands of kilometres further north in Norilsk."

"But surely that's just a reflection of the fact that actually what happened to the remnants of the battle is pretty murky. I mean, they know he was left in the Kessel when it closed, and they have no record – presumably – of him after that. So I suppose it is logical that they just list all the missing there, presuming death if they have nothing to the contrary that has appeared over the years."

It clearly offended his belief in the sanctity of the official records. "Mmm. I suppose so. It just seems a bit strange, without any confirmation."

"But I'm sure they would do that as much as anything else so that people would have some closure about their relatives. I'm certain my grandfather would have liked to have known his son was commemorated there, but I guess all this is from much later than the late 1940s?"

"Yes, it's only really since the end of the Soviet regime that the Russians have opened up at all. The German War Graves people are working in Russia, or in fact all over Eastern Europe; they're finding thousands of bodies a year at the moment. I think there's still well over a million unaccounted for. When you told me about all this, I read some articles I found about it. In my time at school, we didn't really learn this stuff. I found it really interesting, and also quite shocking. The savagery of that war in the East was just unbelievable. It was almost medieval in its barbarity, but added to that were twentieth-century industrial weapons – tanks, shells, machine-guns, flame-throwers and so on. For me, it's just incredible that only two generations away from me Europe was being ripped to shreds by that kind of savagery."

"You're right. We sit here in the comfort of our time, and yet maybe it's so much more fragile than we know. I'm sure around the beginning of the twentieth century they had no idea how their world was going to explode, not just once, but twice in about thirty-five years. They would have been comfortable in their Edwardian stability, but they were actually on the edge of catastrophe. Let's hope we're not lulling ourselves into the same sense of false security."

"That's a fair point, Alex. Look at Bosnia – that came out of nowhere, seemingly."

We chatted on about modern history, but all the while the piece of paper was burning my fingers; I was conscious that in my hand I had the phone number of a man who had probably been amongst the last to see my uncle.

Eventually, Dieter wandered off to get back to his real work, and I pulled the telephone towards me. It was answered by a woman's voice.

I spoke my best German. "Good afternoon. Is it possible to speak to Herr Max Hartmann, please?"

"I will see if he is in. Who is calling, please?"

"My name is Alex Butterfield. I am calling from London, about a personal matter."

"OK, hold on please."

There was a pause, then a man's voice. "Herr Butterfield, this is Hartmann. What can I do for you?"

It was a firm voice, with none of the signs of age that I had been half-expecting.

"This may sound very odd, Herr Hartmann, but I wanted to talk to you about your recollections of your time as a prisoner-of-war in the Soviet labour camp."

There was an intake of breath, and then he spoke in a much sharper voice. "Why would you want to ask me about that? It's not a subject I really have anything to say about. It was a long time ago, and those are memories I do not wish to revive. I don't think I have anything to say to you."

"Wait, please." I probably sounded desperate as I prayed he wouldn't hang up. "I am trying to trace the fate of somebody who I think may have been one of your fellow-prisoners at Norilsk."

"I see. Are you a journalist?"

"No, nothing like that. I'm just a private citizen, but I'm trying to find out what happened to a man called Armin Kuhlmann. I don't know, but I believe he may have been at Norilsk with you."

There was a long silence at the other end. Then, "I remember Armin Kuhlmann. I remember him well. But what is your interest? From your accent, I would say you are British."

"Yes, I am. My mother was Armin Kuhlmann's sister, and on a recent visit to Norilsk I discovered something that makes me believe he was there."

"Your mother was his sister? Yes, of course, they were all in England, so I guess she stayed there. What did you find?"

I relaxed back in my chair. He didn't sound as though he was going to hang up any more. "At my parents' home, here in England, we had some drawings and some paintings done by Armin when he was a child or a very young man. There is a very distinctive signature he put on his work. I was recently visiting Norilsk and I went into the museum there; there I found some mostly charcoal drawings of prisoners and parts of the camp, all with the same signature. With the help of a Russian there, I found Armin's name on a manifest of prisoners brought to the camp in 1943. Your name was on the same list. I then found you on another list, this time of prisoners who were repatriated, but this time Armin's name was not there. So I assume that he must have died in the camp. My mother, her sister and her brother are all dead now, but I want to find out what happened to my uncle. The family know nothing beyond the fact that he was seen still alive on the morning of the second of February 1943, the day of the final surrender. So I hoped you had known him, and that you might be prepared to tell me what happened to him."

"You've been doing some detective work, Mr Butterfield. I'm impressed." There was a silence, then he continued: "Yes, I knew Armin Kuhlmann. I knew him very well, for a long time. We shared a lot of things together." There was another pause at the other end of the line. Then I heard a sigh. "Yes, I knew Armin well. He was a good friend. So they have some of his pictures at Norilsk still? I thought all the ones left there would have been destroyed."

"Yes, they have quite a number. They are exhibited in the part of the museum devoted to showing life in the prison camps, as part of the overall theme of how the city grew up there."

"So the camps are now worthy of museum exhibition, are they? It wasn't the stuff of museums when we were there. It was a cruel, hard place. Well, Mr Butterfield, what do you want from me, beyond the fact that I knew Armin up there in the camp?"

"I'm trying to find out what happened to him."

"What happened to him? He died. He was taken at Stalingrad, and eventually he died in a prison camp. What more can I tell you?"

"Well, I hoped you might be prepared to give me a bit of detail. Obviously, I was fairly sure he had died, but I hoped you could tell me more about his life there, when he died, and things like that. Just more about what happened to him, really."

"It's not a subject I like to think about, frankly. People died, unpleasantly; some, like me, were lucky and came through it. But it can't really do anyone any good to rehash it all, so many years later. Things like that are best left in the past. I'm sorry, Mr Butterfield, I don't think I can help you."

"Please, Herr Hartmann, I want to know what happened to my uncle. I know it's an unpleasant story, but I can't just forget about it. Won't you help me?"

"At the moment, my instinct is to say no, I'm sorry. But I will think about it. Give me your phone number and I will call you back if I can help."

That sounded like the best I was going to get out of him, so I gave him my number and hung up.

Chapter Twenty-Two

The next day, Dieter came into my room to see how I had got on with Hartmann. He made a face when I told him the disappointing news. "That's not good, because I've been trying to get something about the four prisoners who went back to the East and it looks like we have been beaten by events." I looked at him quizzically. He went on. "You remember when the Berlin Wall fell and the East German regime and state collapsed?" I nodded. "Well, you probably also remember reading about how the Stasi records were rifled and burned." I nodded again. "Well, unfortunately, all the records of returning prisoners-of-war were held in the Stasi archive." He held up his hands. "Don't ask me why they thought that information had to be kept secret, but they did. So there is no way we can get any sort of clue about what happened to those four men. All we have are names and the fact that they were released over the frontier at Frankfurt-an-der-Oder in the early summer of 1954. There's absolutely no chance we could find out where they went after that. It's a complete dead-end." He grinned. "You're supposed to be persuasive – at least, all the boys tell me you're good at getting customers to do what you want, so you'll just have to have another go at Hartmann and get him onside."

"Yeah, well, we'll see. Maybe he'll change his mind."

After a couple of days, I was beginning to think the chances of that happening were slipping away as I had had no further contact from Hamburg. I sat with Emily over the dinner table bemoaning the way I seemed to have got so far and then reached a full stop. "The thing is, I've got absolutely no leverage to use to persuade him to tell me anything. But I don't really see why he is so reluctant. It's not as if I'm asking him to divulge secrets; this is stuff that happened years ago, so I can't understand why he's so awkward."

"Come on, you can't say he's being awkward. Somebody he's never heard of calls him up out of the blue and asks him to go back to a very bad time in his life and tell him all the details. You're not looking at it from his point of view at all. You're just thinking of what you want and expecting him to oblige."

I thought about that for a moment. It was true, I supposed; I had simply assumed the man would be prepared to help without even considering why. I was so caught up in my own search that I just expected everyone else to fall into line. Perhaps I needed to adjust my approach.

Beyond Stalingrad

My wife continued: "You need to make him want to tell you the story, not make him think you're just assuming he will because it suits you. Think about it; if someone completely unknown just asked you to tell them the story of your childhood, for example, you'd probably tell them where to get off."

"Mmm. Well, what do you suggest? The truth is, I'm not particularly interested in him, I just want to know what he can remember about Armin. I'm not asking him to tell me anything about himself, for Heaven's sake. Just tell me about my uncle."

"Yes, but Alex, that's the point. You've got to think from his point of view. Maybe he doesn't like the idea that all you want is to know about somebody else. Maybe you have to make him feel important in his own right. I don't know; I haven't spoken to him, but you say he used to own a big company. He's probably got a bit of an ego that you have to work on. Flatter him; let him see you're actually interested in him."

"Can't do any harm, I suppose. That's assuming he's even going to be prepared to take a call from me again." I was a bit down about it, and my pessimism was starting to get the better of me.

"Oh, don't be so negative. You can be persuasive, you're supposed to be good at it. Call him again, tell him you're trying to find out about how life was for them all in the prison camp and also how Armin died. But do it in a way that doesn't make him think you're not interested in him. Make him feel important."

I pondered her advice as I sat in the office the next morning. Maybe I had made Hartmann feel as though I was taking him for granted by just assuming he would be ready to tell me everything just like that. Maybe Emily was right and I should use a bit more subtlety. Well, I'd probably only get one more chance at best. I picked up the phone and dialled the Hamburg number again.

This time it was Hartmann himself who answered.

"Herr Hartmann, this is Alex Butterfield, from London, again."

"Ah, Mr Butterfield, good morning. I didn't expect to hear from you again so soon. What can I do for you?"

"Well, I wondered if I could perhaps explain a little more about what I asked you before. About your memories of the Russian POW camp. I hoped you might give me another chance to explain what I was looking for."

"Actually, I have I have been thinking about your call, and maybe I was a little hasty before. I will listen if you want to tell me what you want and then we can see whether or not I can help. If it suits you, I have time now."

"Sure, I have time now."

I paused to collect my thoughts and put them in order. "I think I explained to you before that Armin Kuhlmann was my mother's brother.

The family know where he was until the Stalingrad surrender; my grandfather received a letter from somebody who was with him in the 6th Army until November 1942 and who also had confirmation that he was seen alive on the morning of the surrender at the beginning of February 1943. From there, he disappeared. After the end of the war, my grandfather tried very hard to find out anything more, but he was unable to get any more information than that. So Armin's parents, his sisters and his brother were left not knowing what had become of their brother. They have all died now but they had all had to suffer the uncertainty. Did he die at Stalingrad? If not, how long did he survive? Was he in a Russian labour camp? They all obviously had their own lives to lead but it must have prayed on their minds.

"Now, I visited the city of Norilsk, up in the Russian Arctic, a week or two ago. I'm involved in the metal business, incidentally, and I was visiting the mines and smelters up there. Anyway, while I was there, I went into the city museum and I found some drawings which were done by my uncle. As I said when we spoke before, I recognised the signature on them. So that made me think that he must have been in the camp there, which was confirmed by the curator of the museum when he found records of the arrival of prisoners. But there was no record of his having left the camp, so the implication of that is that he died there. The curator then managed to find a list of other German prisoners who had arrived at Norilsk at the same time and who were listed as having been repatriated in the early 1950s. You were on that list, so I felt it was worth contacting you to ask whether you remembered anything about him.

"Look, I can imagine that it's not a time which is comfortable to think about. I cannot imagine how conditions were, having to live in that camp. So I completely understand that you would not want to have to relive it, just to satisfy my curiosity and if that's all it was, then I would accept that you wanted to forget all about it." I paused for a moment. This was the bit I had to phrase carefully, to get him onside. "But it isn't just about my curiosity. My uncle just disappeared. I know that doesn't make him or the family unique, but I hope you'd agree that if we can resolve such issues, then really that's the honourable thing to do. Honestly, I'm not after some sensationalist story, or to try and gain anything out of your memories; I just want to know what happened to my mother's brother. He's just one name in all the thousands that are still left in limbo, but I think, with your help, I might be able to close the story, and I think that's a good thing."

"Yes, I can understand your feelings; I agree that the correct thing is to try and put these men to rest, if we can, and I also agree that they all deserve to have their story known. But I prefer not to dwell on the past; when I came back to Germany, I determined that my life started from there, and that what had happened before was a closed book, not to be re-opened. It was a difficult time; we were a defeated nation, and in the eyes of the world the army of which I was a part was reviled. And rightly; what was done in the conquered territories, what was done here at home as well, was despicable, depraved beyond belief. The common guilt was tough, and I didn't want to relive all of that." The voice at the end of the phone paused, then began again, sounding somehow older and less confident. "But, you know, when I listen to you and your desire to know your uncle's story, perhaps I need to tell it. Armin Kuhlmann was a good man; he was no fanatic. Like so many of us, he was a boy, a student dragged away from his studies and sent to war. We were also victims of the craziness of that Nazi period, and I think actually you should know his story and be proud of the fact that even in that dreadful time for my country there was such a thing as a good German. And you're right; whoever these men were, they deserve better than just to be a statistic of the missing; if we can finish their page, it is the right thing to do.

"So, come to see me in Hamburg and I will tell you the story of the Armin Kuhlmann that I knew."

I breathed a sigh of relief. Emily had been right; he'd come round to what I wanted. "Thank you. I could come to Hamburg the week after next, if that would be any good."

"Certainly, that will give me a little time to get my thoughts in order. Let me know when you will arrive and where you will stay and I will arrange everything."

1999 Hamburg, Germany

Chapter Twenty-Three

And so I flew into Hamburg. As the cab took me down from the airport to the centre of the city, I mused on Max Hartmann. I didn't really know what to expect. He had sounded quite chipper on the phone, but he must have been at least in his late 70s, and he had suffered all those years in the Russian prison camp, so it was hard to imagine he would be in good shape. He'd obviously been a business success; 'HartmannLogistik' trucks were a common sight on the autobahns all over Germany and the address he had given me in the upmarket former fishing village suburb of Blankenese implied a fair degree of affluence.

The cab dropped me outside the Vier Jahreszeiten and the doorman took my overnight bag. The pale green leaves were just beginning to show on the lime trees lining the bank of the Binnenalster and the afternoon sun glinted off the smooth water. Hamburg had always been my favourite German city, probably more for its architectural elegance and bustling prosperity than any atavistic throwback to the fact that it was the origin of my grandfather's family, and it was a pleasure to be back again. I had a few hours before my meeting with Hartmann, so after checking in, I decided to take a stroll through the city centre.

At the far end of the Jungfernstieg, I turned to look back across the edge of the lake. In the foreground was the Alsterpavillon, and beyond, over the lake, the hotel. It was the view in one of Armin's drawings that had hung in my parents' house. The pavilion was different, though, this one clearly a construction of the 1950s. My memory of the picture was of a much larger, more ornate building with baroque flourishes; that one had been destroyed in the world war two bombing, but it was surprising how the rest of the scene had changed so little. The Alsterhaus department store was clearly the same, although some of its neighbours had just as obviously been rebuilt after (presumably) bomb damage. I pulled out my camera to photograph the scene, trying to judge as best I could the exact spot from which Armin had drawn. Turning, I walked a few metres down the arcade alongside the canal until the Rathaus came

Beyond Stalingrad

fully into view. I'd been to Hamburg many times, but I'd never really given the towering Victorian building more than a cursory glance. I knew it had been severely damaged in 1943, but had subsequently been rebuilt exactly as it was. Once again I tried to get the angle quite right to photograph what Armin had drawn. On this one, with the arcade behind me, the surroundings looked different. The other buildings were clearly post-war and the whole square was far more open. As I strolled round the outside of the Rathaus, I tried to imagine how it had been for a young art student, caught in the country and knowing conscription must be only a matter of time. This was the Altstadt – the old town – small streets, bars and clubs mixed with shops, less prestigious and up-market than the ones on the Jungfernstieg. The students must have come here for their socialising, the main campus buildings were not far away. Yet I couldn't feel it; it was busy with people, but the buildings were all post-war. Some were obviously copied from what had been destroyed, but it just seemed a modern mid-level shopping centre.

I wandered on and found myself in front of the empty shell of a ruined church. There was no roof, and the walls now enclosed a quiet paved square where the nave and chancel had been. On the back wall was a kiosk, with a sign advertising tickets for the spire, which still stood, one side completely open, in the corner. I paid my Deutschmarks and stepped into the lift. At the top, I came out onto a viewing gallery. At each of the unglazed windows, there was a montage of photographs. I almost recoiled with shock as I looked at them. They were a mixture of old, pre-war Hamburg and pictures taken after Operation Gomorrah in July and August of 1943. I'd heard of the firestorm the bombing had created, but seeing photographs taken only days later brought it home. Comparing the shots of the Altstadt taken before the war with what I had just walked through, I could see I had been right; this was exactly where the students would have gone for their revelry; but it had ceased to exist in July 1943. I spent a while up there comparing old pictures, bombed pictures and the city laid out before me, and two of the captions caught my eye; the first was a quotation from 'Bomber' Harris - "They say the bombing targeted the civilian population - tell me: what war doesn't?" And the second was an explanation of what had happened between 1933 and 1945, finishing with a plea to understand that the German people themselves had been the first victims of Nazism. Well, one of them was incontrovertible; the other, mmm, well, it chimed with the comment Hartmann had made on the phone; it was something I hadn't fully thought of before. I began to wonder also if my grandfather had had to suffer knowing that parts of his family had been in that bombing as well as grieving for his son at Stalingrad.

I went back down the tower and ambled back to the hotel, through the luxury shopping streets behind the Jungfernstieg. The crowds were out on a sunny afternoon, and the contrast of the bright colours they were wearing and the elaborate window-displays with the unbearably grim black and white photos up in the church spire could not have been more marked.

    I'd arranged to meet Hartmann in the hotel bar at seven o'clock. When I walked in, it was obviously him sitting in the corner of the tiny bar by the window, a glass of beer in front of him.

Chapter Twenty-Four

I walked up to him; "Herr Hartmann?"

"Yes, and you must be Alex Butterfield. Welcome to Hamburg. It's a pleasure to meet you." I had expected him to look old, but he was clearly in perfect health, with neatly-cut white hair and a deep suntan on his face. His eyes, behind small silver-framed framed glasses were lively and his smile was genuine. If he was an advertisement for the Russian Gulag, it can't have been that bad, was my unprompted thought.

The barman came over, and I started to order a beer. "No, no," said Hartmann firmly. "It's over fifty years since I last saw my friend, your relative. We must celebrate him with more than a beer. Bring us a bottle of Veuve Clicquot." The barman departed.

"So, my young friend, you are Armin's nephew. You have a look of him, but you're a bit taller. And you're fatter! I never saw Armin when he wasn't starving hungry. We met in the Stalingrad Kessel, and we parted at the Norilsk gulag camp." The smile dimmed for a moment, as if in memory. "He was my best friend, you know." He blinked, as a tear appeared in his eye. He nodded. "But come," the champagne arrived, and the barman poured, "first we'll drink to his memory, then I'll tell you the story." He solemnly raised his glass. "Armin Kuhlmann." I repeated it, clinking my glass against his; finally, I was going to find out what had happened.

"On the phone you said you wanted to know what happened to your uncle. OK, I can tell you very quickly, and that will be the end of it. Or, if you really want the whole story, I can give it to you, but it will take some time, certainly more than one evening over dinner when we have only just met." He looked me in the eye. "I warn you, it's not a nice story; Armin and I were caught by the struggle between the two most evil regimes of the twentieth century - one could almost say, of any century. There was little to choose between Nazism and Stalinism. They were both determined to crush individuality and impose total domination by the party. They were so similar, yet they fought the bloodiest war that's ever been seen. That war was what we were caught up in. It's your choice: the simple fact of when Armin died, or the full story."

I didn't even hesitate. I had to hear it all. "The full story."

"OK, then I suggest that this evening we just get to know each other, and you come tomorrow to my house out at Blankenese and I'll fill in all the details I know, or at least that I can remember." I nodded my agreement, although I was slightly disappointed that he wouldn't just get on with it. He must have seen that disappointment in my face, for he continued, "My friend, don't worry, I will tell you everything I can, but you must understand it's difficult for me too, to go back to those times." For a moment, his eyes took on a haunted look, then the sparkle came back and he went on, "Come, let's get the rest of this bottle taken through and have our dinner."

He led the way across into the Grill Room, where we were shown to a table in the window. The room was art deco, with dark, shiny panelled walls and a black and white chequerboard parquet on the floor. The lamps, the balustrade around the raised part of the room at one end and the decorations on the wall were all flavoured with 1920s elegance.

"So," he said, as we sat and were handed menus by the waiter, "the food here is very good. It's mostly German style, which I understand you sophisticates from London may not regard as a gastronomic experience, but try the schnitzel or the liver, and remember you are really more in central rather than western Europe here, at least where the food is concerned." He said it with a twinkle in his eye; I was already beginning to warm to Max Hartmann.

I nodded, and said, "OK, I'll go for the schnitzel."

"Perfect. And perhaps a game terrine to start. And we can have any wine you want – and this restaurant has a fantastic list – but I'm going to suggest a German red, a Spätburgunder. That's a Pinot Noir, and we grow it very well. Not entirely the same as Burgundy, but good."

I smiled at him. "Sure, I'll leave it to you. You're the local."

"True, but your grandfather's family came from here, although Armin grew up in the south-east, near Czechoslovakia." His face became serious again. "We spoke a lot of our homes and families during the years over there. Sometimes it seemed the only way to keep our sanity."

We sat in silence for a few moments. Then he started again. "It's quite difficult to think back to that time. When you first rang, as you know, I wasn't sure if I wanted to open it all up again in my mind. The day I came back I put it all behind me and concentrated on the future. But then, I thought I couldn't just ignore my old friend by refusing to talk to you so here we are.

"You know, I came back to Germany in 1954. I was one of the last survivors to be repatriated. What I returned to was really a strange country. In fact, the first thing to get used to was that it was effectively two countries, even though the Russian Zone was not yet completely cut off. So, remember I was born in 1920. From the age of thirteen onwards, therefore, I had known only the totalitarian state and what we experienced in Russia was yet more of that. What I found here was a democracy, trying to find its way back to acceptance. Of course, I missed the very worst of the privations here, immediately after 1945. By the time

Beyond Stalingrad

I was back in Hamburg, the reconstruction was well under way so I didn't see the total destruction the bombing had caused. It wasn't my home city either; I come from the Ruhr. But I found out that my parents had been killed in the bombing there, and my sister had married an American GI in 1950 and gone back to the States with him. So when the vagaries of 'the system' dumped me here in 1954, I had no reason to go elsewhere, so I stayed. With all the building and the new factories and the constant movement of people, there was an obvious demand for transport. I had nothing but the small cash payment the state made to me as a returning prisoner but that just about covered the down payment on a clapped-out 1930s truck. There was a lot of scrap metal in Germany at the time, as you can maybe imagine, and I got work mostly delivering it into the copper smelter here, the Norddeutsche Affinerie. They were good people; they saw I was ready to work hard and they gave me a lot of business. As they started buying more and more from outside the immediate Hamburg area, so my business also spread out over the country. I could afford soon to have three or four trucks, and in 1959 I founded HartmannLogistik. By the early sixties, I could buy new Mercedes trucks instead of old wrecks, and we branched out into general transport, not just the scrap metal. It became a very successful company." I looked at him and tried to imagine the polished, prosperous old man with the twinkling eye as a returning refugee, effectively scrambling to try and make a living from his beaten-up old truck

"But back to 1954. People didn't want to know about what had happened at Stalingrad and afterwards. I don't mean there was any antipathy, but if ever I started to speak about it, there were just blank stares." He sat back in his chair, gathering his thoughts for a moment. "But it was difficult to adjust, at first. I understood why people were anxious to move on from the war, and they had all had nine years already to get used to it. For me, though, the war had only ended the day I got back home to Germany, and so I still needed to understand how it was to live in a defeated nation; until then, I had been a foreign prisoner in a camp. Here, I was among my countrymen, at home, and yet it was all strange. When I left, at the beginning of Barbarossa in 1941, there had been some kind of certainty. Now, it was no longer there." He glanced across at me. "Don't get me wrong. I, and people like me, had not all been rabid Nazis – and by the way, Armin most emphatically was not; you don't have to worry about that one coming to haunt you – but that had been the reality of life. All my adult life the state had dictated what I did and how I did it. Now, I had to get used to being free." Again, he looked at me, this time with a smile on his face. "It was a great, liberating feeling. Of course, it was not the same for everybody. Those prisoners who were released but then ended up in the Soviet zone, and were caught there when the Wall was built, they went straight back into the arms of the state. In that way, I was one of the lucky ones. It was no more than a lottery; I was put on a ship that took me back to Hamburg; I could just as easily have been put on a train that would have dumped me on the Polish/German border, then who knows? I may have ended my days in the East and never have known freedom." He looked older, suddenly. "We never know where life will take us, Alex. Some are lucky, some not. All we can do is take the chances we are given." He paused again, as if collecting himself. "But it was difficult, as a thirty-four year old man, to have to pay electricity bills for the first time, to have to deal with all the utilities and the minutiae of normal life. For most people, the war had stolen five or so years of their lives; for us, it was fifteen." He chuckled. "I remember when I first tried to organise my telephone with the phone company. I had no idea how it worked and the people from the company thought I was an idiot, and treated me like that; well, you can imagine: here's a thirty-plus year old man, having to have everything explained to him as though he were a teenager. And it was like that with everything. Imagine it, Alex; all the years when I would normally have learned all this stuff had disappeared."

I ate my food almost mechanically, absolutely fascinated by his story. Like the letter from Krumm I had first read at my parents' house, it was compelling.

"So, anyway, I managed to work my way through all those little problems, and I built my business; it became very successful, one of the foremost logistics companies in Germany. I married and I have had a good life. As I said, I was one of the lucky ones. It didn't seem so when we were in the Kessel, or in the camp, or working down the mines or in the smelter, but, you know, I kept my health and my sanity and when I got back, I could surf on the economic miracle. I sold the company in the late eighties, for a lot of money. After that, I was only involved as the Honorary President, a purely ceremonial role, just to keep the name alive." He sighed. "We didn't have any children, though; I don't know if that may have been an effect of the privations of the captivity. I would have liked to hand the company on to another generation."

He looked at me, apologetically. "But I'm sorry, I seem to be telling you my life story, when you really want to hear about Armin. We can talk about how it was in the camp tomorrow, but perhaps I could start this evening by telling you how we first met. First, though, let's have another of these" – he pointed at the wine bottle and gestured to the waiter to replace it.

"OK, it was only a short while before the surrender. I was a sergeant with a German officer and a company of HIWIs in the reserve line in the northern sector of the Kessel. I'd originally been a tank man, but the tanks were long gone." He glanced at me. "You know HIWIs were the non-German 'volunteers' we had in the 6th Army with us?" I nodded

Beyond Stalingrad

– I'd read enough about the battle to know that one. "Well, the ones with us were mostly Ukrainian. They were a fairly sullen lot, but then I guess they knew their fate would not be good. They had joined us to fight against the Stalinism that had taken their country, but by now they knew they were on the losing side and that their fate would not be pretty, because to the Russians, they weren't just enemies, they were traitors. My officer was another young guy, from a very wealthy, traditional family, and he found it very hard, harder than the rest of us. His nerves had been failing for some time, and the command of the company was effectively left with me, even though I was only the NCO. Anyway, in the end, he just couldn't take it any more, and he shot himself." He glanced across the table. "It wasn't that unusual. Even some of the senior officers took that way out, particularly in the last few days, when the surrender became a virtual certainty. So I was left holding the position for a couple of days with my HIWIs, until Armin arrived to take over. He was different from his predecessor. He was frightened – we all were. But he knew what his duty was and he did it. He did his watch-keeping with the HIWIs, he patrolled with them and he made sure that everything we had in the way of supplies was shared fairly and equally between us all. He only had a few words of Russian at that stage, but I was reasonably fluent – I'd picked it up as we advanced the previous year – and the Ukrainians all spoke it; they respected him, though. In fact I'd go further and say they liked him." He smiled at a memory. "He made a good first impression. He arrived on a pony-drawn cart, and we got to shoot the pony for food. That was the first meat we had had for some time and it meant the HIWIs were already well-disposed to him. We'd had no meat for days, if not weeks, so Armin was already a hero compared with his predecessor when he arrived with the pony.

"Anyway, the Russians bit by bit squeezed the Kessel, and we got orders to fall back when the attack came on our sector. Well, we didn't really get specific orders, the contact with HQ was very difficult then. We were actually part of a mob, not an army by then, and street by street through the suburbs we retreated back to the centre. Armin looked after his men, like the best officers do, and we didn't have many casualties in that phase, unlike some of the other companies. Anyway, we finally ended up in the Tractor Factory, with our backs tight against the river. Under the grey overcoats, Armin and I were still in our black Panzer uniforms, and when they saw that, we got taken in to form part of the guard for Groscurth's bunker; he was functioning as Strecker's second-in-command at that time, in the northern sector of the Kessel." He grunted; "Huh! Those black uniforms were a curse in the end; we didn't know it at the time, but the NKVD troops were specifically told to take the 'Nazis' amongst us, by which they meant the SS, the Feldgendarmerie and the HIWIs, for special treatment. We knew the difference between the black of the SS and that of the Panzer troops, but they didn't, as we found out to our cost later.

"The fighting in those last few days was if anything the fiercest we had encountered. The shelling was constant, the rockets were coming in on our bunkers all day and all night. We all knew this was the end, but Strecker had decided we should hold out as long as we could, to give the armies in the Caucasus a chance to retreat." He glanced across at me, lost in his memories. "Strecker was a good General – far more competent than Paulus, and Groscurth, who was his second-in-command, was actually a fine man; they weren't Nazis, they just had to play the hand they'd been dealt by the crazies back in Berlin. There was a story – I think the details are still a matter of debate – that at a small town in Ukraine, in the initial advance, Groscurth put his Wehrmacht soldiers between the SS and some children marked for execution, to protect them. Anyway, in those last few days, he and Armin spoke a lot; strangely, as one was a senior officer and the other just a company commander, they became a sort of friends. But the end came. Paulus surrendered and we could only hold on for another day or so before Groscurth finally called a halt to it." His face took on a far-away look. "I remember that morning, 2nd February 1943. We climbed out of the bunkers to face the Russian troops surrounding us. We looked what we were – a totally defeated army. To be honest, they didn't look much better, except for the faces. Ours were tired, frightened, sick and starving. They were probably as tired and starving, but their faces had the look of victory. To begin with, we just sat in the ruins, waiting for something to happen. So in the afternoon, they kicked and prodded us to our feet and marched us down to the river. Then we were taken off to the northern part of the city where we were held in some sort of ruined factory buildings as a kind of holding camp. I'm not sure how many of us there were there, but that's where they began sorting us into groups. The HIWIs were led off separately. I don't know what happened to them, but the rumour was that most of them were summarily executed pretty immediately. In fact, though, I think some of them were actually finally shipped out to work-camps in far eastern Siberia. Probably nobody will ever know their true fate." He shook his head. "They made a bad decision when they decided which side to join. And I remember while we were in this place, we had to listen to a speech by a man called Walter Ulbricht. He subsequently became the head of the DDR – I'm sure you've heard of him. He was a German communist, who had been broadcasting on behalf of the Russians from behind the front. There were a couple of others, but I can't remember their names. I think one of them was a poet, or a playwright or something. Ulbricht spoke for some time, a real harangue, but I can't remember a word of it now. Just propaganda and Soviet triumphalism." He shook his head sadly. "But you know, what he subsequently created in East Germany, that was the same totalitarian, corporate state that the Nazis had made. Crazy. All that rhetoric, and yet what was really the difference between the Gestapo and the Stasi?" He looked across at me. "You've probably worked out I hate politicians, especially the totalitarian ones.

"For the first couple of days in that bombed-out factory, the NKVD gave us no food. We didn't know what was happening. Were they intending to starve us to death? Wait for the typhus to claim us all? We just sat staring into space, hardly talking, trying not to think of our situation. Armin and I sat together, occasionally trying to give each other an encouraging smile. At that point, it was just clinging on to someone you knew – the real friendship came later.

"So we spent a few days – I'm not sure really how many – in those ruins, with no roof and shattered walls giving us no protection from the cold and the snow. Men were dying in the snow and were just left lying where they fell. Some men determined they would not lie down, because to lie down would risk never getting up again, so they just stood together, determined to sleep like horses, on their feet, with their overcoats stretched over their heads. Others just curled up in the snow; they mostly never got up again. Visions of hell in our western minds and art usually have raging flames and burning bodies, but this one just had cold and snow and dying men. Anyway, after a few days there, we were marched off to Beketovka."

He looked me straight in the eyes. "This has been a pleasant meal, in a wonderful restaurant in a free city in a free country. I'm not going to spoil that with Beketovka; that hell can wait till tomorrow. Come, let's finish the wine and have some desert."

Half an hour or so later I was seeing him out to his car in front of the hotel. "So, Alex, I will collect you here tomorrow morning and we shall drive out to my house. About 9:30?"

"No, don't be silly. I can take the S-bahn directly from here. Then if you give me directions, I can go to your house from the Blankenese station. You don't want to drive into town and then straight back out again."

He nodded his agreement. "OK, that's good. But I will meet you at the station; it's quite difficult to describe the way from there to my house by foot. So, I bid you good night, my friend." Solemnly we shook hands, and he got into his shiny black S-class Mercedes and drove off.

I went back into the hotel and up to my room. Idly, I flipped through the TV channels. Nothing of interest. German TV tends to be less than riveting. I tried to read, but thoughts of what Hartmann had told me kept spinning through my mind. It was impossible to imagine what they had gone through. Yet, he had come out of it and built a successful life afterwards; he seemed happy with his lot and certainly many would envy him his lifestyle. One thing that had struck me was the lack of bitterness.

Fifteen years of his life had effectively been taken from him, yet he said not a single word of blame. He seemed just to accept it as his lot to have been caught up as a piece of driftwood in the ideological struggles that had gone on. I sat, half thinking and half reading, eventually going to bed, after first checking my S-bahn route for the next morning.

I slept, but not well; in my dreams, the soldiers kept coming, the endless columns of shabby zombies, heads down, starving empty faces marching, stumbling, past me, heading for nowhere, all under the pitiless eyes of their guards. The steady tramp of their feet went on and on and on.

Chapter Twenty-Five

The next morning, after breakfast, I crossed to the Jungfernstieg S-bahn station and picked up a train for Blankenese. After the first few stops, the train emerged from its tunnel to run on above ground and I called Hartmann to let him know my arrival time. Once we had left the inner suburbs, pretty much like the inner suburbs of any European city, seen from the railway line, the houses on either side got bigger, with more extensive gardens around them. The river wasn't quite visible from the train, but I knew from previous visits that the big houses along its banks on the Elbchaussee were traditionally the homes of some of Hamburg's richest citizens. Likewise the former fishing village and now commuter suburb of Blankenese, which we reached after half an hour or so. Hartmann was waiting in his car outside the station. I got in and he drove off, very shortly turning off along a narrow street that curved and twisted along the side of the hill. We drove down through a gateway onto a drive that dipped sharply, ending in front of a square white house.

Going in through the front door, I found a stunning interior. The house was built on the slope, and we had come in at the top, with the rest of the house below, following the drop in the land. The whole of the top floor, once through the entrance hall, was a single open space, with floor-to-ceiling windows forming the entire wall facing out over the river. Below us were the roofs of the old houses of the fishing village. The other walls were white and the floor was of a blond wood with three large Afghan carpets. There were black and white leather armchairs and a telescope on a tripod was positioned in the corner, up against the window. But what then caught my eye made the rest of it seem insignificant. On the bare white wall to my left was a group of four line drawings. Each showed a figure, unshaven, gaunt face with drawn eyes. They were arresting in their starkness; and in the bottom right-hand corner of each was the 'AK' signature, familiar from my parents' house and the museum at Norilsk. As I walked across for a closer look, Hartmann said "Yes, those are the ones I managed to bring out with me when I left. The one at the bottom left is me, the others are fellow-prisoners." I looked closely; the features were recognisable, but this was a tortured Hartmann, not the healthy specimen I was coming to know. "Two of the other three died, and the third – who was a Russian political prisoner – was taken away to another camp shortly after Armin drew that picture. If I had to guess, he died as well. If anything, the politicals were treated even worse than we were. They were Russians, you see, so they regarded them as traitors, and reserved their special hatred for them. Those clothes we're wearing – they were the prison uniform. I wore that from 1943 until 1954. Eleven years of the same thing, every day. Same clothes, same inadequate food, and very similar work. Hard, brutal work; our miners here in Europe have a tough life, but let them try hard rock mining in perma-frosted ground." He gave a smile. "Nowadays, you know, I'm told the miners up in the Arctic there are amongst the best-paid manual workers in Russia." He shook his head, for a moment an old man trying to get to grips with the peculiarities of modern life. "How it changes. But come, let's get some coffee and I'll tell you about Beketovka." He called down the stairs "Marthe, can you bring us some coffee up here, please." He gestured to the armchairs looking out across the river. "Let's sit here; a pleasant view, at least, while we talk of savage times."

As we sat looking out through the huge windows, a loaded container ship came into view from our right, heading upriver to the port of Hamburg. Hartmann gestured to it. "There's a constant stream of them, in on one tide, out on the next. Container ships bringing consumer goods in, car carriers taking the cars for export going outwards. It's a far cry from 1954, when I came back and the country was still rebuilding. It's been a staggering achievement; how good could it have been, though, if all those good men - like Armin - had still been here?" He sighed. "Twice in two generations. 1918 and then 1945; we had to start all over again. Let's hope we don't have to do it again." He paused, turning towards the staircase. "Here comes the coffee." A middle-aged woman appeared up the stairs carrying a tray. "Put it down here, Marthe," he said, gesturing to the low table in front of us. She served us each a cup, and retreated back down the stairs. Hartmann picked up his cup and sat back in his chair.

"OK, yesterday evening we left us in Stalingrad; the next move was the march to Beketovka."

I interrupted. "Before you carry on with that, there's one thing I don't understand. Yesterday, a couple of times you mentioned that you were in Panzer uniform, and I understood from what I had learned before that Armin was a panzer soldier." Hartmann nodded. "Well, from what you were saying yesterday, at Stalingrad you were infantry. What happened to the tanks?"

1942 Russia

"Ah, the mighty Panzer armies……….Well, OK, let's make a little detour before we get to Beketovka." He sipped his coffee, lost in reflection for a moment. "When Barbarossa started, at first we swept over everything in front of us. The Russian resistance was stubborn and they were very brave soldiers, but they were totally outclassed by our equipment. There

Beyond Stalingrad

were some vicious battles, but we had overwhelming superiority, with the Stukas in the air and our Panzer IVs on the ground. The T-34 was a good tank, but we held an advantage at that stage with our longer-range gun. So in that first summer and autumn, we just rolled through Ukraine and Russia in our tanks, with the infantry frankly struggling to keep up with us. The winter caused us problems, and we suffered big set-backs; we had outrun our supply lines and the snow and the cold compounded the difficulties. That was really the first time we had known anything but total success and we were pushed back further away from the Don. But we regrouped, and when the spring of 1942 brought its thaw, we started to advance again. The Army was still broadly intact, we had re-established our supply routes and we could feel in our bones that our target, the Volga, was achievable.

"So on we went again, our morale high and expecting total victory. Armin and I were not in the same unit, but we were amongst the same divisions dashing across the Russian countryside. He would have been commanding a troop, a group of tanks, and I was commander of my own vehicle. Honestly, whatever we thought of the whole stupid war faded into the background at that point. You've got to try and imagine the feeling; we were young men, riding in the turrets of big, powerful pieces of machinery, racing across the empty landscape. They were heady days." He paused for a moment, staring back in time to the wide open Russian steppes.

"We felt invincible; any resistance, we just hammered it with our tanks' guns. Farmhouses, villages, towns - anywhere where the Russian soldiers tried to hold on, we just swept over them. We weren't aware of the killings and all that that went on behind us, with the SS and the Einsatzgruppen, but we destroyed a lot as we swept on. I'm not proud of it, but we did what we were told and we just streamed forward, blasting everything that blocked our way. Later, of course, we paid for that youthful exuberance.

"Anyway, at the Don crossing at Kalach we met some stiffer resistance." He was lost in his memories of fifty-odd years ago, and for a moment I tried to imagine what it must have been like for a young man in his early twenties. I believed him when he had told me that these elite front-line troops knew nothing of the barbarity being carried out by other elements of their army behind them; they must have felt like gods, riding in their open turrets across the steppe with the plumes of dust trailing from their clanking metal tracks. Had Armin felt that as well? Or had he been wishing himself back in England with his family? Sadly, I reflected that we would probably never know.

Hartmann was nodding his head, like old men do at their memories. "Kalach was where it began to change, at least for me. There had been bitter fighting elsewhere, at Kiev and Smolensk and others, but I hadn't been part of that. I and my group had had an easy time really, but now life got much, much tougher. The Russians had a lot of T-34s there, and the terrain on the Don steppe was not so helpful to the attackers. It's a flat plain, but it's littered with deep cuts, almost like small ravines, which made it far more difficult for us to advance at the pace we had been. The Russians were also well dug in, their tanks protected by these great cuts in the land. We began to lose tanks to their guns." He looked across at me. "I guess you have never seen a tank take a direct hit from a high-explosive shell." I shook my head; of course I hadn't. Hardly any of my generation had. "Well, it's not pleasant. Remember, we carried all our ammunition with us, so if a tank was hit, there was always the risk that its own shells would also ignite, turning the whole thing into a massive fireball. I think the English called it 'brewing up'." He smiled thinly. "It was very rare for any of the crew to get out; well, that must be obvious. For protection, the way into a tank is small and protected, so for the men inside, when they took a hit, they had only seconds to try and scramble through the tiny hatch. Mostly they died in the fire. And then after the skirmish, you try and find anyone alive. When you open the hatch of the wreck, the stench is dreadful, a mixture of charred flesh and high-explosive. And all you can see are burned corpses with the metal bits of their uniform fused into the remains. However many times you see it, it's difficult not to throw up. Kalach was my real introduction to war. For the first time, I lost a significant number of friends, and what made that worse was that I knew how they had died. I didn't have to write the letters to their families, like the troop leaders did – that's a job Armin would have had to have done. They lied, of course, and said the men had died quickly and painlessly; you couldn't tell a mother her son had been roasted to death inside a petrol can full of high explosive. That would have done nothing for morale.

"Anyway, we won the battle at Kalach, but it cost us a lot, of men and of tanks. They had to re-equip many of our groups, and that meant there were some Panzer troops who were remustered as infantry. The rest of us carried on with the advance towards Stalingrad and the Volga. Well, in the late summer we got there. We who still had our tanks at that point had a piece of luck, then. They decided that the assault on the city should be undertaken by the infantry, and that actually tanks would be of limited use in the street-fighting, so we were stationed out on the steppe as a screen while the attack was happening. And that's where our tanks stayed, mostly. As the fighting got more and more intense, and then eventually as the door was shut on us and the Kessel sealed, we had to abandon more and more of them, mostly from lack of fuel or our inability to make them function in those temperatures. So then most of the surviving Panzer troops were attached to infantry groups – I was sent to a HIWI company, which, as I told you yesterday, was where I first met Armin. He had been put in command of a group including some Wehrmacht troops and the remains of his Panzer group at the airfield at Pitomnik before he joined us.

"So that's the story of how the Panzer troops lost their tanks."

He leaned forward and felt the coffee pot. "Cold. Shall I get Marthe to make us some more?" I shook my head. "Not for me, I'm fine, thanks."

"OK, then let's get back to the main story after our little detour. So, we were marched away from Stalingrad towards Beketovka. I don't honestly know how far it is – I guess today, in a car, it would take no more than a few hours. We marched for about four days. Well, I say we marched, but it was really just shuffling along following the man in front. We had no strength left to march. It wasn't like one of those tales you're fed about brave, defeated troops proudly holding their heads high as they leave a battlefield; we were a shattered, destroyed bunch of zombies. And as we left the holding camp, there were crowds of people, a mixture of the civilians who had somehow survived the battle and Russian soldiers guarding the route. They were jeering and spitting at us, then they began throwing stones. Anything we were carrying they grabbed from us – blankets, mostly. That's where Armin lost his case of drawings; he had it slung across his shoulder and as we stumbled through the rubble, someone reached out and snatched it. He'd carried it with him all through the battle, and those pictures were a record of the decline of the 6th Army. Historians now would love to have them, but I guess they went to start a fire in the ruins of the city. The measure of our condition was that Armin didn't even try to struggle to retain the case; he just tramped on ahead of me. I suspect you don't know too much about lice, but as we walked, we warmed slightly, which made them more active, which just made the discomfort worse. You could feel them all over your body. Some men got used to that – or claimed to – but I never could. That was one of the worst parts for me.

"Anyway, we trudged on. Anyone who faltered, or fell out of line, the guards just shot. They shot them and left them there, lying in the snow. There were a lot of groups taken on that march, and I believe well over half of the men died before they even reached Beketovka. Our column was less than half in number by the time we got there and many of those were on their last legs, being dragged or carried by their comrades. We'd been given no more than a few chunks of mouldering bread to eat, and virtually nothing to drink. Men were grabbing handfuls of snow to try and get some liquid. It seemed an endless march.

"Looking at it from fifty years later, it seems incredible that such barbarity could exist between two nations, but in a way I can understand. We were the front line troops, if you like, as we advanced across Russia. We fought the Red Army, and pushed them back to Stalingrad. We had little to do with the civilian population directly" – he held up his hand, as though to stop me interrupting – "I know, we destroyed their country and their lives, but we were fighting a war. But what happened behind us, that was something else. We only really heard rumours of the activities of the SS and the Einsatzgruppen, but there is no question that they introduced a savagery, a racial and political hatred that was unimaginable. It was the counterweight to that brutality that we were caught by." He shook his head sadly, an old man lost in his memories. "I don't know how many millions of people were killed in that campaign, but we have to accept that the extermination of parts of the civilian population was a horrendous crime. Looking back, now, I would have behaved as those Russians did towards us in the immediate aftermath of the battle. You couldn't expect them to distinguish between different Germans - to them, we were all guilty and should be treated accordingly. At the time, of course, after the weeks spent squeezed in the Kessel, we had almost lost our humanity. It was just survival. On that march to Beketovka, we didn't think, we just shuffled one foot in front of the other.

"Anyway, we survived the march, Armin and I, and found ourselves in the camp at Beketovka. There was a fence of barbed wire, with quite low watchtowers at intervals along it. The main camp consisted of wooden huts, badly constructed, unheated and with rows of wooden bunks as the only furnishing. When we arrived, after that dreadful march, we had to stand outside for several hours while we were counted. The number must have changed quite a lot while they were counting, because men were dying as we stood there in the snow. That pointless counting became the main feature of our existence – every day, out there in front of the huts, we stood for hours. And what difference it made, I have no idea. They certainly didn't need the numbers to arrange their catering! We got a bowl of greasy black 'soup' each day, and untreated millet; you probably don't know anything about that, but it's very difficult for humans to digest, especially when they are already suffering severe malnutrition. It just made our condition even worse, if that were possible. We had to try and heat the snow to melt it to provide water, but you can probably imagine that with the rampant disease and death, the snow itself was stained and filthy and poisonous."

He looked at me, and must have seen the sheer horror of disbelief on my face. "Alex, are you sure you want me to continue? This story does not get better. There is a happy ending for me" – he gestured around him, at his house – "I'm comfortably here at home in my expensive house in Hamburg. But I'm one of the very, very few survivors."

"I've come so far in trying to find out what happened that I think I need to hear it through to the end. I know it's not pleasant, but I can't just let my uncle disappear in such a hideous place; he's part of the family. We need to remember him."

He nodded his understanding. "I knew from Armin how close his family were to each other. So different from my own. You seem to carry it to the next generation."

"Yes, I think we're all quite close. But I don't know yet whether or not I will tell them all the detail. But I have to know."

"OK, but let's take a break. At my age, I don't necessarily walk far, but I like to get out each day. Shall we take a walk, and I'll show you a bit of the village?"

"By all means."

1999 Hamburg

We wandered down the narrow passageways with their cobblestones and uneven stairs and came out finally right down by the river front. As we walked, an old man out for a stroll with an acquaintance, Hartmann chatted on. "You know, I saw the land for this house years ago, long before we could afford it. There was an old cottage there, and eventually in the late seventies I bought it, so that my wife and I would have somewhere to retire. Then the business really took off, and we bought the big house on the Elbchaussee. But we always dreamed of this place, because of the view and the way it's a little village, although it's so close to the city. So eventually, after selling the company out, we had time and we started planning to demolish the old cottage and build the new house that we had designed by one of Hamburg's best architects. Eventually it was finished, we moved in, and then six months after that, my wife died, so I've lived here alone since." He shrugged. "You know, things never work out as you want them to, and Russia taught me to be grateful for every good thing as you enjoy it. And my wife was certainly a good thing. It's sad we never had any children, though, to pass things on to. I would have liked to see my company go to another generation; but life is how it is."

He led us over to a bench on the river bank, and we sat looking at the view. I felt sorry for him then; all the suffering in the war and afterwards, and then the retirement with his wife he had looked forward to had been cut off. Somehow, it almost seemed worse than the camp, perhaps because it was final. He glanced at me, and must have seen something in my face. "We had six happy months here, you know. It's not as if she had a long illness. It was a sudden heart attack – alive and happy one day, gone the next. Really, after all the starvation and illness and so on in Russia, you'd have thought it would have been me with the weak heart. In fact, in the camp it was the big, strong guys who went first, on the whole. Smaller, less well built people like me were more able to adapt to the lack of food. Armin was in a bad way at Beketovka; he was a tall man, almost as tall as you, and had obviously been fit and sporty before. But we got him through it. We met up after a few days there with another friend of his, all the way through from university, called Klaus Müller. He'd been taken at Pitomnik airfield and had already been at Beketovka for a couple of weeks before we got there. You know, telling you all this is bringing things back to me. It was Klaus who first told us about the black uniform thing. He had been in the same Panzer regiment as Armin, but in Beketovka, he was wearing a grey infantry uniform; he had taken it from a body when he realised that they were weeding out the black clad soldiers. We didn't have a chance to do that, and anyway, in the end it made no difference. I heard that Klaus died in a work camp near Moscow about a year later. By that time, we had been moved up to Norilsk – Norillag, as we knew it – with Ukrainians and Russian politicals as well as Germans." He stood up. "Come, let's go back up to the house and have some lunch, then I'll tell you the rest of the story. You may have to give me your arm up the steep bits of the path."

1943 Russia

Chapter Twenty-Six

The remnants of the 6th Army sat dying at Beketovka and the other camps. Kuhlmann and Hartmann had managed to stay together while on the nightmare march from Stalingrad, even though Kuhlmann was barely hanging on. In the camp, standing out in the freezing air at one of the seemingly endless counting parades, they had met up with Kuhlmann's old university friend, Klaus Müller, who had survived the fall of Pitomnik a couple of weeks earlier. Over the next few days, the other two had kept Kuhlmann alive, sharing their meagre rations with him and hunkering down when possible in a corner of their hut to try and preserve some warmth. There were dead and dying all around them. The Russians hardly bothered to move the corpses and the dead and the waste products created a foul stench that permeated the whole camp. Apart from the parades, the Russians kept to the outside of the barbed-wire fence. There were two doctors in the camp, but with no access to drugs, food or clean water, there was frankly virtually nothing they could do to ease the suffering of their comrades. There were around 50000 prisoners there, and to be fair, even had the NKVD wished to do anything to alleviate conditions, it would have been nigh-on impossible; nobody had ever thought of what might happen at the end of the battle, in the sense of making logistic plans. The result of the lack of planning and indifference to the suffering of the prisoners meant that Beketovka would come high on a list of the most evil places on earth.

Then the dividing began. First, the NKVD troops came in and separated the prisoners by nationality. The Romanians and Hungarians were weeded out and moved to their own huts. Then, the Austrians were separated; it was an irony not lost on the Germans that the Austrians, followers of the Austrian, Hitler, managed to differentiate themselves and enjoy marginally better treatment; how easily the popular acclamation of the Anschluss in 1938 was forgotten.

Finally, the Germans themselves were split. Those who aroused the biggest antipathy amongst the NKVD, that is, the SS and the Feldgendarmerie, who had been complicit in the vile activities of the SS-

Sonderkommando of the Einsatzgruppen, were put in separate huts from the ordinary Wehrmacht soldiers. Kuhlmann and Hartmann, along with many others, found themselves caught with the hated ones, thanks to their Panzer uniforms; Hartmann's protestations in Russian earned him no more than a smash in the face with a rifle butt and they were moved into the other huts in a separate part of the camp. It was the last time Kuhlmann saw his friend Klaus Müller, with whom he had been through university and the whole war until now. Officers, NCOs and other ranks were theoretically put into separate huts, but Hartman was supporting Kuhlmann, who was still bad, and was simply swept with him into an officers' hut. All the uniforms with their badges of rank were shredded and filthy, and nobody really cared who went where, so the two stayed together.

In late April, as the spring finally started to arrive on the steppe, the Russians began the monumental task of rationalising the prison camps. All in all, in the twenty or so camps around Stalingrad there were about 235000 prisoners. There were the remains of the 6th Army, including Romanians, Hungarians and other allies and members of the 4th Panzer Army, most of whom had been taken during Manstein's abortive attempt to break through to the Kessel during the winter.

First of all, bizarrely in view of the notional egalitarianism of Stalin's Russia, the senior officers were taken off to a camp near Moscow, where they benefitted from far more civilised conditions than those they left their men suffering. A far higher percentage of senior officers survived than of any other ranks, including Paulus himself, who was finally repatriated to the Soviet Zone of Germany where he penned his account of the disaster that had overtaken his command. The junior officers, NCOs and ordinary soldiers were seen as a labour force, desperately needed in a country whose male population was almost completely under arms. Regardless of any conventions concerning the treatment of prisoners of war, Stalin intended to use this by-product of the battle to sustain basic Russian industry. When they were being sorted, many of the Germans described themselves as 'agricultural labourers', in the expectation that life on the land would be the least of many possible evils. To little effect; some were sent as far as the Pamir valley, in modern-day Tajikistan, to build a power station; many went to factories in the Urals; some, indeed, remained in the Stalingrad area and formed the labour force for the reconstruction of the city. Some few did get their wish and worked on collective farms; working conditions may have been marginally preferable, but in the end, it made little difference: the survival rate was pretty much the same.

By early May, Kuhlmann's condition had stabilised. They were all still suffering disease and severe malnutrition, though, and the death rate had hardly reduced; every morning, their first task was to remove the dead from the hut and stack the bodies by the burial area. The work-parties were constantly digging mass graves, throwing the bodies in and then covering them with a layer of lime before putting the next batch of bodies on top. Those in the burial parties themselves were particularly vulnerable through constant exposure to decomposing bodies. For the rest, there was no occupation at Beketovka; they simply sat, mostly in silence, still struggling to comprehend what had happened to them. As the numbers in the camp decreased, through death and the trains rolling out to other camps across the Soviet Union, the amount of food available for those remaining increased marginally, which contributed to Kuhlmann's improvement. Then, half way through the month of May, it was their turn. After the first counting parade of the day, the inmates of half a dozen huts in their part of the camp were marched off the main camp square towards the railway sidings. There were a number of trains there, all made up of a locomotive and a string of enclosed wagons. Russian soldiers were loading columns of men into the trains, prodding those that didn't – or couldn't – move fast enough with their bayonets or striking them across the back of the head with their carbines. They were allotted, a hundred at a time, to a wagon. As they were forced up through the door of the wagon, Hartmann managed a smile. "Train journeys always lead somewhere, Armin. It must be better." Kuhlmann nodded his agreement, and indeed that was the general expectation amongst them all. They had been defeated and then suffered the horrors of captivity, but at least they were leaving the hated Beketovka. Surely for a more conventional prisoner-of-war camp?

By the time there were a hundred men in the wagon, it was cramped. Pots of a rough porridge and chunks of salt fish were thrust in after them and the doors to the wagon were closed. They stayed there in the dark, most sitting, some standing, for hours before the train – obviously now fully laden – eventually began to move forward. They ate the food; there was a single hole in the middle of the floor through which they could urinate and defecate. Soon, the atmosphere in the wagon became foetid and dank. They had no water and the salt fish exacerbated their thirst. The train rolled on through what must have been a day, when it braked to a halt. The doors were pulled open and a voice in pigeon German called out "How many dead?" There was no answer, and, cursing, three Russian soldiers clambered in and began checking. Out of the hundred, after the first day, ten had died. Their bodies were unceremoniously dragged out and dumped through the wagon door. More porridge and salt fish was put in, this time accompanied by a couple of drums of water. The same routine was repeated, and after four days it had begun to dawn on the prisoners that this was not in fact better, it was simply the same as Beketovka with the added discomfort of being in a bare, ill-sprung moving prison. They had no idea where they were going, but after seven days, their number was down to around half what it had been. It was also getting colder again, and eventually, on the eighth day, when the train stopped instead of the usual call of "How many dead?" the Russian soldiers swung up into the wagon and started to prod them out through the door. Stumbling out, their eyes were initially blinded by the white snowy landscape. Some of them grabbed handfuls of snow to thrust into their mouths to alleviate the thirst that had never really left them on the journey, others just dumbly fell into line at the side of the rail wagon. Glancing along the train, Kuhlmann could see it was a lot shorter than it had been when they had boarded it; clearly some wagons had been dropped off on the way. He nudged Hartmann and gestured. "Stopping train; leave when you want to," he said. Hartmann replied with a wan smile. The two had come to depend on each other to get through by now. The guards prodded them into line; only about half the hundred who had been packed into each wagon at Beketovka remained. The rest lay beside the railway lines where they'd been thrown en route. They would never have a grave; just more of the detritus of the war. Under the attention of the guards' rifle stocks, the column shambled along a rough snow-covered track, each blindly following the row in front. Those who fell were dragged out of the column by the guards and shot, the bodies left lying in the snow.

Finally, they were brought to a halt in front of a broad pair of gates in a barbed-wire fence. Their guards carefully counted them, and then the NCO in charge marched forward to the gate. The prisoners could see that beyond the first set of gates there was a space and then a second pair set in an inner fence parallel to the outer one. As the NCO moved forward, the first gates were opened; from the second ones, another soldier advanced towards him. When they met in the middle, the guard NCO saluted and handed over the paper with the number of prisoners he was delivering. The prisoners were then made to move forward, so that they were in the space between the two fences and the gates were closed behind them. A second squad of soldiers now counted them, and, the numbers seemingly agreed between the two, the inner gates were opened and the prisoners marched in. As the gates closed behind them, their original escort marched off back to the train. They had another journey awaiting them.

1943 Siberia

Chapter Twenty-Seven

Slowly, the Germans began to take stock of their surroundings. This was home, now, the last home most of them would ever know, even though they were almost all young men in their twenties. They could see row upon row of wooden huts, a few barred windows on each side. They stood on a path of packed cinders which led to a parade ground dividing the rows of huts in two. Between the huts, the ground was covered in hard-packed snow. There were tall posts with lamps on them around the edges of the parade ground and running in rows down between the huts. The fence was punctuated by squat watchtowers, each topped with a searchlight and with a couple of soldiers on the observation platform, hunched against the cold.

As they stood there, their senses slowly beginning to return after the nightmare of the train journey, they felt the air catching in their throats. Kuhlmann looked up and beyond the far perimeter fence, he could see tall chimneys belching out a thick yellowish smoke. He nudged Hartmann and pointed; "You're from the Ruhr; that must be like home from home." Hartmann started to laugh, but it quickly dissolved into a fit of coughing. The guards came amongst them, splitting them into groups of forty and then pushing and shoving each group towards one of the huts. There were doors at both ends, and each hut was divided across the middle by a shoulder-height partition of thin planking. In each half, there were ten bunks down either side, a bare mattress on each one. Bare bulbs hanging from the ceiling provided a dim light, not really helped by windows which were grimy and barely translucent. The walls were blank wood, broken up only by the regular wooden piles supporting the roof beams. They stared around them; it was better than the filth and squalor of Beketovka, but it was still unspeakably bleak. The guard in charge of the party that had escorted them in told them they would be summoned to parade in one hour, when the commander would address them. Then they would be fed. Meanwhile, they should allocate bunks and generally "settle in and make yourselves comfortable", he said with a sneer. They'd been in the train for days and sheer exhaustion overcame even hunger, as the men lay down on the straw mattresses and slept.

A loud hooter sounded an hour later, waking them from the escape sleep had given them. Guards flung open the doors to the huts of the new prisoners and started yelling at them to get out on parade. Befuddled, cold, hungry, they stumbled out and the guards made them line up, hut by hut, on the parade ground. It was by now pitch dark and the electric lamps cast a harsh white light over the camp. As the last stragglers were pushed roughly into their places, a small group of uniformed men marched out in front of the parade. The man in the middle, shorter than those surrounding him, stepped forward. He began speaking to them, in fluent, unaccented German.

"You are in Siberia. The town you can see over there with the factory chimneys is Norilsk. This camp is one of a series that make up the Norillag correctional facility. You are all prisoners of the Soviet Union, who have been captured after invading the country, killing many thousands of countrymen and destroying many cities. Particularly, you are responsible for the almost total obliteration of the city of Stalingrad. Thanks to the heroic efforts of the Soviet Army, you failed in your mission to subjugate the people. The war continues and will not finish until we have left Berlin in the same state as Stalingrad is now. Many of your comrades who were captured with you are still in Stalingrad and will be used as the labour to rebuild the city; that is justice.

"You, however, have been selected to undertake different work. Under the ground here is a mining complex which produces valuable metal ores, which are then transformed into the metal we need to build tanks and guns to drive the invader from the land. You will be aiding the production. You will work in the mines, in the smelters and on the construction sites in this city we are building here. You will be fed according to the amount of work you do. Each team is allotted its work for the day and that work must be done. If it is not, then your food ration will be decreased by the same percentage as your failing in the work.

"Your routine is simple; you will parade here at 6:30, and you will be counted. You will then eat breakfast and be issued your food for lunch. You will then parade again and march to your work task of the day. You will break for twenty minutes for lunch and then you will be marched back here at 6:30. When you return, you will eat supper. Behind me, beyond the accommodation huts, is where you will find the refectory building. When you are to eat, you will stay together in your hut groups and queue until the guards tell you to go in. You will then collect your bowls and pass in front of the hatch where your bowl will be filled. You will sit in hut groups and leave when the guards tell you to. For us, the time you spend eating is wasted time; you will obey the orders of the guards and be in and out of the refectory as quickly as possible. One day a week you will not work; for this part of the facility, that day will be Saturday. For those who are confused, today is Thursday. On Saturdays, you will have some educational classes conducted by political commissars. We believe that all men are saveable; with Soviet re-education perhaps even members of the SS and Wehrmacht can again become useful members of society.

"You should also know this is the last time you will be addressed in German; from now on, you will have to understand Russian, except for the re-education which may continue to use German. Now, the guards will escort you to the refectory to eat. Please remember what I have told you. Infractions of the rules will result in punishment. Punishment will not be pleasant." He paused, and then spoke again. "Ah, I almost forgot. Before you eat, you will be taken to the delousing showers and then issued with your prison clothing. You will no longer wear that uniform." In fact, the uniforms they were wearing, once-proud clothing of the German Reich, were shabby, ripped and mixed with all sorts of the warmer Russian uniforms they had taken from bodies to try and keep warm in the Kessel.

The guards marched them to the far end of the camp, stripped them, sprayed them with a foul-smelling chemical and then made them walk through the showers, where the water was barely above freezing. They were then all handed the rough padded two-piece uniform of the Gulag; there was a number stencilled on the back of every one. They were also given their foot-cloths and a pair of felt boots. Their heads were shaved. Then, like cattle, they were herded to the refectory. The food consisted of a bowl of thin cabbage-flavoured soup and a hunk of hard bread. They were given no more than a few minutes to eat it, group by group and were then marched back to their huts.

A general lassitude took them that first night; it was difficult to come to terms with this reality. Conditions in Beketovka had been worse, but it had been the end of the battle, the end of the struggle. Now, here in the Arctic, they were faced with the reality that this was the future. It wasn't going to change, not for a long time. Their experience had convinced most of them by now that they were going to lose the war; all they could cling on to was the hope that when it ended, they may be sent back home. Lying on his back in his bunk, staring into the darkness around him, Kuhlmann couldn't believe where he was. All through the campaigns there had been a thin, tenuous thread that had connected him to his family. He'd been on the wrong side, but at least he'd understood it. Now, he was somewhere in Arctic Siberia, cut off twice from those he loved – once by being in the wrong army, and once by being a prisoner. His mind wandered back into the past, dreaming of the little sisters who had meant so much to him, and he wept, lying in a prison bunk, wearing the rough uniform of a Soviet political prisoner. Whatever hopes any of the others may have harboured, he knew the Russians were never going to let them go. The Geneva Convention precluded using prisoners-of-war as forced labour, so they'd never be released to tell their tale. They'd just work until they became too weak to be of any use, and then they'd be left to die. He let his mind take him back to the dream of the happiness of the past, and eventually he slept.

1999 Hamburg

Chapter Twenty-Eight

By the time Hartmann had finished telling me about the early days of their captivity and their arrival at Norilsk, lunch had long gone and we were again sitting in front of the big windows looking over the Elbe.

"You know, after the first shock of finding ourselves slaves, it kind of settled down, just into a routine. You got up in the morning, you ate the swill they gave you and you marched out to wherever that day's work was to be. Most of the time, at least in that first year, we were above ground, but sometimes we were sent down the mine to haul trucks of ore back from the face to the bottom of the elevator; that was hard work. It was the worst job; I remember pulling the trucks, a rope tied round your waist, your back always bent and in that terrible atmosphere down the mine. The miners blasted the ore body to break it and there was always a haze of dust that got into your lungs, your eyes, your ears. You were down there for eight hours, and the targets they set for the amount of ore you had to haul were big. Mostly, we couldn't achieve them, so we had reduced food rations.

"But let's not get ahead of ourselves. I'll try and tell it chronologically. First of all, we got to know the others in our hut. They were a mixture of SS and Panzer troops, like us, also caught by the black uniform issue. But these SS men weren't really the ones the Russians wanted, either. These were SS troops, caught with us in the Kessel. The ones they wanted revenge on were the Einsatzgruppen, and they had always been behind the front, doing their filthy work when the front line troops had already moved on and taken the battle further. There were few of them in the Kessel because that was on the front line. These SS guys were soldiers, not the thugs and murderers the Russians really wanted. It was just the way the conscription worked. Some were conscripted into the Wehrmacht, like me and Armin, others into the SS. The hard line Nazis who chose to join the SS for ideological reasons, they never put themselves in danger in the advance across Ukraine and Russia, nor in the trenches or the street fighting at Stalingrad. Some of those guys in the camp with us were only eighteen or nineteen years old. He shook his head sadly, a far-away look in his eyes. "When you get to my age, you ask yourself, why do societies send their young men away to war? They're the future, or they should be, so why send them to be killed? It's crazy.

"Anyway, in our section we were all Germans; in the other half of the hut, there were a few Ukrainians as well and the camp as a whole at the beginning was about half and half German and Ukrainian.

"I should explain that the Norillag camp network had been in existence since before the war; Stalin had been sending his own citizens there since the early thirties, but our particular camp was new. We were amongst the first arrivals, and it slowly filled up over the next few weeks as more drafts were brought in. I'm not sure how long before the war they'd started the mining, but all of that was already developed by the time we were there. There was a smelter there, as well, which was where all the filthy smoke and pollution came from, but it was being extended and we were most often working either at the smelter or on the construction site of the extension. I don't know why, but mostly they made the Russians do the underground work; for us that was quite unusual. But whatever particular task we had any day, it was all heavy, hard labour. We were just the brute force they needed to do a lot of what frankly in Germany would mostly have been done by machinery. It was an incredibly wasteful process."

He looked at his watch. It was six-thirty, and the view outside was fading in the dusk. "I think it's time we had a drink. And I'll tell Marthe to prepare us some dinner; you will stay?"

I nodded. "Thank you. Of course, as long as you are prepared to go on telling me, I'm ready to listen."

He stood up and went across to a cabinet of drinks. The old man with the distant look in his eyes who was telling the story morphed back into the urbane, wealthy host. "What would you like? Beer, gin, whisky, glass of sekt? Anything else?"

"I'll have a gin and tonic, please."

He smiled at me. "Of course; very English. I'll have a beer."

He busied himself with ice and glasses and bottles for a moment or two and I reflected on how it must feel for him, to remember the nightmare of the past from the comfort of his luxurious home. He'd clearly managed to put the horrors behind him and forge a normal life here in Hamburg. I wondered how many of his fellow returnees had been as lucky.

"Max, are you in touch with any others who came back from Russia?"

"No. I didn't want to be in the army, I didn't like the Nazis and all I feel about that time is that fifteen years of the prime of my life were stolen from me. I thought very hard before I agreed to see you, because I knew it would re-open the past and really I was reluctant to do that.

But then, I thought of Armin, and that he had died unmourned and his grave was unmarked, and I couldn't ignore the chance to finish his story for his family.

"So far, I haven't really talked specifically about him; I've just been telling you how it was generally, for all of us. Perhaps it's time to concentrate a bit more on him particularly." He paused, then handed me my drink and went across to the four pictures on the wall. He stood in front of them for a moment, seemingly lost in his thoughts.

"Where to begin? OK, well, here, with the pictures. You've seen these, and you've seen the ones in Norilsk. The first thing you should understand is that he was a genuinely talented artist. Friends from galleries in Hamburg who have been to this house and seen these have begged me to sell them; obviously, I can't do that, they are more to me than money. But I tell you that so you can understand.

"But I have not been able to look at them; they don't normally hang there in this room. That would have been too much of a reminder of what I wanted to forget. They've been kept in a cupboard, all these years. I just brought them out yesterday, so that you could see them. These four, and whatever there still is in Norilsk, these are the only surviving pieces of Armin's work in the world."

I interrupted. "No, we have a few still in the family. But these and the ones in Norilsk are different. The others are from when he was a teenager - they're good, but they don't have the power, the rawness of these. The experience changed him as an artist."

"Yes. Look, I have these on my wall today, but they are disturbing pictures. The suffering of the victims is so visceral, it's difficult for me to look at them." He pointed at one of the four. "That's me. That tortured face is me in my mid-twenties, when I should have been at my peak. But Armin has caught the horror of our lives so clearly. He drew that in the evenings, after we had returned from work and from our feeding." A memory clearly struck him. "You speak German – you know the difference between essen and fressen; for us it was the latter – it was a feeding time, not a mealtime." He sat down again, facing the huge windows.

"But to begin. So there we are in our camp, we are malnourished, we are working harder than anyone has a right to ask of us, and we can see no end to this life. At that time, in the first few months of our captivity, despair was probably greater than at any time before, in the Kessel or at Beketovka. We knew we were forgotten, that the Germans could do nothing to bring us home and that for the Russians we could conveniently be worked here until we died. We were no longer people, we were just totally expendable cogs in Russian industry. When we had gone, there would be replacements immediately there to take our place. In short, there was no hope.

"In those circumstances, you can probably understand that there were quite a lot who tried, and in many cases succeeded, to take their own lives. I said before there were boys of no more than eighteen or nineteen, and they were the most likely to take that way out. Later, the camp became our life, and our society and relationships ordered themselves to that reality. For the first period, though, that hadn't happened. In our hut, there were no suicides, but nevertheless everyone had to find their own way to adapt to the life. Some of the men turned inward, and would hardly speak. Others spent all their time writing letters home; although the Russians took the letters, I doubt if any of them were sent. Why should they bother? But for some in those early weeks, that was the only thing they could cling on to. Armin and I spoke a lot together, mostly about our homes and families." He smiled. "You know, I probably know more about your mother as a child than you do! We came to rely on each other; just knowing there was somebody you could talk to made such a difference; otherwise, you had to bear it all alone. I envied him; obviously, his father was a rich man and he had grown up in big houses, with servants and cars and lots of holidays, but it wasn't that. It was the family that made me jealous. Whenever he talked about things he had done, he was always saying 'we', not just 'I'. I had a sister, three years older than me, and I was fond of her, but we lived our separate lives; she had her friends, I had mine. We lived in the Ruhr, where my father was a manager at a steel foundry, and my parents made a good home for us. But when Armin described his life at home, it seemed idyllic. Although we'd known each other for a while now, it was only then that he told me how split the family had become, and how the rest of them were in England. That was awful, and I then understood that his separation from normality was at two degrees, unlike the rest of us. That bit I didn't envy so much.

"Anyway, that talking about our lives before the war was how he and I got through that early period at Norilsk. Without his company, I think I would have gone mad. And it did me good to see how a man who had been dealt such an unfair hand could bear it with such dignity. Look, we both wanted desperately to go home, but whatever we said to the others, to encourage them, to each other we were honest that we thought we would die there.

"I already knew he was an artist, because I had seen the drawings he had made in the Kessel, and some of those he still had from before, during the advance through Ukraine. They would have been a fantastic historical record, they showed the deterioration of the soldiers from the good days at the beginning through to the end. I still remember the drawings he did in Groscurth's bunker in the final hours before the surrender. Those would have been gold-dust to historians - the photographs of the battle are one thing, but you don't see the faces in detail. Armin's pictures showed the men, the tension, the fear."

He stopped again for a moment, as if trying to make sure he got his thoughts in the right order. He took a swig of his beer, and then began again, his voice quieter, as if the memories swirling around in his mind were taking him back to that bleak place of fifty years ago.

"All the huts in the camp had a stove, and we were given a certain amount of fuel - I imagine you can already guess that the supply was inadequate, especially when it was still cold outside. So we used to smuggle any bits of wood we could back in after our work parties so that we could keep warm. We picked them up during the day and hid them under our uniforms, or grabbed as we saw anything lying on the ground marching back to camp. I remember a few beatings from the guards when they caught any of us doing that. Well, Armin started his camp drawings by using the charcoal those bits of wood produced to sketch on the blank wooden walls of the hut. He drew the faces of the men around us, and I think it was a real shock for some of the men to see how they now looked, according to his drawings. We all saw the deterioration in our fellows, but we all nevertheless expected ourselves to look as we had done before all this started. Seeing the truth of what the war and then captivity had done to us was frightening.

"Most of the guards just ignored the drawings on the wall – I suppose they just wanted a quiet life, and although their superiors would probably have objected, just to be unpleasant, they turned a blind eye. There was one guy, though, who was interested in the drawings and he started talking to Armin about it. That was unusual; mostly, the guards would have nothing to do with us individually – they just treated us as an amorphous mass. The only real exception to that was if they thought you weren't doing what they wanted - you were marching too slowly, or talking when you weren't supposed to, or something - and then they'd hit you, either with a fist or a rifle-butt. But this guy could only have been about twenty and he was clearly unsuitable as a camp guard, from the point of view of the authorities. I guess their conscription was as much of a lottery as ours. He started speaking quietly to Armin when we were being put back in our huts for the night, and eventually he smuggled in some paper so Armin had more than just the hut walls to draw on. Armin was almost manic in those early days; every moment he wasn't working or sleeping or eating, he would be sketching. It was almost as though he was desperate to make sure he had recorded everything. He drew men working in the mine, at the smelter, he drew us marching in our squads from the camp to our work, and of course he drew the faces of the men, mostly just staring into nothing. It was fascinating, after the first few months to look back through those pictures and see how the expressions changed, from what looked like stupefaction to just resignation. The faces got more and more cadaverous, if that was possible, because they were slowly starving us to death, as well. The daily calorie intake - although I didn't know it at the time; then it just seemed insufficient - was only 1200 a day. Then you have to remember that was reduced whenever your team did not fulfil its quota, so overall we were well below an adequate intake, particularly given the hard physical labour we had to undertake. But at least the disease that had been rife in the Kessel and then at Beketovka was nowhere near so prevalent."

He stopped, took a long pull at his beer. His face looked tired and drawn, exhausted by the effect of the memories. "Alex, if you don't mind, I'd like to stop this now. It's a strain going back to that time and I need a break. Dinner will soon be ready, and I suggest you stay overnight here, rather than go back into Hamburg and then return again tomorrow morning. You will find we will have anything you may need, so is that OK with you? Then we can talk of some lighter things this evening. You can tell me more about yourself, your family."

"Well, that's kind, but are you sure it's not too much trouble?"

He waved my protests aside. "Of course it's no problem. I have all this space here, I have good food and wine; please, feel at home. You will be doing me a favour, as well. I like to have company."

He pointed through the window where it was now fully dark. A huge shape, lit with what seemed like hundreds of glowing light bulbs was moving up the river towards Hamburg. "Container ship. That's one of the really big ones, coming in on the full tide. When you see that, and you realise how peaceful Europe is now, with the ships coming in constantly from all over the world, perhaps all the sacrifices did mean something. But I don't know. It all seemed just such a waste." He sighed, and he looked an old man. "As long as it never happens again………. but they said that all before, in 1918. Anyway, come on, let's have another drink and we'll go downstairs and see how Marthe is getting on with the dinner. Then I'll take you right down into my wine cellar and we can choose something good to accompany it."

This time, instead of the stairs, he went to the lift and we went first down one floor to the kitchen and dining room, and then, having learnt we would be eating fish, down another two levels to the wine cellar, where he chose a couple of high-class white burgundies from a large selection of bottles.

The dining room shared the same view over the river as the room above, and the table was angled to the window so that we could both see the passing ships. With the high tide, there were lots of them during the evening. The walls of this room were hung with much brighter pictures, a couple of impressionist-style Provencal landscapes and a striking Caribbean sunset. Presumably, from the gallery owners who had praised Armin's work.

Beyond Stalingrad

It was a relief to me to talk about other things; the unremitting bleakness of Hartmann's tales from the camp was making me depressed. God knows how hard it must have been for him, having lived through it and now retelling it all. It was only then that I began to realise how much I owed him, that he had been prepared to go through it all to try and help me understand what had happened to my uncle.

Away from the talk of the camp he regained his effervescence and was an entertaining companion, with a host of stories about the ups and downs of running his logistics business. He was widely travelled, as well; it seemed to me that he had embraced life to the full having escaped the fate of so many others in the camp. He had healthy appetites, too; a bottle each was clearly his normal expectation of wine at dinner, and then afterwards, sitting back up in front of the windows watching the ships pass, he was very generous with the bottle of Asbach Uralt. It was well after midnight when I made my way down one floor to my room. Sleep didn't come easily. In my mind, I kept seeing the prisoners tramping back and forth to work, struggling to get food, sitting staring hopelessly into the distance with empty eyes. I was grateful not to meet them in my dreams when I did finally fall asleep.

Chapter Twenty-Nine

The wine and brandy combination obviously had no harmful effect on Hartmann; when I came up to the main room around eight thirty the next morning, I met him just coming in through the front door, having been for a walk around the village. "My wife made me promise to get out for a walk at least once a day," he said. "It was one of the last things she said to me; she was worried I would get fat and idle, left to myself." He laughed. "That won't happen. I like my food and drink, but you can see, I'm in pretty good shape. Come, let's have some breakfast. I'm sure Marthe could do you some English bacon and eggs."

We went down to the dining room, where I resisted the temptations and settled for orange juice, croissants and coffee. It was a beautiful sunny day, the light reflecting off the calm surface of the river and the blossom on the trees in the village making an idyllic picture. I pointed out through the window. "That's the sort of picture of Armin's we have at home; pretty landscapes, bright colours and lots of light."

He nodded. "Yes, that's the side I've never seen. By the time I knew him, the art was dark and tortured. There were no colours in the camp and the light was always filtered through the smog of the smelter's pollution. And I guess you think of snow as sparkling white, like it is on your ski holidays or in your English countryside. Well, at Norilsk it was always grey, covering the ground for eight months or so every year." He took a sip of his coffee. "You know, I've tried to block the camp out of my mind, but now as I think back to those times, the more the memories all come back to me. Things that seem so trivial now, and yet were so important then. Those first pictures of Armin's, the ones I was telling you about, they were all destroyed. That happened because of one of the really petty things. You see, we weren't allowed to have any possessions. Everybody did, of course - you might find a bit of a broken tool that you could whet into a knife, for example, or you might keep a spoon, or anything. But you had to hide it, and every so often the guards would come in and search the huts, turning over all the bedding and stuff just to make sure there was nothing hidden. For them, it was no more than a game, but for us, it was real. These things we hid, we did it because we thought we might be able to use them, or for bartering, but really just so that we could have some kind of individuality. If we're all the same, but I've got a little blade that I can use to whittle sticks, say, and you haven't, then that kind of asserts that I'm different from you, that we're not just the mass of the labour force they want us to be. Saying it now, in this big house so many years later, that sounds crazy, in a way. But then, it was the truth; these things were important out of all proportion.

"So, Armin had drawings hidden under his mattress, and the guards came in to search. He'd avoided it a couple of times before; although they were supposed to search everything, sometimes you got lucky and they missed you. Armin had a top bunk at the end of the row, and they'd just been lazy. This time, though, he was out of luck and they pulled his mattress off and saw all the drawing paper. From the comfort of Hamburg now, we can say: would it have mattered to them to leave them there? And the answer is, of course, logically, no. But logic had nothing to do with it, and they dragged him out to the camp commandant, who immediately gave him five days solitary." His face darkened. "Five days was just about bearable. Ten days was at the maximum, and those who got more, fifteen or twenty days, they almost without exception either came out crazy or, within days, killed themselves. Or both. Solitary was an inner circle of hell, an experience even worse than the camp itself. I only had one three day sentence in all my time there; I'm not sure I could have taken any more."

1943 Siberia

Chapter Thirty

Two of the guards dragged Kuhlmann across the parade ground and through the first wire to the commandant's office, situated in the area between the two barbed-wire encirclements. A third followed behind bearing the drawings in his arms. The commandant listened to the guards, then, without bothering to ask Kuhlmann anything, immediately sentenced him to five days solitary confinement and told the guard to put the drawings straight on the stove. They did that in front of Kuhlmann, before dragging him round to the solitary cell, which was built on behind the block containing the commandant's office and the other administrative functions of the camp. It was a small, square concrete room, not quite big enough for someone of Kuhlmann's height to lie out flat. They were lucky in one respect in this camp, though. At least here they had sufficient headroom to stand up; at some of the other camps, the solitary cells were only around a metre and a half high, meaning any time there guaranteed serious pain in the back. There was a concrete seat set into one corner, and a lockable hinged flap on the door to enable the guards to put the food through without opening it. A hole in the floor provided the only other facility. The only light came from a narrow slit just below the roof on two sides. True daylight never really penetrated, and the thickness of the walls rendered it virtually silent.

Kuhlmann picked himself up from the floor where the guards had thrown him and sat resignedly on the seat. Since Beketovka, he had had no time alone. They had been crammed together, in a camp or on the train, constantly. Individuality had not existed; the effect of the camp, in fact the intention of the camp, was to make every one of them identical, to make them all just the same unit of labour. So for the first day or so of his solitary, Kuhlmann actually enjoyed the sensation of being alone. He was able to ignore the physical discomfort and lose himself in the bliss of silence and solitude. But the mind is a dangerous place and later his thoughts began to wander back to the past. Then the mental torture started; images from his pre-war life swirled around his mind, tempting him back to try and regain those happy times. He let his thoughts drift through the sunny days in the big house in Aue. But then reality always came back, from the pain in his body caused by the confined space or the rattle of the flap as his meagre rations were thrust through or just the dim light and damp, cold atmosphere. Trying to focus his thoughts on reality didn't work – his mind kept floating off to the past. He found himself thinking of that last conversation he had had with his father, back in early January 1939. He had been so sure that the older man had been exaggerating the dangers of going back to Hamburg. And he himself had been so sure, in the arrogance of youth, that he would be all right. It wasn't self-pity, but the torture of feeling that he had let down his parents - his last meeting had been an argument, and now he would never have the chance to put things right. Trying to lose himself in comfortable memories failed, as that last disagreement kept spinning around in his head and then the discomfort and infinite misery of the present intruded again, bringing him back to the torture of the present. That was the true horror of the solitary cell, the way it played with the mind and twisted past and present together, never allowing the prisoner any peace from his thoughts. That was far more telling than the physical discomfort, which was finite. The mental pressure was truly disturbing. Kuhlmann was one of the lucky ones who managed to keep his brain from scrambling under the strain of the blurring of reality and imaginings.

1999 Hamburg

"Of course, you must remember that at this time, the war was still going on," Hartmann continued. "It was just after that spell Armin did in solitary, in around October 1943 that we were visited by Seydlitz." He saw my questioning look. "He was a Wehrmacht general. Although the war was still on, the mixture of our camp was changing. As I told you before, we started off as mostly prisoners-of-war. But during those first six months or so, the number of Russians – political prisoners – increased a lot. I don't really know how, but with the greater number of Russians, we became more aware of the news – of what was happening outside. I suppose they had communication with people outside – letters and so on – which was simply not possible for us. But, you know, when we were outside at work, or queuing for the refectory, they'd pass on the news: it was strange, we were on opposite sides, effectively, but we were all in the same prison. Anyway, we knew the war was going badly for Germany and that the Russians were beginning to advance, although so far of course there had been no invasion by the British and Americans on the western front. The political re-education sessions, which took place every week, consisted of no more than the commandant or one of his political commissars haranguing us about the evils of capitalism and the innate superiority of Soviet socialism. They never gave us any true news, as far as we could tell, compared with what filtered in to the camp, so you can imagine that nobody paid a great deal of attention to them. But then, as I say, Seydlitz appeared one day. Now, he was a controversial character already. We knew that he had bolted from our lines over to the Russians in the last few days of the Kessel. The Russians had accepted him by now, and he had been one of the founders of the Bund deutscher Offiziere, which was an attempt to gather an army of German POWs to join the Russians and fight against Nazism. He came and made a passionate speech about how Hitler and the Nazis had poisoned our nation and told us how true Germans would join him and fight to rid the country of the cancer. He told us he was going to raise an army of 40000, who would be airlifted to attack from behind German lines. Looking back at it now, he was totally delusional. He obviously had no idea how many had died after the surrender, in Beketovka and the other camps, on the rail journeys and then in the work camps. He must have thought the whole 6th Army had survived. But then, it was different, and you could tell from the reactions of some of the others that they saw it possibly as a way out. But Armin put it in a kind of perspective. He stood up, and looked straight into Seydlitz's eyes. 'You're mad,' he said. 'The Nazis got us here, I agree with that. They did poison our country. But are you stupid enough to believe that this alternative is any better? Look around you. You have been cosseted by your captors in your comfortable senior officers' camp. The state of the men you see here is a truer reflection of the power you now want to serve. Don't you understand? We've been lied to, sent into a hopeless war, starved, tortured and abandoned, and you think we are going to start all over again, to repeat all that in the name of another vicious dictatorship? Do you really propose handing our country to another bunch of greedy thugs like before? Do you want the camps to continue, the people to be treated like this?' He gestured around him, at the state of all of us. 'You're just trying to save your own skin because you can see the way this war will end. Do you really think we don't understand that we are the ones suffering here while you and the other senior officers are well looked after, in your special camps? Why would we believe anything you or your sort have to say to us?' By this time, quite a number of the others were muttering in agreement with him; then the guards weighed in and dragged him out of the room. I was worried that he would be going straight back to solitary, but they just took him outside and gave him a beating this time. Seydlitz got no volunteers from our camp, though, and in the end he did himself little good with the Russians, either. They played with him for a while, but then after the war they convicted him of war crimes and then he had to suffer in a camp. Eventually, he was released around the same time as me; he was shunned when he got back to Germany, though. However much people hated what the Nazis had done in their period, Seydlitz's alternative was no better."

He sighed, staring out of the window. "You know, after those first few months in the camp, it all kind of blurs together. We worked every day, long hours, underground or in the factory, we ate inadequate food, we slept. Men died, mostly from the combination of overwork and underfeeding, but also suicides and killings." He saw my sharp look. "Oh, yes, killings. Those little sharpened knives I spoke about earlier, some men used those to cut throats. We were kept cooped up and imprisoned; it's not really surprising that arguments and fights broke out. They were generally about what to you - or to me now - would seem nothing. But then – these were things that could be life and death. Stealing food, stealing tobacco, but most important was not working properly. That may sound odd: why should we care about the work? But that was the cleverness of the system. We worked in teams, normally hut by hut. The work was given to the team leader each day, and he had to ensure that it was finished by the end of the day. If it wasn't, then the whole team would have reduced rations. So everybody had to work to make sure the quota was filled, and if anybody slacked, then the whole team suffered. So persistent slackers could cost the rest of their team dear. It was very simple, but invidious, because when one of your team was ill, maybe, or really couldn't work flat-out, then the lot of you would suffer. And the targets we were set needed flat-out effort to satisfy. If anybody did not contribute fully, the whole team had to exist on even less food than normal. That could create a lot of tension, and it provoked a number of killings over the years we were there.

"To begin with, when we first arrived, one of the SS, a major, was our team leader. But gradually it became clear that he was using the team leadership as a way of trying to duck out of some of the work himself. The Russians left us to choose our own leaders, and we threw him out; two or three others tried, but in the end couldn't command the respect of the rest. Then, after that meeting with Seydlitz where Armin had really made himself much more obvious, we chose him as our leader. The men really came to trust him as a fair man, with enormous personal integrity. It was the same reaction I had seen in the HIWIs back in the Kessel. People respected Armin; I know that sounds strange in a prison camp where we were all first and foremost looking out for ourselves, but the way it was structured, as I said, that meant we were all also dependent on each other.

"I can see us now, on that parade ground, with that brooding, ugly Mount Schmidt looming over the scene, grey snow on its face and peak, cinders under our feet, freezing while the work detail was given to each team leader. Then we march out, through the two barbed wire fences, down the track to the mine combine. Some go underground, some stay on the surface. It's crazy, you know. I was going to tell you about the work how we slaved over it, the day-by-day drudgery of it, but now I come to it, it's just a blur. So many years of my life and I can tell them in one sentence: I worked, I was underfed and I slept. There isn't anything else.

"Armin, though, was different. After the solitary, he still persuaded that guard to bring him drawing materials and this time he was far more careful about keeping them hidden. He had loosened one of the floorboards of the hut and was able to put things down there. Everybody had a place to hide the little possessions they somehow managed to hang on to - I had hollowed out one of the joints of my bunk and I could keep stuff there. Most of us had only one purpose in our lives - to stay alive. But Armin had something else, as well. He made it clear to me that he was drawing because he needed to make a record of what had happened to us. Like me, he thought that ultimately we would never get out of the camp; we didn't believe the Russians would let the world know what they had done. Of course, what we missed was that they were doing the same to their own citizens – it was part of their system. So finally, the few lucky ones like me did get away in the early mid-fifties. We had no idea how the world would get to see the pictures; we just knew he had to draw them and we had to keep them secure. After the manic drawing before the first ones were burnt, he did less, but these were searing images of a group being worked to death. I know you've seen some of them at Norilsk, but there were a lot of others they wouldn't put on show, even now. It became his obsession to bring what was being done to the world's notice." He shook his head sadly. "In the end, I failed him. All I was able to bring out with me were those four, and I couldn't bring myself to show them to the world. I kept them here, hidden even from myself. There've been books written about that time, but you can't put the awfulness of it into words easily. The pictures showed it much more – the bleakness, the zombie faces. I know the world doesn't owe any sympathy to the German army of the Second World War, but we were young men dying as slaves. I was lucky - so very few of us came back."

I interrupted him. "Max, I'm sorry. I shouldn't have come. You've got your life and it's not fair of me to make you go back in your mind to that time. I should have left things alone. I can't change anything by making you relive it."

"No, no, no, Alex. Armin has no marked grave. He has still a family who need to know what happened. I know your mother and your aunt and uncle have all died, but his memory deserves to be kept alive and his soul to be set to rest. I need to do that for him. I should have done it long ago, but I didn't. Now, as I come to the end of my life, it is the time."

1945 Siberia

Chapter Thirty-One

He sat back in his chair, and stared through the window. Now I began to grasp why he shown such initial reluctance to talk to me. When I came here, I hadn't even considered the strain I was going to be putting him under. I had just thought I was asking him to tell me his war experiences, rather like my father had done. It was only listening to him that I had begun to realise that this wasn't like that; I was asking him to talk about almost being starved and worked absolutely to death, while years of his life were stolen from him. Could I really justify that, simply to satisfy my curiosity, or should I let sleeping dogs lie and go back to London, leaving this old man to enjoy the remaining span of his life without driving him back to those unhappy times? As if reading my mind, Hartmann continued.

"I've gone so far with the story, Alex, that I've got to finish it. I can't leave it hanging there.

"So we got to the end of the war. We were getting pretty up to date information by this time, and we knew the end was near. The Russians had told us as each town fell as the Red Army moved westwards; of course, we knew very little of what was happening in the west, how the British and Americans were doing. That I think was pretty generally censored throughout Russia – the people had to be made to believe victory was all the work of their great leader, Stalin. Then suddenly one day there were huge outbreaks of firing as the guards emptied their guns into the sky and great cheers and shouting. When we reached camp that evening after work, the guards were all yelling at us Germans that they'd defeated us and that our country was destroyed. Even some of the Russian political prisoners joined in, although it was difficult to see what they had to celebrate - Stalin was the one who had put them there, after all. The next political re-education session, they made us watch newsreels of the Red Army rolling into Berlin. Those of us who had seen Stalingrad now knew that Russian soldier had been right when he told us as we were marched away that what we had done to their city, they would do in spades to our capital. Armin and I stood together at the back of the room where we were shown this and talked quietly about it. It was a two-edged sword. On the one hand, we could understand the rejoicing at the fall of the Nazis - in fact, we could have joined in with that - but the destruction of one of Europe's great capital cities was horrific. We couldn't imagine how it could ever recover, nor the population. And then, we didn't know about the personal revenge taken by the Russian troops - the rapes, the indiscriminate killings, the looting. I only heard of that when I got back all those years later.

"Some of our fellows, particularly the youngest ones, thought that the end of the war would mean the end of our captivity. There were a few more smiles around, at least for a few days. That expectation didn't last long, though; the commandant called all the German prisoners together on the parade ground and spoke to us. By that time, there weren't actually that many of us. We'd been there for about two years, and the death rate had been horrific. Anyway, he told us that he was very sorry to have to say that we would not be going home; he told us that part of the agreement made by the victorious allies had been to the effect that German prisoners of war could be regarded as part of the economic reparations for the devastation of so much of European Russia, and that we would be staying to continue our work in the rebuilding of the Soviet Republic to atone for what we and our fellows had done. That wasn't news really to me or to Armin - as I said before, we were already resigned to the fact that we wouldn't get out. But for some of the others it was devastating. They had built their hopes on repatriation, and to find it wasn't going to happen destroyed them. The number of suicides went up. Armin was very good with those young guys. He was like an elder brother; he watched over them, he listened as they wept about their future and he gave them his own strength to help them through. I think that period immediately after the war ended was the worst of all, because that's when we found out for sure that we were truly forgotten and abandoned."

"Is that true, that the allies made that agreement then?"

"I'm not sure. I think there was a tacit acceptance that Russia had probably suffered worse than anyone else in the war – on the allied side – and that nobody was going to make too much fuss over a few thousand remnants of a German army."

I nodded. "Mmm. I do know there were some strange things then. I know the western allies sent back a lot of people to Eastern Europe, knowing their fate was extremely dubious. And of course the original tinder-point of the war was the invasion of Poland – well, I guess the Poles would have been disappointed to have been 'rescued', only to be overrun and dominated by foreigners again."

"Sure. The politics between Churchill and Roosevelt on one hand and Stalin on the other were messy. The greater good demanded sacrifices, and we were one of those. As I said, there weren't really many of us by then, and we were well integrated into the Soviet labour system. No, we were an embarrassment to the west and best forgotten.

"Anyway, Armin helped the younger guys through that period, and we had no suicides on our team. The work carried on exactly as before and we started to get a new influx of prisoners. These were Russian soldiers who had been held as prisoners of war by the Germans. They were released as the war finished, but the paranoia at the top of the Soviets was such that they were automatically suspected of having been collaborators with the Germans so they were immediately shipped out to work camps as soon as they got back home. They were utterly bemused when they arrived at Norilsk. They thought they had been freed by their own comrades, and yet here they were imprisoned as slave labour by their own side. If anything could sum up the lunacy of the politics, it was that.

"So in the end, we were quite a small minority, amongst the politicals and now the returning Russian soldiers. There was one difference, though; they had all been given a specific sentence. We hadn't; we were there on an open-ended ticket. For the next few years, the deaths were frankly from overwork and starvation. Those who would kill themselves had done so, and the remainder just did the work and tried to stay alive. In the end, I guess almost anything can become a routine. Our lives were what they were. We worked, we slept and we ate inadequately. There was no future other than that."

Again he paused, and I thought of the true horror of that statement. He was saying that they had given up all hope of what to the rest of the world was normality and become just what their captors wanted them to be - compliant, disposable cogs in the industrial machine. But it was the logical conclusion for the system; people were infinitely replaceable - so why not use them up? For every one that was expended, there would be another. Unshackled by the conventions of humanity practised mostly in the west, the masters of the Soviet Union could spend their human capital freely. And for the Germans, well, their own leaders had been doing the same thing; they were the truly unfortunate ones, caught from both sides and with the sympathy of neither.

"That young guard, the one who had originally given Armin drawing things, he was still there. You know, things are coming back to me: I haven't thought of him for fifty-odd years - now I remember, his name was Pavel. He spoke to the prisoners more than the others, and he seemed to have a bit more humanity in him. I don't want to make it sound like there was a stereotype of the brutal guards, but in truth it was mostly like that. The only contact we had with them was marching back and forth to our work each day, and then they patrolled inside the compound after we got back from work and during the night, to make sure that all prisoners stayed inside their huts. That meant that while we were queuing for food and then returning to our huts after eating we were together in the compound with the guards. Mostly, they were just a threatening presence, always keeping together in at least twos, always holding their guns at the ready, even when they were lounging by the gates, smoking. One or two of them would occasionally give cigarettes to prisoners, but there was no kind of black market or anything like that, like you see in films or on TV. Frankly, they wanted nothing to do with us, particularly those of us who were German."

"How did they know who was who?" I asked, curious. "Surely you were all wearing the same prison uniform, all had shaven heads? Was it possible to distinguish Germans from the others?"

"It was in the number. All prisoners had a number stencilled on their uniform, and the letter in front of the three digit number determined your origin. So they knew who was who, and we were right at the bottom of the pile for them."

He got up from his chair and stretched his arms. "The days ran into months and the months ran into years. We heard about the great events that were happening, but they never impacted on us. The Berlin airlift, the beginning of the Korean War, all we heard just reinforced the idea that the world had split into two, and we were caught on the wrong side of it. The political indoctrination went on; I don't know what they were hoping to achieve, because even if we had become converted to Stalinism, they weren't going to let us go.

"But then, in late 1950 and early 1951, they did begin some repatriations. We heard through the grapevine that prisoners from the camps around Stalingrad, which was where the bulk of the Germans were kept, had begun to be sent home. Then a couple of months later, a trickle of men from the Norillag system started to be sent back. We were surprised, given our scepticism about ever being free again, but it seemed that some movement was taking place. I still have no idea what prompted the Soviets to change their minds, but I can only assume there was some hidden political agreement between east and west and this was the outcome. In fact, between then and around 1954/55, pretty much all the survivors were sent back. There was a lot of arbitrariness, though, and where men ended up was very mixed. The lucky ones got to Western Germany – but there were a lot who ended up in the East. Of course, at that time, there was still a degree of free movement between the two halves of the country, not like it became later when the borders were effectively sealed."

He stared off into the middle distance, remembering. "It was in winter 1952 that Armin died."

Beyond Stalingrad

January 1952, Siberia

January 22nd 1952 started like any other day for the prisoners at Norilsk. The klaxon blasted out at six a.m., on a cold, cold day. There was a thin drift of snow in the air, but during the night it had clearly snowed more, because the parade ground was covered in a new fall. The cold white lights up on their poles shone brightly; daylight would not come for many hours yet, so far north in mid-winter. Pairs of guards, muffled from head to toe in heavy clothing to ward off the cold, rifles slung across their shoulders, marched across from the perimeter to the doors of the huts, which they unlocked and flung open. Inside, the prisoners were hurriedly donning their padded prison uniform jackets and wrapping whatever pieces of cloth or fur they had managed to beg or steal from the guards around their shaven heads; they scrambled to get out through the doors, despite the cold. The sooner their hut got to the refectory, the better; the food was hot for the first inmates, but if they were unlucky enough to be at the back of the queue, not only did they have to stand in the bitter cold waiting while others ate, but the likelihood was also that the porridge they were served would be no more than tepid. Kuhlmann and Hartmann jogged with the rest of their hut across the frozen ground. They were in luck; their hut was first to the doors of the refectory, which meant they would be the first ones in for breakfast. As they made to go inside, though, a group from another hut arrived and began trying to jostle and barge their way through the group of Germans. The newcomers were a mixture of Russian politicals and former Russian POWs and as they pushed and shoved their way forward, some of the Germans reacted angrily to the breaking of accepted camp behaviour. Soon the two groups were scuffling; one of the Germans fell to the ground, and as his fellows stepped forward to protect him, suddenly both groups were lashing out at each other. The guards, who normally stood back and watched as the prisoners meekly filed through the refectory to get their food, weighed in with their rifle butts to try and separate the fighting prisoners. They didn't hold back at all, and in a couple of minutes there were about half a dozen men lying on the ground clutching their bleeding heads. The NCO of the guards shouted orders at his men, and they separated the two sides. He called for the two team leaders and they were roughly dragged in front of him. One thing the authorities were seriously worried about was an uprising amongst the inmates of the camp system; there had been a couple of instances elsewhere and they had been stamped on hard. The NCO left the two leaders, Kuhlmann and a Russian political, standing in the snow while he went to seek instructions from the commandant. Four guards kept watch on them, while the remainder chivvied the prisoners through the refectory and off to the parade ground to prepare to march out to work. Kuhlmann and the Russian were still standing there in the bitter cold when the rest of the prisoners set off to the mine combine.

They were there for around an hour and then the commandant marched out of the administrative building and through the inner gate into the camp compound. He stood in front of the two. "Under the NKVD code for the behaviour of prisoners in work-camps, it is forbidden for prisoners to fight amongst themselves. It is further forbidden to permit other prisoners to do it. You are the team leaders of your huts and it is your responsibility to maintain discipline among your men. I cannot accept prisoners behaving as happened this morning. There will be an example made. Kneel down." Both men knelt, and the commandant walked round behind them. Pulling out his pistol, he put a bullet in the back of each of their skulls. They pitched forward, blood and brains pouring on to the grey snow. The bodies were left lying face down in the snow.

1999 Hamburg

Hartmann walked round the room a couple of times, then he continued.

"When we got back from the mine that evening, there was no sign of Armin. His bedding was still on his bunk, and I quickly checked his hiding place; the drawings were all still there as well. I assumed that he had been sentenced to a spell in solitary again, but then the young guard, Pavel, whom I spoke about before, fell in beside me as I walked back from my evening meal. He described what had happened. I broke down. I sat on my bunk in the hut weeping. Armin and I had been constant companions for nine years; we had known nothing but a losing battle and captivity in each other's company, but through that he had become the best friend I have ever had. We'd struggled through all of it together. The Kessel, Beketovka, years of slavery in the Norillag; he'd got through all of that, and then to die for something so stupid as a petty squabble about who got to eat first. And he wasn't even involved in the squabble. Face down in the snow, the back of his head blown away. It was the arbitrariness of it that seemed so futile. On a different day, he may have got solitary, or maybe even the guards would simply have beaten up a couple of the fighters to show the rest of us. But this day..........I have no idea why, but the commandant for his own reasons decided that the sanction had to be the death of two men.

"And that was it. If I had been an automaton doing my work before, now I became like a zombie. My mind closed in on itself. My only wishes were to get some of Armin's work out for the world to see and to tell the story to his family. Pavel was a decent man; he made sure I had time to hide the stuff again before Armin's bunk was reoccupied, and in fact he smuggled some of it out. I guess the drawings you saw in Norilsk were those; either that, or they found the rest after I had gone."

Somehow, I hadn't expected the end to have been like that. I don't know what I had been prepared for, but the story was unsettling. To have gone through all the hardships, to have suffered the battle, the prison camps, the slavery, and then to have died alone, shot on a whim, seemed worse than anything I could have expected. Hartmann must have seen something of that in my face, for he sat down again next to me. "Alex, I told you it wasn't a pretty story. But you know, there are a lot of good things despite the ending. Remember your uncle as a fine man, a talented artist, but above all a decent and honourable man in the most trying of circumstances. He was loyal to his friends, he thought of his family to the last. You should all be very, very proud of him. My friend, it's trite to say wars are awful things, but unfortunately they shape a lot of men's lives. What you should remember, and cherish, is that through all of the war and its aftermath, he remained the most steadfast of friends. I still miss him, even after all this time." He paused. "And I'm more sorry than I can tell you that I didn't come and find his family many years ago. I let him down."

"I don't think you let him down. Life let him down; nobody should have to live and die like that. You suffered it as well. As you yourself said, you were one of the lucky ones. When you got back, it was perfectly natural that you tried to catch up and live your own life. Everybody would have done the same."

"Well, what's done is done. But now you know the whole story, Alex. I told you it wasn't pretty, but at least you now know for sure what happened to your uncle."

"Yes; I think I'm glad my mother and her sister didn't find out the truth. It was probably less painful for them to be able to convince themselves that he had died in the battle rather than that he had lived through the camp and then died there. And my grandmother, of course. Losing a son in war would be bad enough, but to know that he had become a slave and died just on a vicious whim would be far worse."

"Worse than uncertainty? I don't know; I should have told them when I got back, but, you know, I just wanted to put all of it behind me and restart my life."

"So finish the story, Max. Your story. How did you get back to Germany?"

Chapter Thirty-Two

Hartmann's eyes got that far-away look again, remembering. "By the spring of 1954, there were very few of us left who had been there from the beginning. Mostly they'd died, although a few had for some reason been sent to different camps. As I said, I don't know what triggered a change in the Russians' attitude, but they started releasing people, or, more correctly, repatriating them. Some went in March and April, and then at the beginning of May I was told to be ready to leave in two days time, when I would be sent back to Germany. I was to travel with one other prisoner, who had been in the same batch as me on the train from Beketovka, all those years ago. But he'd been in a different hut from me, and always on different work details, so although I was aware of whom he was, I didn't really know him at all.

"So anyway, on the day of our departure, after the first roll-call, the two of us were marched over to the administrative building between the two wire fences; there we were finally able to take off the prison uniforms. What we were given to replace them was pretty basic, but you have no idea how good it felt to be out of the uniform. Until then, I hadn't really believed that we were going to be able to leave. But we did. We were put in the back of a truck and it delivered us to the port of Dudinka. They put us in a guardhouse there, and we waited, getting more and more impatient. In the camp, the days just passed at their own pace, there was no room for emotions, like boredom, or patience, or hope. You just worked and ate and slept. Nothing else mattered. But now, when we could see that we were on the verge of going back to the world, suddenly that waiting became almost impossible to bear. It was as though something was awakening that had been hibernating inside us. We started to talk about the future, which never happened in the camp; there, there was no future, nor any past. Everything was just survival in the present. That's when I discovered that I didn't like the man I was with. He was a genuine SS man, not like us caught out by the black uniform. He was a Hauptsturmführer, which I think to you would mean captain, or maybe senior lieutenant, something like that. Anyway, he was an SS officer and even after eleven years in the camp, he still needed to make me understand that I was his inferior. I had been a sergeant, but I'd forgotten all about that kind of thing years before; in the camp, rank meant nothing. You worked the same, whatever you had been before; well, anyway, this man, Rolf Dietzer was his name, was still determined to follow the rules of the third Reich. He called me Hartmann and expected me to call him 'Sir'. Well, I wasn't going to jeopardise my trip to freedom by arguing - although had he tried this in the camp I would have hit him - so by the time they took out us on the ship, I was just not speaking to him. We were locked in a small cabin with no windows, a light on twenty-four hours a day. The ship was one of the regular ones that transported the nickel to Europe; it took about four weeks, through the Barents Sea and round the North Cape at the top of Norway. At first, we weren't allowed out at all; we stayed in our cabin, two meals a day, and that was it. Then, after three or four days, we were let out during the day and ate with the seaman in their mess. They were all Russians and actually they treated us fairly well. For us, the big deal was to get enough food, because we were given the same rations as the sailors. That was incredible." He stopped and looked straight at me. "You must remember, we had basically not eaten properly since 1942, before the Kessel closed. Anyway, our metabolisms had to an extent adapted to the lack of food, so after the first full meal we had, we were both violently sick. Funnily enough, that made Dietzer a bit more human; he toned down his SS superiority a bit after that, and we reached a kind of armed truce where we could speak to each other, as long as we kept off the war, the Party or the future of the world. That suited me anyway; I didn't know what I would be coming back to. We knew - obviously - that Germany had lost the war, but we didn't know the extent of the bombing and the destruction, nor how much reconstruction there would be going on. The Russian sailors told us a bit – they made the voyage to Hamburg, Rotterdam and Antwerp regularly, but of course in those days on a Russian ship they weren't allowed to get off while they were in a western port, so their knowledge was limited.

"It was quite boring on the ship; we saw the North Cape as we passed quite close, but most of the time all you could see was the empty sea and the horizon. The voyage took about four weeks, and I was really excited by the time we were coming down the Danish coast. Well, we came into the river past Cuxhaven, and that's when I really began to understand that finally I was going to be home. Dietzer and I sat on the deck all the way along the Elbe to the city." He pointed out through the window. "We came down past here in broad daylight and with the sun shining. Lord knows, the Germany we'd left, the Nazis' thousand-year Reich, hadn't been my idea of heaven, but to be home! Alex, you have no idea. We docked in one of the basins and the captain called us both into his cabin. There he gave us the travel papers that would let us into Germany, and bade us farewell. We walked down the gangplank, carrying nothing but a small bag each with some odd clothes in it. We went into the Port Authority office and announced ourselves. We were obviously not the first, because they knew exactly how to treat us.

"First of all, they welcomed us home - and hearing that word 'home' just made my eyes well up - and told us we were back amongst our own people. They gave us a temporary pass, and a sheaf of documents to complete to get our registration done, and our identity cards and all that sort of stuff, and they gave us some money to see us through the first couple of weeks. By then, they said, provided we dealt with all the forms they had given us promptly, we would be in position to receive our former soldiers' pension, which would help us to get started in our new lives.

"So an hour later, there I was, in company with a largely unreformed Nazi, walking down from Altona into Sankt Pauli. Today, by our standards now, we would describe it as a drab mess, bomb sites mixed with new construction sites and the very occasional surviving pre-war building. We got to the Reeperbahn in the early evening; now, you know what it's like today." I nodded. "Bright light, clubs, shows. Well then, it was different. It was still the genuine seaman's red-light district. There were dive bars, whores on every corner and an overall feeling of life on the edge. But to us, that day, it was incredible, just indescribable. We found the Seamen's Mission, dumped our pitiable possessions, and went out and hit the night. We hadn't drunk alcohol for twelve years or so, and we ended up in some sleazy club. Somebody could easily have taken all our money off us - not that we had much, just the bit the Port Authority had given us - but they didn't. We told them our story and where we'd come from, and they stood us drinks all night, and the whores took pity on us. We stumbled back to the Seamen's Mission with the dawn, and stayed there with the mother and father of all hangovers until the following morning.

"Dietzer came from not far away, in Bremen, so he set off to find his way home. I didn't know whether I had anything to go back to in the Ruhr, so I went and found myself a room to lodge in in Altona and set about getting all my papers in order, so I could finally start my adult life. I'd left in 1940 as a twenty-year old apprentice; now I was an adult, but there was fifteen years missing." He paused for a moment, and then went on. "So that's really the whole story, Alex. As I told you before, when I started making enquiries, I found that my parents had died in a raid in 1944 and my sister had married a GI and gone off to America in 1950; I had no reason to go back to the Ruhr, it had probably suffered even worse damage than Hamburg. So I stayed, made my life here and the Gods smiled on me; HartmannLogistik became a great success."

"It's an incredible story, Max. You've had a remarkable life."

He shook his head at me. "No, no, not really. Don't forget that even in the mid-fifties there were still thousands of what were called Displaced Persons all over Europe. The combined efforts of the German army and then the Red Army had decimated most of Eastern Europe, and the population movement was incredible. Any ethnic Germans, for example,

Beyond Stalingrad

in Poland, or Czechoslovakia, or Hungary, were simply expelled. So from there alone, there were thousands upon thousands of refugees who arrived in Germany as the Russians tightened their grip. There was still a huge unsettled population swarming around the country. I was just another one of those."

"I didn't really mean that. I meant to have experienced everything you did in the war, Stalingrad, the battle, the surrender and then years in the camp. And still to come out alive and healthy. That's what is incredible."

He looked out through the huge window, over the sunlit river, the big trees lining its bank ruffled slightly by the gentle breeze. "Yes. Well, we were just the flotsam of the war. We were caught in the cogs of the sausage machine. Some lived, some died; it was totally arbitrary; it wasn't the good who lived and the bad who died, or vice versa. It was a total lottery. I could have been killed in the Kessel, I could have died at Beketovka; but I survived. I survived and made lots of money and had a comfortable life. If Armin had survived, he would have been recognised as a great artist. Which is of more use to the world?" He shook his head. "I'm sorry, Alex, I haven't thought about all this for so many years. It's quite tough to relive it all."

"No, I'm sorry I put you through it. But I'm really grateful that you told me the whole story. At least Armin won't just be a name, a forgotten man."

Max Hartmann insisted on driving me back to my hotel to collect my things and then on to the airport to catch my flight. As I got out of the car, he came round to my side and hugged me. "Alex, I know initially I was reluctant to meet and tell the whole story, but actually it's a relief to know that Armin's family now finally know what happened to him. Please keep in touch; I'm an old man, with no family of my own, and after all we went through together, I learned so much of Armin's family that I feel you're almost my own. You are all always welcome here in Hamburg."

1999 London

Chapter Thirty-Three

When I got home later that evening, my wife was sitting with a book and a glass of wine. "Was it a good trip? Did he know what you wanted?"

"Yes, he and Armin met at Stalingrad, and then were in the same camp together until Armin died – or rather, until he was killed. Do you want me to tell you the story?"

She looked astonished that I should even need to ask. "Definitely. Pour yourself a glass of that" - she pointed at the open bottle – "and tell me all of it. Oh, but before you start, you had a phone call this afternoon from a man called Khorsky. He said he was calling from the Norilsk museum, so I guess it's all about the same thing."

"Yes, he's the Russian who was helping me - you remember? - I told you about him."

"Yeah, of course. But come on, sit down and tell me what Hartmann said."

I looked at my watch. It was too late, with the time difference, to call Khorsky back this evening. So I started retelling the story Hartmann had told me; I didn't spare her any of it, although I couldn't give it the same brutal, realistic detail as Hartmann. By the time I finished, it was well after midnight and the first wine bottle had been joined by another. Finally, she sat back in her chair. "That's an amazing story; but it's so sad. He got through all the fighting and the surrender and then years in captivity and was just killed on what seems like a whim. You've done really well to get to the bottom of it. In some ways it's a pity that it didn't all come out until after your mother and Elisabeth and Franz had all died, but on the other hand, I suppose it's maybe better that they didn't have to know that he lived for so many years as a slave." She paused for a moment. "It's awful when you say it like that – a slave, disposable labour. While the world is supposed to be civilised."

"Well, yes. I think Max said it about right. They were caught in between the two most oppressive and vicious regimes of the twentieth century, and were just pawns in the struggle. You know, we've always known about the German camps, in Poland and so on, but this stuff about the Germans in Russia has never really been well-known. I suppose they were the losers, so naturally they were kind of overlooked."

"History is always written by the victors. I can't remember who said that, but it's true."

"Churchill," I replied, automatically.

"Ah yes. So what are you going to do? Are you going to tell your sisters and all the cousins? "

"Yes, I think so. But I'm not sure what we should do. He's got no grave that we know of, and his only memorial is in that cemetery that Dieter discovered - I told you about that - miles and miles from where he actually died and with a wrong date on it."

"What about the memorial you saw in Norilsk? Doesn't that commemorate them all?"

"Well, I suppose it does. But it's not like our war memorials here or in France. There are no names carved on it or anything, and it's actually, as far I could understand, a memorial to all those who passed through the Gulag, not specifically all those who died. But on the other hand, we should also remember that although it's a big deal to us, there are still about a million other German soldiers from the Russian Front unaccounted for. It's tough being the losers. I mean, think about the First World War memorials. The German cemeteries are all well kept and cared for, for sure, but they don't have the same power, the same presence as the Allied ones. Think of Thiepval, or Tyne Cot, or the Canadian one at Vimy. Compare them with the German one at Langemarck. You can understand why, but for the first time this has made me think about the other side of it. Thousands of German families must be in the same position of not knowing what happened to their relatives who marched off to invade Russia. "

"Yes, but don't get sidetracked. You have found out what happened to your uncle, and you can put the uncertainty to bed. Speaking of which, it's about that time. We've both got to go to work tomorrow morning."

Next day, when I got into the office, I called Khorsky straight away.

"Ah, Alex. Thank you for calling back. I called you on your home number yesterday; I realised that with the time difference, I should have called the office anyway. But then your wife said you were travelling, so I thought best to wait for you to call me back. I have some good news."

"So do I. I have been in Hamburg, where I spent a couple of days with Max Hartmann - you remember, one of the repatriated prisoners you found in your searching. He was able to tell me pretty much the entire story, from their capture at Stalingrad, all the way through the camp until Armin Kuhlmann died and he - Hartmann - was sent home."

"Well, that's fantastic. I'm so pleased the research was worthwhile. So I may have the last part of the jigsaw puzzle. I have found somebody here in Norilsk who was a guard at the camp in the late forties and early fifties. I spoke briefly with him and he certainly remembers the German prisoners who were here, so I have arranged to go and see him the day after tomorrow to ask him to tell me all he can think of about that time. But from your side, what did Hartmann tell you?"

"It's a long story. Let me give you the main points now and I'll fill in the details later."

So for the second time, I retold Hartmann's story, although this time missing out some of the detail with a promise to fill it in next time I saw him face-to-face, rather than over the phone.

At the end of it, there was silence for a moment or two. Then, "Wow," he said. "That is fantastic. I had hoped we may find something of the story, but I never imagined we would get everything like that. You did well to trace Hartmann and we are lucky he is still alive and clearly mentally still so alert. I was worried you would either not find any survivor or if you did, that they would be unable to remember what happened so long ago."

A bit more mutual praise for our forensic investigative powers, and he rung off, promising to give me a call to report his conversation with the ex-guard.

1999 Siberia

Two days later, Mikhail Khorsky drove in his Volvo across the town to the address the former guard had given him. It was an apartment block dating from the 1960s, dowdy and drab. He parked amongst the mounds of discoloured snow lining the roadside. The apartment number he'd been given was on the fourth floor; the door was opened by an old man, with bristly white hair, an unhealthy grey complexion and a limp as he walked. He wheezed as he welcomed his visitor. "You must be Mr Khorsky. Please come in."

The main living room of the apartment into which he led Khorsky was neat, tidy and clean, in surprising contrast to the corridor and stairwell which were in keeping with the shabby exterior. "Please, sit down." He waved his hands expansively, and Khorsky sat on a firm wooden chair. "You wanted to ask me some questions about the camps here, and particularly the artist prisoner, you said on the telephone."

"Yes, that's right. But first of all, I'd just like to ask you some questions about yourself, so I know what your background is." Khorsky pulled a notebook out of his briefcase and a pen out of his pocket. He went on:

"I'm one of the curators of the museum here, so I just like to get all my facts right."

"Of course. I have visited the museum several times, but not for many years now. To be honest, I find it quite difficult to get around. My health is not so good." He smiled, a sad smile. "I have spent too many years breathing in the atmosphere of our beautiful city. My lungs have long suffered for it. I don't go out that much any more. My daughter comes here and checks on me most afternoons.

"So, about me. My name is Pavel Dashkevitch, and I come originally from eastern Belarus."

"From Belarus? You've come a long way from home to live up here in the Arctic."

"Yes. Like with many others of my generation, the war sucked me out of my ancestral home and spat me out up here. You're from the museum, a historian. Let me tell you my story, which will explain to you what I was doing in the camp – if you have time, of course."

Khorsky nodded enthusiastically. Anything that built on his knowledge of the development of the city and its population was grist to his mill. "I have all afternoon. I would be fascinated to hear your story."

1941 Belarus

The old man settled himself back in his armchair. "I was born in a small village in the north-eastern corner of Belarus, near the town of Vitebsk, in 1923. There had been a lot of fighting in the area during the Civil War, and indeed I believe there was still some skirmishing with odd Whites who were still in hiding even in the first few years of my life. My father and his father before him were peasant farmers and all of the lands in our region were collectivised very soon after the end of the Civil war by the Bolsheviks. My father became one of the workers on a collective. It was a hard life; the targets that were set were hard to achieve and we rarely had enough food. I understand things were far worse in Ukraine, where they had real famine, but they were tough enough for us anyway. But there was no alternative. Nobody seriously thought about trying to change anything - the memories of the older people of life under the previous regime did not make that sound any better, so the world just carried on as it was."   His eyes took on a far-away look. "It was primitive; we were ignorant of things outside our immediate surroundings, and we had no real understanding of what was happening when the war in Western Europe began. The commissars promised us that we were safe, that Comrade Stalin had had the foresight to make an agreement with the Germans that would prevent us from becoming involved in their war. We believed it. I was a teenager then, but a man because I had already begun working with my father on the collective. Growing crops was in my blood; fighting wasn't.

But then, one day in 1941, the story of the Commissars changed. Despite Comrade Stalin's brave efforts, the Germans had cheated and attacked us with a massive force and were advancing from Poland into our country. We began to see the Red Army soldiers marching westwards to meet the invader. The news was uniformly bad. The Germans were approaching us at a great speed; we heard of towns being captured, and then Minsk, closer and closer to our own land. It was July; the crops needed tending until they were ready for harvest, but the Commissars called all us younger men to the side, and told us our duty lay in joining the militia to fight the invader off, while our parents brought in the harvest. We were not moved by the political speeches, but it was our land - the land of our forefathers, for generations. What could we do? To a man, we all volunteered, and the older ones had to be restrained and made to stay to finish the harvest, or they too would have joined us. I was just eighteen years old. We were hurried westwards; some of us had uniforms given to us, many didn't. The weapons we had were old - many of them rifles left over from the Civil War. Our training was basic - there was no time for anything but teaching us to handle the guns, to fire them, and to obey what our sergeant told us." He looked across at me, seriously. "As a historian, you will know that the purges of the thirties had decimated the officer class of the Red Army; at that time, in the desperation of the first attack by the Germans, it was the NCOs who held the army together. But anyway, we were marched westwards, towards the enemy, to start with. Then, before we had arrived anywhere, we were hurriedly turned around and sent back to Vitebsk, just to the north of our village. There we were made to dig our defensive trench lines and take up our positions. We sat there, in the trenches, waiting. We didn't notice, at first, that there was another trench line behind us, with men positioned in it. Later, we learned they were NKVD troops.

"Well, we didn't have long to wait. The tanks appeared on the horizon and our artillery opened up from behind us. It was the first time any of us had experienced warfare, the noise, the dust, the fear. The Germans halted in the face of our heavy guns; we began to think Vitebsk would be the turning point, that we would repulse them and clear them from our land. Such is the optimism of youth.

"Then they began firing, and it wasn't long before they had the range, and the shells started dropping all around us. Some of our men couldn't stand it - we were farm boys, after all, not real soldiers - and they scrambled up out of the trench to run away, behind us, towards the town. That's when we realised why the NKVD were behind us. Every man who tried to retreat was shot by our own side. They had machine guns to use on their own men - we had old rifles to use against the German tanks.

Beyond Stalingrad

"For a while, though, it was stalemate. Our anti-tank guns were effective in holding the Germans, and with their tanks unable to advance, the infantry were pinned down behind them. We sheltered in our trenches from the bombardment by the German guns; we'd learned the lesson of attempting to retreat through the NKVD lines so we just stayed put, waiting for it all to finish. We knew nothing of tactics, of the way a battle develops, we just knew that we would have to keep shooting at the German soldiers when they came forward, until our ammunition ran out. It was simple; we were defending our land, not State, or Party, or Red Army, or anything like that. It was the most basic emotion; this was our land and our people. We would fight until the end for it.

"Well, for me, the end came even quicker than it did for my comrades; I was caught in a shell-burst and badly injured. Although I later heard stories from other places that the NKVD forced the wounded to stay in the line and fight on, in my case I was rushed back to a casualty clearing point by stretcher bearers and then evacuated many kilometres behind the fighting to be operated on. My comrades were not so lucky; it was only a matter of a couple of hours later that it became apparent that our guns were beginning to run out of ammunition and then the German tanks began to move forward. The infantry were behind them, and within a very short space of time, they had taken the city." He shook his head, as if in wonder at the naivety. "Sitting in our trenches, we had had thoughts of a heroic defence of our city, throwing back the invader. In reality, it was a tiny skirmish which barely held up the relentless progress of the Germans. The NKVD troops mostly escaped, though, falling back to the east as it became apparent that the militia line was not going to be able to hold.

"So they swept on, the Nazis; there was a great battle around Kiev, where there were huge casualties, and of course the massacre at Babi Yar. But the fighting in that first year of their Barbarossa operation was in vain for us Russians. The Germans just rolled across our country and Ukraine and into Russia itself. I heard all this only in scrappy news reports at the time and then with more detail later, but, as you know, they reached the Don and then, after the setbacks they suffered in our Russian winter, got as far as Stalingrad in 1942.

"My wounds were quite bad; you see, even now I still walk with a limp. I was sent to a hospital in the Urals to recuperate, along with many others wounded in those dreadful battles. However, they could not get me healed enough to send me back to the Army - if they had, I doubt I would be here talking to you today, for those few of my comrades from home who survived and escaped from Vitebsk were later sent as reinforcements to Stalingrad. None of them survived that, so I can safely say that this" - he tapped his hand against his leg - "saved my life. It still gives me a lot of pain, though.

"Anyway, once they decided they could not use me back again as a soldier, they had to do something else with me. I was transferred to the NKVD, which made me feel very uncomfortable, after what I had seen with my own eyes at Vitebsk; I'd heard similar stories from other Army men I had met subsequently, as well. But there was nothing I could do. I was sent for training at a barracks in Yekaterinburg, where it became obvious I was not to be a soldier of any sort. I was to be a prison-camp guard. Well, it was never what I had dreamed of as a boy on the collective in Belarus, but I can't deny that I was relieved not to be going back to the shellfire again. My NKVD training consisted mostly of political indoctrination, rather than any sort of military work. They were anxious that those sent to guard the captives would be ideologically sound. Well, I never had too much time for all of that, but I was smart enough to work out that if I let them know that, then instead of being a guard, I might rather end up as a prisoner myself. Anyway, everything was in such turmoil with the war that we all just did what we were told. We wanted the invader out of our country and that gave the authorities enormous power to do what they wanted with the population, all in the name of defeating Nazism. And I couldn't go home, even if I had been allowed to, because it was still occupied at that stage. So, like everybody else, whatever our misgivings, I just submitted to what they wanted." He passed for a moment, and sighed. "You're too young to know how it really was in the Stalin period – the whole population was under control, there was no individuality. And it was that feeling, that one could do nothing that wasn't ordered by the regime, that made me wonder a bit about the German prisoners.

"First of all, I was posted to a regular prisoner of war camp, a little to the east of Moscow. The prisoners there were mostly Germans, with some Rumanians, all of them ordinary soldiers. They were put to work as agricultural labourers, the sort of work I had been familiar with at home all my life. From what I saw later, I know they were some of the lucky ones. Sure, they were forced labour, but somehow it's always easier on the land rather than in a mine or a factory. They were hungry and over-worked, but they spent their days working at something I knew. Compared with what came next, it was almost normality. After all, don't forget we were often hungry at home as well, what with the toughness of the quotas we had to meet. I was at that camp in 1943, after the Stalingrad surrender, and prisoners taken there began to arrive in around April of that year. They were in a terrible state – starving, lice-ridden, diseased. I had no sympathy with the way they had invaded our country and killed hundreds and thousands of our people. But seeing them in that condition was awful; they were like me, most of them, just in their late teens or early twenties. I know that there were horrible atrocities behind the front line as they advanced, but these were just accidental soldiers, like me, or so it seemed. When you saw them, you didn't think of invaders or killers; you just saw farm boys, like me, caught up in something they didn't understand. Many of them spoke some Russian, and although we were forbidden to speak to them, I did. All they wanted was to go home, to be away from the war and the guns. Sure, there were some who were Nazis and spouted all that rubbish about the master race and Lebensraum and so on, but most of them were just young men, lonely, hungry and thousands of kilometres from home. I could sympathise with them; I knew that some of the boys I had grown up with were in the same position on the other side. And I wanted to go home, too."

Chapter Thirty-Four

"Well, I stayed at that camp until the beginning of winter that year, 1943, and then I was told that my duties were going to change. At the camp near Moscow, the guards had been a mixture of Army and NKVD troops. Now, they'd decided things should be more formally arranged. The Army would guard regular prisoner of war camps and the NKVD would have sole responsibility for political camps - what is called the Gulag. So I, together with some others, was transferred to the camp here in Norilsk, which was designated as a Gulag camp for dissidents and criminals. We arrived here in November of that year. As soon as we got here, it was obvious that this was not just a place for Russian politicals. As you know, the camp was split over many sites, both directly in or around the city as well as much further afield serving other industries. More than one of the camps in fact contained almost exclusively Germans, although in overall numbers, there were perhaps hundreds rather than thousands of them. When we were addressed by the commandant, he told us that these Germans were clear Nazis, who had been in the SS or similar units. As such, he told us, they were the worst of the Germans, which is why they had been sent to this camp system rather than left with the ordinary soldiers. We should have no sympathy for them, they were the type who had committed the worst atrocities against our people. He said they were here to be used up as labour in the mines and factories associated with them and that frankly they were not expected to live; welfare was only to be a concern if it appeared to impinge on their ability to work.

"So, we all expected to find the bogie-man figure we had seen in the cinema propaganda, the brutal fascist killer of men and rapist of women. But actually, they were in an even worse condition – if that were possible – than the ones we had been guarding before. They were in a pitiful state and as successive groups arrived on the trains and we had to move them into the camp huts, we could see why. Or in fact, we could see and smell why. The stench of death and disease when we opened the doors of the train wagons was horrific. The men had been crammed in there with little food and water and no sanitation for days, and they were diseased before they were loaded. Our first task each time a draft arrived was to clear all the corpses so we could see how many men we actually had. I don't know how many died on that train journey, but it was many; many.

"Well, the routine soon settled down. We marched them down to work each day and back again in the evening. Our food was frankly not much better than theirs, but we had more of it. It was a tedious life for us; we were just there with our guns to make sure the work got done. Very often, the teams did not achieve their quotas, which meant less food. It was a paradox of the system; if they were too weak to fulfil their work quota, then they were fed reduced rations, thus making them weaker which again made it more difficult to achieve the next quota. As the commandant had told us, they were literally being worked to death. Many died in their first few weeks here; I think they just gave up. But then, once they had got through the initial period, they stabilised a bit and settled to their inadequate diet and the work details.

"Well, we'll come to the man you were interested in in a moment. But first, perhaps you would like some tea?"

Khorsky nodded. "Yes, please." While Pavel was out of the room in his tiny kitchen, he pondered the story the guard had been telling him. It was fascinating to be hearing at first hand such an everyday story of how the camps had been. Even if the search for Kuhlmann didn't get any further, he had an amazing source of new information for his museum.

Pavel returned, clutching two cups of black Russian tea. "So," he began again, "the artist." He paused again for a moment, as though gathering his thoughts. "Every morning, at the sound of the klaxon, we had to get the prisoners out of their huts and down to the refectory where they would get their breakfast and their bread ration for lunch. At the same time, we had to check over the huts to make sure none of them were sick or dead overnight and to do spot checks of whether they had managed to conceal anything in the hut. If there were dead bodies, we dragged them out and dumped them in the burial pit, if they were sick we really just kicked them until they followed their comrades out to work or if they couldn't, we assumed they'd be dead by the next day and left them there. Searching for contraband was arbitrary – whether or not we could be bothered. But anyway, I began to notice charcoal drawings appearing on the walls of one of the huts. Some of my fellows wanted to rub them off, but I persuaded them to let them stay; I didn't say this out loud, but I thought, the prisoners had nothing at all positive in their lives, so maybe we could leave them this, at least. So the drawings stayed and over a few weeks it became obvious that they were actually quite good. They were pictures of some of the men in the hut, and even in charcoal on a background of the wooden wall of the hut, you could see how the artist had captured the despair and hopelessness in their faces. Well, there was the same old regulation that we guards were not supposed to communicate with the prisoners except to give them their orders, but we were rarely supervised on a day to day basis, so it was easy enough to find out who was the artist. It turned out to be a man called Armin Kuhlmann, and I started talking to him quite frequently, as we were moving the prisoners around the camp. He was quite a tall man, like them all painfully thin and sallow-faced.

" But look, don't get the wrong idea. We didn't have cosy fireside chats or anything like that. We exchanged words as we were marching them to work, or waiting for the gates to open or whatever, mostly about his drawings. It was my idea then to suggest that I could try and smuggle him in some paper of some sort, which he may prefer to the walls of the hut. Smuggling them things wasn't difficult. In many ways, the camp authorities didn't care: their job was to run the camp in such a way as to get the necessary work in the mines and smelters and so on. As long as that happened, the commandant and his staff kept their jobs and their lives." He glanced across at Khorsky as he said that. "Oh yes, consistent failure to achieve targets could result in a death sentence for the administrators of the camp; actually, the state didn't care who it killed as long as it got what it wanted. It was truly a time of the end justifying the means." He took a long swig of his tea, which must have been getting cool by now.

"Anyway, so I - and some of my fellows – got to know a bit about some of the prisoners. The one thing we did learn was that, contrary to what we had been told, these men were not rabid Nazis, they were just soldiers on the other side, who had been doing what they had been made to do. I began to feel sorry for them. There was one particular incident with the artist that gave me a bad feeling. One day, some of my comrades searched the hut Kuhlmann was in and found some of his drawings hidden amongst his bedding. They dragged him off to see the commandant, burned his pictures in front of him and then stuck him in solitary. That was just mean and vindictive; there was no harm, his drawing didn't affect the work." He shrugged. "But it was a brutal place. How do you rank the petty bullying against working men to death as slaves? Anyway, he withstood the solitary, and life went on, such as it was.

"The war ended in victory, but it didn't really change anything for us. I got word from home that my parents and both my brothers had been killed in the fighting, and we began to hear stories of the savagery of what had gone on during the occupation. Some of my fellows wanted to take their revenge for the atrocities, but in truth the number of German prisoners was dropping anyway; they were dying. To tell it honestly, they were part of the industrial machinery that was wearing out. They were replaced by Russians, and people from the occupied states, who were there for political crimes, on the whole. They all still ended up with the same look of hopelessness on their faces, though, wherever they came from.

"In the years immediately after the end of the war, I applied several times for permission to leave the NKVD service; I wanted to go home, even though I had no more family there. But permission was not given;

Beyond Stalingrad

I had to stay up here, doing my job. In the end, I felt I was as much of a prisoner of the system as those I was guarding. I married, the daughter of another NKVD man in the camp, and we were given living space in the city, which got me out of the guards' barracks, at any rate. But I'm sorry, it's not me you want to hear about; you want to know what happened to the artist, Kuhlmann.

"Well, it was in January 1952. By now, the number of Germans had declined so much that they only occupied two or three huts. As there got to be fewer and fewer of them, so they became more and more a target for some of the other prisoners, particularly those who had seen what had happened to the land they had occupied. There had been quite a few fights between the two sets of prisoners, which we guards had to break up. The commandant had told us that this fighting had to be stopped – it was potentially detrimental to their ability to do their work – and that he would take severe measures against any prisoners involved. Well, on that particular morning, I was on duty in a watchtower, rather than inside the camp, but we could see a fight broke out at the door of the refectory. By the time the guards down there had separated the two sides, there were quite a number of men lying on the ground bleeding - mostly, I think, from the effects of the guards' rifle butts rather than the actual fight. Anyway, the team leader from each group was separated from their men and made to stay on the parade ground while the rest of them were marched off to work. They were there for some time, and then the commandant came across.

"We were watching from the tower, and we expected him to order them to solitary or to have them beaten. Instead, he simply walked behind them, made them kneel down and shot both in the back of the head. Even by the standards of that place, it was a brutal act. Up in the tower, we were shocked; we were inured to a lot after so many years in that place, but what happened that morning was simply murder. Sure, many died from the effects of the camp, but this was just one-on-one killing by a man with a gun on men kneeling in front of him. Kuhlmann was the team leader of the German group and he was one of the men shot.

"The bodies were just left there lying in the snow for a couple of hours, by which time it was fully light - or at least, as light as it ever got in winter. Then, when I and my fellow guard were relieved by our replacements in the watchtower, we were ordered to collect the two bodies and take them to the burial pit. We slung them onto a cart and pushed them through the gates and around to the east perimeter where the burials were at that time. We helped the two guards who were on duty there to pitch them into the pit and then cover them with lime. In the winter, there was no urgency about covering recent corpses with soil - everything was too cold for any risk of infection; burial duty in the summer was probably the worst job in the camp - so they were probably covered later that day or the following one." He sighed. "I know it sounds callous, but that's how it was, in the camp, at that time. Kuhlmann had seemed a decent guy, and he was certainly a talented artist. I knew one of the other Germans was a friend of his, I can't remember his name, and the next day I spoke to him about the drawings. He told me I could take some of them, if I wanted, because he knew it was me who had given Kuhlmann the materials. So, surreptitiously, over a few days, or weeks even, I took a few out of the camp when I had the chance. That was my downfall, really. After a while, one of the other guards noticed what I was doing and reported me. A couple of NKVD officers came round to my apartment, terrifying my wife and our baby daughter, and ransacked it. They found the pictures, and I was brought before the commandant. I was guilty of three things, he said: fraternising with the prisoners, bringing contraband into the camp and taking things out of the camp. For any one of them, he said, I could have been sentenced to serve a term in the camp myself, as a prisoner. However, he was going to be lenient on me. I was to be dismissed from the NKVD service - you can imagine how pleased I was to hear that; I'd been asking for it for a long time - but I was also to be restricted to the region, the Krasnoyarsk Krai. That was a blow, as it meant I couldn't go home to Belarus. But on the other hand, my wife and I had started to build our life together up here and things were for sure tough everywhere in the country.

"I feared at first that the NKVD would make it difficult for me to get any work in the town; they had the power to do that. But actually, they didn't. They didn't pursue me at all, which was a relief. So, we stayed here and I worked at many things. My wife died five years ago, my daughter is now married to one of the management of the mine, and I have never left here since that day in 1943 when I arrived. But anyway, that's not what you came for, to learn about my life after the camp. I have told you what I can remember of the artist, Kuhlmann; I wish they had let me keep at least one of his drawings, but you could never really understand what they would allow and what they wouldn't, sometimes." He stopped speaking, and sat back in his chair, a frail old man far from the land of his birth.

"Thank you," said Khorsky quietly. "That was a very interesting story. There is an Englishman I know who knows something of Kuhlmann. I will pass on what you told me; I am sure he will be interested. And, perhaps I can come another time and listen to more of your memories; I am anxious to learn more about that period, to add to our displays in the museum."

1999 London

Chapter Thirty-Five

"So, that's the story Pavel Dashkevitch told me," said Khorsky. I think it finishes it all off for us."

"Yes, and it fits with what Max Hartmann told me in Hamburg. I've got pretty much the whole story of Kuhlmann's life, from the last days in the Stalingrad Kessel up to his death in the camp. I suppose the only thing I don't know is where his grave is. Do you think Dashkevitch knows that?"

"I did ask him, but he seemed very unsure. He referred to the eastern perimeter of the camp being the site of the burial pit, but that doesn't really help. Although theoretically we should know the sites of all the camps, it's actually almost impossible to find any way of being precise enough to locate anything. The landscape has changed so much, with new buildings, tracks becoming roads or disappearing and very few traces of the old framework. No, I think you will have to be grateful with how far you have got, and accept that you will not find the actual grave."

"Yes. Well, I want to thank you again for all your help; without you, there is no way I would ever have managed to discover the story. You have really been helpful and I appreciate it."

"It's kind of you to say so. I'm thinking now of how to use this new detail in the exhibits here. So whatever background you have about Kuhlmann before he was in the camp would be really helpful. It's always easier to frame displays if there is a real human angle to them, and this would be a classic way of using the individual to tell the story of the camps in general. I'm looking forward to getting to work."

I chuckled at his enthusiasm. "I can actually give you a lot of background. I have not told you this until now, because I thought it might muddy the waters, but Armin Kuhlmann was my mother's brother. My uncle, except he was dead before I was born."

There was a silence. Then, "But you're British?"

"Yes, but my grandfather was German and my grandmother English; the family lived in Germany until the rise of the Nazis, and then moved to England. Armin got trapped in Germany and conscripted there."

"Wow. That sounds to me like another story to tell. So you will have real detail about him, before the war."

"Yes, from my mother and my aunt." So the phone call went on a lot longer as I gave him a précis of Armin's life and the full story I had heard from Max Hartmann.

When I had finished the call, I sat back in my chair, staring at the ceiling.

A lot of the story was corroborated by two totally different people, and they agreed pretty much completely so that I could say now with certainty how and where my uncle had died, and what had happened to him between the end of the Stalingrad battle and his death. I was glad I didn't have to sit down with my mother and my aunt and describe to them how their brother's life had ended; they had both lived such full lives that the contrast would have been painful. I would tell my sisters and cousins the whole story. None of us had ever known him, and yet he'd been a presence in our lives, as his sisters had often referred to him when talking about their own childhood. My mother hadn't told me of the darker side of their life in Germany when I was a child, but she'd certainly told me lots about the fun times they'd all had together. It seemed that maybe I'd got the chance to lay the demon that had haunted them all since 1943. It wasn't immediately obvious how, but in some way we had to commemorate him, a young man who had died a squalid, pointless death so many thousands of miles from home. He'd been one of so many, and the story Khorsky had just told me kind of emphasised that. The guard, Dashkevitch, had been dragged away from his home as well and left marooned thousands of miles away to live his life in the alien surroundings of Arctic tundra. In his way, he'd been just as much a victim as those he'd been guarding. Everything I had learned, from Hartmann as well as from Norilsk, had taught me more and more about the barbarity of that war fought out on the Eastern Front. All those young men had been caught up in a struggle between two monolithic states, fighting for their very lives against each other, and yet ironically, as Hartmann himself had said, the true differences between them were no more than nuances. Corporate state against corporate state and the individuals were minced up in the middle of it and spat out arbitrarily, dead, mutilated or alive.

But it felt good to have achieved my aim. I was already thinking that perhaps a small exhibition of Armin's pictures would be the best way to commemorate him. Probably best in Hamburg – I was sure Max Hartmann would be prepared to lend his, as a starting point. So what I had to do next was think of a way to persuade Khorsky to get his superiors to agree to lending some of the ones in Norilsk to us to show them.

I was in high good humour when I got home that evening; I regaled Emily again with how clever I had been in my detective work, and had a long telephone conversation with my sister Isobel talking about how we could present Armin's pictures to the world. We wouldn't be offering them for sale, of course, they would be simply on exhibition. I was sure that we could generate interest not just in Germany but probably internationally in such a visceral picture of recent history. Isobel was keen too, and we agreed to talk to all the cousins to make sure everybody was involved.

The next morning I called Max Hartmann and he was happy to agree to lend his pictures. More, he suggested that he could arrange with a friend of his who owned a gallery to give us space to mount an exhibition. We would have to pay, of course, because it would occupy the gallery for a week or so, but that wasn't going to be a problem. Everything looked good.

But all the while, the past was unclenching its icy fingers and stretching them out towards the present. Later on that day, I got a call on my mobile; the screen showed it was from Andrey, in Moscow.

"Andrey, hi, how are you? It's a while since we spoke."

"Alex, yeah. Listen, this has to be a quick call. I was called in by my boss yesterday and told not to deal with you any more. You've really upset somebody."

"Hey? How? What have I done?"

"I was not told. He just said to me that you were not a suitable person for us to deal with and that I should make no more contracts with you. If I had to guess, I would say it was what I told you before, that your investigations up in Norilsk were seriously pissing someone off."

"No, that's ridiculous. I've just been trying to discover what happened to my uncle. And now I've got the whole story, anyway, so I don't need to dig any more. But nobody could be worried about that."

"I think they are worried, Alex, and somebody definitely doesn't want whatever you know to become public. Look, I'm just standing out in the corridor; I can't really speak. I'll call you later on, at home."

And the line went dead.

I put the phone down and leaned back in my chair. What on earth was he talking about? How could there be any problem with what I'd been doing? Sure, it wasn't a pretty story, but it was all a long time ago. A full generation ago. What had happened then was in a different time, a war; the whole world had surely moved beyond that. All I'd found out were facts, the story of one life and death amongst the millions. I glanced at my watch. I needed to call Khorsky to see whether he was aware of any of this, but with the time difference it was too late. It would have to be tomorrow morning.

My thoughts were broken by one of the junior traders coming in. "Alex, I've just spoken to Andrey at Arctic Mining. I gave him a bid for some metal but he said he couldn't sell to me and that I should come and see you. We don't have a problem with them, do we?"

I shook my head. "No, not really. There just seems to be something they are a bit touchy about. I'm sure it will sort itself out, but for the moment, see if you can get the metal from the Canadians. I'll get Andrey sorted out, but maybe not today."

He looked quizzically at me. "Honestly," I said, "I really don't know what their issue is. Andrey called me about ten minutes ago. You know they can sometimes be a bit funny; we'll be able to sort it out."

Shaking his head, he went out. Mmm. Clearly, what Andrey had said was true. There really was some sort of issue. We were a big customer of Arctic Mining and stopping the relationship would have an effect on both of us, so whatever they didn't like, they were prepared to lose money over it.

I left promptly that evening, to make sure I was at home by the time Andrey rang. I got caught by train delays, though, so I was just walking in through the door of my house when my mobile rang. Gesturing to Emily, whom I could see in the dining room, I went straight through to the study.

"Andrey, hi. What's going on? I understand you refused to sell to us earlier today. Is this all serious?"

"Yes, it is. I was not joking before. I have been told your company is no longer an acceptable contract partner. Somebody is very annoyed, but so far I'm not sure who. The instruction has come from very high up."

"Well, I don't really know what to say. I've never come across this before; we have a really good relationship with you. I can't believe that the fact that I have been pursuing what is after all a purely personal – or family - piece of history could create waves like this."

"Alex, I understand that to you it makes no sense. Frankly, to me it's as stupid as you think it. But you have to understand the previous generation in my country - or at least, some of them. We can laugh and joke about the way things were here in the middle of the twentieth century. They can't. For them, it was a deadly serious time. Some would rather forget what was done to them and theirs, others would rather forget what they themselves did. I don't know why, but in this case I have a strong feeling it's the latter. Nobody will say in two words that is your delving into the past which is the problem, but reading between the lines I'm pretty sure of it."

"Well surely that implies somebody within Arctic Mining was somehow involved?"

"Alex, I don't know and I don't know what you have discovered. But I guess it's something about the camps, and yes, there are people at the company who were involved in the camps. That's inevitable; the whole city was involved and there are still quite a lot of people – and their children or grandchildren – who were part of the system."

"But it must be somebody quite senior in the organisation."

"Yes, that's probably true. But look, Alex, you know I'm happy to help you, but my first concern is that you are an important customer for us. I'm anxious to sort this out so we can start selling to you again."

"Me too. Maybe I should give you all the background."

"OK, that might be a starting point."

So I told the story again, or at least the important bits. Emily came into the study while I was talking and gestured at her watch. The children had been visiting friends and she had to go and pick them up. She went out and then came back with a gin and tonic for me, before I heard the front door bang behind her.

Andrey listened without interrupting, then when I had reached the end, he said, "Mmm. You've done pretty well in following the story through."

"Well, a lot of it was Khorsky, the museum guy. He helped a lot. Without that I wouldn't have got anywhere near the truth. But it was also good for him because it's given him plenty of material."

"Yes. I think maybe you should talk to him again, and see if he knows any more about annoyance at you delving into things. He would probably be aware of any real official concerns. I'll see what I can do internally, within Arctic Mining, but you should definitely talk to Khorsky again. When you call me, only use the mobile; you're seriously persona non grata, so the office landline wouldn't be a good idea." He rang off.

I sat back in my chair, the remains of the gin in my hand. My first task tomorrow was going to be to talk to Khorsky.

Chapter Thirty-Six

That didn't go as planned. I called his number at the museum first thing in the morning, but got no answer. I kept on trying through the morning, and eventually the line was picked up. I asked for Khorsky, but the voice at the other end just repeated "Gone away, gone away." That wasn't particularly helpful, and when I carried on asking, the line went dead. This all seemed to be getting way out of proportion. At that moment, my boss put his head in through the door and asked me to come into his office for a minute. I sat across the desk from him.

"Alex, what's going on with Arctic Mining? I understand they've decided they don't like us all of a sudden."

"I'm not sure exactly what the problem is, but Andrey tells me he has instructions not to deal with us for the moment. I spoke to him yesterday evening and he said he was trying to find out a bit more. He's as much in the dark as we are, I think."

"Mmm. It needs to be sorted out. That business is worth a lot of money to us. We've got a strong relationship with them and I don't want to let our competitors get their foot in the door. Should I speak to them? Ask them what the problem is?"

"No, leave it to me. I'll talk to Andrey again and see what I can get out of him. I'm sure we can work it out." The last thing I wanted was him speaking to Andrey's boss before I'd had a bit longer to try and clear the air. As far as I was concerned it was a private matter and didn't need all this corporate involvement.

I wandered back into my own room and called Andrey's mobile. I told him about my failed attempt to get hold of Khorsky and that I was trying to keep personal and business affairs separate; I asked him for the moment not to make mention of the fact that my delving into history might be connected to the trading ban.

"I won't, but I don't know about anybody else. If anybody speaks to Lev" - his boss, and the head of the sales organisation - "about it, I imagine he will probably mention your name. But he's off to Hong Kong and China for a week this afternoon, so it should be OK for a bit."

"Good. Andrey, I know I have no right to ask this, but could you call the museum in Norilsk and see if you can find out what is happening with Khorsky?"

There was a pause. "OK, I guess we're good enough friends for that. I'll see what I can do. I'll call you back later."

He called me back within half an hour. "OK, when I called the museum, they told me the same - that he had left and didn't work there any more. But I persuaded them to give me his mobile number and I have spoken to him. He was at home, and sounded pretty depressed. He has been suspended from his job and forbidden to go into the museum. They are going to investigate him for showing classified papers to someone not authorised to see them. That's you, Alex. You seem to have stirred up a real hornet's nest. Anyway, he's feeling very sorry for himself, but he doesn't appear to know who is behind all this. I can give you his mobile number, if you want to call him, although I'm not sure he'll be too keen to talk to you. If they really decide to go after him about that classified document thing, that's pretty serious."

"Thanks." I took down the number and after Andrey had hung up, I sat thinking for a while. I needed to think about how to approach Khorsky, because it seemed pretty obvious to me that I wouldn't be his favourite person right now.

1999 Siberia

Mikhail Khorsky was still pretty shell-shocked as he sat in his flat in Norilsk. In his mind, he kept running through the interview with the director of the museum. He knew that maybe he had got a little carried away in helping the Englishman Butterfield with his searches, but to be accused of releasing classified documentation? That was a serious offence, one for the security services. But anyway, part of his job, part of what he'd been hired for, was precisely to open up some of the history of the camp times. Why was it suddenly an offence?

Another thought struck him forcefully. He wasn't the only one. He grabbed his car keys and went out to the old Volvo. He had to go to see Pavel Dashkevitch. He needed to warn the old man that he should keep quiet about their conversation.

When he got to the old man's flat, the reception this time was very different. Dashkevitch didn't invite him in, just stood with the door ajar and waited for Khorsky to say what he wanted. It was obvious from the old man's demeanour. "So they've been to see you?" Khorsky asked. Dashkevitch nodded.

"They asked you what you had told me?"

He nodded again.

"What did you tell them?"

"Just that you had been asking about the camp, and that artist prisoner. They wanted to know if you had asked about how he died. I just told them I told you the story. They told me not to talk about it any more, or it could affect my pension or my apartment. They threatened me. Please go. I don't want anything to do with this. I thought I was just telling you a story. I didn't realise I would get into trouble. Go, and don't come back again."

"I'm sorry," said Khorsky. "I didn't know. I didn't want to cause you problems." He turned and left. He heard the door of the flat close behind him.

As his front door closed, the old man glanced across at the leather-coated man sitting across the room. The latter nodded slowly. "OK Pavel, that was very good. Just remember that's all you have to say. I don't want to have to come back and visit you again – and neither do you want me to."

Khorsky sat in his car before starting it up, thinking about what Dashkevitch had said. It made one thing clear. Of course it was about the camp, but apparently more specific than that. They had asked the old man if he had talked about Kuhlmann and particularly his death, so it wasn't just the investigation of the camps that was the issue, it was rather something to do with Kuhlmann. Presumably, his death. But why? It was all so long ago; it was just history. Then he shook his head, as if to clear it. Something was wrong, but that wasn't his problem. Best stay out of it; it already seemed to be creating difficulties for him and his work. He'd been interested in helping the Englishman find his relative, but enough was enough. He wasn't going to jeopardise himself if he could help it.

He drove slowly back to his flat. As he went in through the front door, the telephone was ringing.

1999 London

I was on the verge of hanging up, when he picked up.

"Mikhail, it's me, Alex Butterfield. I understand there have been some problems with our investigation."

"Problems? Yes, you could say that. I seem to have lost my job; certainly for the moment, even if not necessarily permanently. But for now, I am forbidden the museum and I have been visited by some very disturbing men who advised me not to talk to you. So maybe I should just hang up now."

"Mikhail, no, don't do that," I said, hurriedly. "I'm really sorry if I'm responsible for this, but I just don't understand what's going on. I thought you might be able to help me."

"Alex, helping you seems to be at the heart of the problem. Look, I'll tell you now what I know, but then that's got to be the end of it. I can't risk my whole career over this." He paused. "OK, so I was called in yesterday by my boss who had two heavies there with him. He told me that he understood that I had been showing documents that were technically classified and the property of the Security Services to a foreign visitor. He told me that that could not be tolerated and that they were going to have to investigate my conduct. In the meantime, I was suspended from my work and forbidden to come in to the museum. He said that if I was lucky, I would be posted to another museum and if I was unlucky I would be prosecuted for passing classified documents. I tried to explain that I was just doing some research to improve some of our displays about the 1940s and 50s, but he was not prepared to listen to me. I was told to go home immediately and wait until they had decided what action to take."

"That sounds pretty heavy-handed."

"Yes, it's how they behave when they really don't like something. Anyway, this morning I have been to visit Pavel Dashkevitch - you remember? - and I have found out that he too had had a visit. He was asked specifically if he had discussed Kuhlmann and his death, not just the camp in general. So it's pretty clear to me that it is your specific rather than general enquiries that are the issue. But Alex, I know no more than that."

"But…"

"No, Alex," he interrupted me. "I don't know any more. I'm sure you were going to say it makes no sense. I agree with you. But that's all I've got to say." And the phone went dead as he hung up.

I sat staring into the middle distance, trying to make sense of it. Why should anyone be upset by me looking at the events of fifty-odd years ago? Sure, it wasn't a pretty story, but it began in total war and finished under a repressive regime that had been overthrown by now. I could see that the Soviets would possibly have been sensitive about it, but Russia now had turned its back on that totalitarianism. Khorsky had originally told me that one of his specific tasks was to show more of the gulag time. So why were they now turning on him? And thousands of people had died in the gulag. Russians, Ukrainians, Poles, Lithuanians, you name it; from any of the Russian-dominated republics, there had been victims. So why would the death of one German soldier concern anybody? In a perverse way, it was more excusable - Germany had at least been an enemy in war, so you could argue Germans were more legitimate targets than the poor politicals.

And then a thought struck me. I picked up the phone again.

"Hi, Andrey, it's me, Alex. I've got a question for you. When the gulag system was finally closed down, were there ever any trials or prosecutions for crimes of any of the guards or commandants or anything?"

"No, of course not. The system changed, the camps were closed, but there was no backlash towards the people who had been operating it. At least, not in general terms. I'm sure there will have been some cases where a specific crime may have been committed where there would have been action taken. But not just for having been part of that system; that would not have been right."

"So nothing like Nuremberg, or any of the trials of Nazis that there have been since then?"

"No, the two things were different. One was extermination, the other was a system of forced labour. Look, Alex, I'm not saying it's right, but you have to remember one thing. The trials in Germany were of a defeated people. It was a chance for revenge. Here, it was not the same. There was no conqueror to come in and exact vengeance. People were just grateful the terror time was over and wanted to forget it."

"So what happened to all the guards?"

"Mostly, they were pensioned off. Look, you know a lot was based on the labour camps. You saw yourself up at Norilsk how the city and the mine and all its ancillary works were built by slave labour. We don't like it, we try to keep it hidden, but we know the truth of it. But why are you asking this?"

"Because it is the only reason I can think of for the reaction to my investigations of my mother's brother's life up there."

"What do you mean?"

"I think there must be somebody who is still in a position of authority who was involved with his death. My looking into it would not be good, because, after all, the way the story seems, it was frankly cold-blooded murder."

"Yes, that's true; but it was fifty-odd years ago, in a time when political killing was almost normal. I know that sounds dreadful, but it's the truth. I know you have a particular interest, Alex, but you have to remember how many people died under that system. I can't believe there would be such concern about one individual, however seemingly arbitrary the circumstances."

"Mmm." I paused for a moment, thinking."How easy would it be to find out the name of the killer? I mean, he was the commandant of the camp, so presumably his name must be recorded somewhere?"

"Yes, I suppose that's probably right. Frankly, I've never needed to find out anything like that, so I'm not sure how you would begin. But seriously, do you really want to carry on with this? You've found what you wanted - how he died. Do you really need to keep digging? I don't think it's going to do you any good. I mean your relationship with Arctic Mining; they don't like it."

"You know what I think? I think that either somebody at a high level in the company is somehow linked to the camp, or somebody in the local authorities who can put pressure on the company. It can't be the commandant himself, I'm guessing he couldn't really still be alive after this time. My guess is it's a relative of some sort, who wants to protect his father's or uncle's or whatever's name."

"Well, it's possible, I agree. But if it is true, then these are powerful people you're talking about. Look, the relationship we have with your company is an important one to us; there are very few people here who would have sufficient power to cut that relationship like they have. It's got to come from right at the top level. So I would suggest you leave it alone. Carrying on investigating will cause nothing but more difficulties."

A thought struck me. "Andrey, you're not hiding something, are you? You don't already know who it is, do you?"

He sounded hurt. "Of course not. We're friends, Alex. I'm not keeping anything from you; I don't know what is going on. I just know that you won't do yourself any favours if you keep on digging."

"OK; but can you do one more thing for me? Can you ask somebody you know well from the previous generation in the company if he knows whether any of his colleagues were involved in the camps? You'd just be asking out of interest, just to learn more about the history. That can't be too bad."

"Alex, you're not listening. This is a big deal for somebody. If I go stomping about asking questions I'm going to become as unpopular as you are with whoever it is. Besides, all those old-school guys keep close together. If I ask one, it will get round them all in no time and that won't help you at all. I really think you should leave it alone. You know the story now, just go back to your own life and - I was going to say forget about it, but I don't mean that. You won't forget your uncle but carrying on now will not help him and will only harm you. You've done everything you can."

"OK, I take your point. I'll think a bit more about it all."

We finished the conversation and hung up. In one sense I knew he was right; I'd got pretty much the whole story: Armin Kuhlmann, from Stalingrad to death. Any more I learned wasn't going to change anything. Did it really matter which Russian guard had actually pulled the trigger? Armin had effectively been killed the moment he was taken into the system as a prisoner.

Sometimes you don't see the wood for the trees. When I got home that evening and told Emily about the dead end I seemed to have reached, she gave me the obvious answer. "Why don't you ask Hartmann? He was there for years, after all. He must know about the commandant, I would have thought."

I gave her a kiss. "Why didn't I think of that?"

"Because you're getting too close to it. You're not thinking. Go and call Hartmann now, and see what he has to say."

Actually, what he had to say wasn't that helpful initially, once I'd explained where my investigation had got bogged down. They'd rarely seen the commandant, and had no idea of his name. "The guards always referred to him as 'commandant', or 'the boss', or something else like that. He only came into the main part of the compound a few times -

that I saw - in all the years I was there. But you could tell the guards were frightened of him."

"Well, do you know how old he was, or anything like that?"

"Very difficult to tell. I mean, this is a man I saw a few times, a long time ago, in a very particular situation. He wasn't old, like a different generation from us, I don't think. I did see him once, close-to: when he sentenced me to solitary. All I remember is that he looked like most of the guards - very short, military-type hair cut, NKVD uniform and he had the power of life and death over me. I'm sorry, Alex, but I can't help on this one." He paused for a moment. Then, "Alex, don't let them put you off; what you're doing is right. If you can find out the name of the man who pulled the trigger, then you should do. You can't change anything, but we should finish Armin's story properly now, if we can."

I thanked him and hung up. He'd reinforced what I really thought myself, that whatever difficulties may be created - and Andrey was probably right about that - I had to try and solve this last piece of the puzzle. They'd been wartime enemies, but what the commandant had done that day had been no more than a petty murder, just because he had the power to do it with no retribution. Well, we couldn't change that, but we could make it known.

Two minutes later, the phone rang again. It was Hartmann.

"Alex, there was one thing about the commandant. He spoke perfect German, without any trace of Russian accent. I don't know if that is significant - at the time, the peculiarities of the guards was not something any of us had the energy to think about."

That was interesting. Could the man actually have been a German? In my experience, the Russian accent in German is as distinctive as it is in English. There were certainly Germans involved with the Russians at the time, in just the same way as there were Russians in the German army; Hartmann had himself mentioned how Walter Ulbricht had harangued the defeated Germans after the battle. Ideologues from both countries had positioned themselves with the enemy. The absurdity of it struck me again - in reality there was barely a cigarette paper between the two authoritarian regimes, both utterly committed to controlling all aspects of their citizens' lives, and yet there were so many who had managed to convince themselves that it was a battle of opposing world views. It was almost a separate war from the one waged between the western allies and the Nazis. In fact, as I found out that evening as I did a bit of research, the Comintern had instructed the German communists to co-operate with the Nazis against the social democrats in 1932 and Ulbricht and Goebbels had both addressed the same transport workers strike meeting; the co-operation didn't last long, and Ulbricht was not the only German communist ultimately to take refuge in Soviet Russia and support the Russian war effort. That was all sort of macro stuff I found quite easily

Beyond Stalingrad

in reference books; what I didn't get from there was the lower-level kind of information I was looking for. I couldn't find any trace of individual Germans serving in the NKVD, let alone running labour camps.

1999 Monaco

Chapter Thirty-Seven

And there it stayed for a bit. I knew what I wanted to find out, but I didn't know how to set about it. Being an NKVD guard was hardly anything to shout about, neither was it the sort of subject on which there was too much research available. Finding out the names of the guards seemed to be just a difficult as finding those of the prisoners; they were locked together in their own dark world of the past.

A few days later, I headed off to Monaco to attend a conference discussing the nickel business. As I got off my flight at Nice and walked through into the airport hall, I glimpsed Andrey by a carousel with a group of others - unmistakably Russian - waiting for their bags. He saw me, and gestured with his phone. I had only hand luggage and as I stepped into a cab to take me down to Monte Carlo, sure enough, my mobile rang.

"Hey, Alex, if you hadn't made yourself so unpopular you could have come with us; we're just waiting for the helicopter."

I laughed. "Yes, I suppose I could. But now I just have to slum it in a cab. Am I still invited to your dinner tomorrow?"

"Yes, I believe you are, despite everything. You may find yourself sitting down amongst the also-rans though, rather than up with us. But look, I have got something to tell you. My colleagues are all off to the casino this evening, so perhaps we could meet around nine. But let's get away from the hotel. I assume you staying at the Hotel de Paris?"

"Yes."

"OK, well, look, you know the Place Ste Devote, where there is the statue of Williams in a Bugatti?"

"Yes," I said again.

"Well, behind there is a small bar, I can't remember the name, but you won't miss it. I'll see you there at about nine."

"OK, I look forward to it."

"Got to go, my helicopter looks like it's ready!"

Beyond Stalingrad

Sure enough, as my cab wound its way along the Corniche before heading down the hill into Monte Carlo, I saw the helicopter passing, out over the sea.

Monte Carlo is a strange place, hemmed in as it is by sea and mountains; during the season, I was never a fan - too crowded, and by people I didn't really want to know. But out of season, which is when the conference was held each year, without the crowds, the old belle époque architecture has a beauty of its own. I strolled down the hill the racing cars roar up in the Grand Prix and wandered slowly down towards Ste Devote. I knew the Williams statue and the bar was obvious just across the road from it. I walked in just before nine to find Andrey already there with a bottle of wine on the table in front of him. He poured me a glass and raised his: "Cheers. I hope you like this."

I tasted it; it was a beautifully chilled white burgundy. "Mmm; very good. So have your boys all gone to the casino?"

"Yes; same every year. First evening here - off to the casino, then the next one is our dinner. The third one normally gets a bit messy, just with all the Russians together and then we leave the next morning." He grinned. "I told them I had a bit of business to deal with this evening, and they looked at me as if I was crazy. Business before casino? Whatever next? But I never win at blackjack, anyway. There was something I found, though, that may be of interest to you."

"I'm all ears," I said.

"But before we get on to that, how much do you know about him?" He pointed through the window at the statue of the man at the wheel of his Bugatti.

"Williams? Not much. English guy who won one of the early Monaco Grands Prix."

"Yes, he did. In fact, he won the first one, in 1929. He was a very successful racing driver in the late 20s and early 30s. But there's a much more interesting part to the story, given that we've been talking about world war two and people dying in camps."

I looked quizzically at him.

"Williams lived in France - he was married to a French woman - but he went back to England in 1940 and joined the army. He must have been about 40 then. They realised that he was a fluent French speaker and could easily pass as a Frenchman and they got him transferred to the SOE - the sabotage group that worked with the French Resistance. He was captured in France in 1944, and eventually sent to Sachsenhausen. He seems to have been executed there in 1945, very shortly before the camp was liberated. At least, that's the official story; there are others who claim that he escaped and lived under an alias under the protection of the British MI6. So it's a bit like what you've been looking at - a man who disappeared into a world war two prison camp, and somehow died, but the details are murky."

"Interesting. I have to admit I didn't know that. But surely there must have been survivors who knew what happened to him?"

"Just like with your uncle? That's the point, Alex, this stuff is so lost in the confusion of war and its aftermath that all sorts of claims have been made. And the contemporary witnesses all remember just parts of the story; the difficulty is piecing it all together."

"Mmm. But why would he use an alias after the war?"

Andrey shrugged. "Who knows? But the general consensus is that he was executed and the alias story is just romanticising. Anyway, I just thought you might be interested in the story. That's not really why I dragged you out here this evening.

"I had to go up to Norilsk for a couple of days last week and I went along to see your friend Khorsky. He's feeling a bit less twitchy now, and he seems to be less frightened of being prosecuted for giving away state secrets. He's worked out it was just a threat to stop him helping you. They've told him he will have to leave, but they're going to post him to another similar job somewhere else. He's pretty relaxed about it all now. So we had a look at some records, he and I, to see what we could find. Incidentally, I hope you appreciate all this on your behalf." He grinned. "It's amazing how you can be intrigued by a mystery and not want to let it go."

"I do appreciate it; without all the help, I wouldn't even have known where to begin."

"Well, anyway, we looked through the records of the camp, and it seems that the commandant at the period in question was a man called Grabel. We couldn't find any details about him; where he came from, what happened to him later or anything like that. But that's possibly an interesting name."

I just stared at him.

"Come on, Alex. You're fluent in German. What does 'Grab' mean?"

"Grave," I said immediately. "But 'Grabel' isn't a word."

"No, and I know I may be stretching things, but just bear with me for a bit. At that time, there was still a hangover from the Bolsheviks and their thinking. You know that plenty of them adopted assumed names; well, Stalin himself was one of them. They chose names to give a feeling of strength, or mystery, as well as to hide their identity from the Tsar's secret police in the old days. You know that, right?"

I nodded, and he continued. "Well it occurs to me that this could be one of those. I'm thinking, 'grave', 'death', just right for an NKVD labour camp commandant. And if I'm right, then it's a good possibility that he was a German, hence the use of a - slightly corrupted - German word."

"So you're suggesting that a German, for some reason a member of the NKVD, came to be the commandant at that Norilsk camp, using an alias to conceal his real identity?"

"I think it may be a possibility, yes. But there is something else, as well."

"Before you go any further, when I spoke again to the German ex-prisoner I tracked down in Hamburg, he told me that he recalled the man speaking German without a Russian accent. That kind of suggests he may have been one."

"Ah, well that backs up my theory. You see, there were actually quite a lot of German communists floating around at the time - they had mostly escaped into Russia during the 1930s, but then during the period of the Molotov-Ribbentrop pact, they had to lie low, because they were frightened that they might be handed back. That's where I think the alias may have come from. And then, when the Germans broke the pact and invaded, that was the name he was known by. But look, I think I know who Grabel's son is."

I waited.

"I think you'll know the name, and you may understand why they want to hide the fact that his father was a German camp commandant and a petty tyrant and murderer." He paused for a moment or two, and then told me the name.

I stared at him. "Are you sure?"

He nodded; his expression was deadly serious. "It's not something I am about to shout from the rooftops, and I couldn't objectively prove it if you asked me to, but I'm pretty sure it's true. He's from the Norilsk region, and he's always been a bit vague about his background. We just know that his father was 'an official' in the area, who died when he was still very young, and his mother remarried and moved to Moscow. He took the stepfather's name. It all certainly fits and it also explains why you've run into so many obstacles. It's a story they don't want told."

I tried to get my mind round what he was telling me. "But is it so damaging? I mean, nobody is responsible for their parents' actions, and anyway, you say he was brought up by a stepfather. So nobody can blame him.'

"That's true. Look, it would be very unlikely to do serious long-term damage; his career is secure enough for that. But it's not the kind of thing anybody would like to become common knowledge, and this guy is in a position where he can prevent it. He can, and so he will. That's just how it works. But I think you'll find this is what is behind the change of attitude to your enquiries. And it's not just me that thinks it, either," he added. "Khorsky and I discussed it at some length. He's obviously concerned that his part in helping you doesn't cause him problems, but he's quite well attuned to what goes on up there - far more than me, even though

I have some relatives - and while we talked about it he became more and more sure that that was the case. It seems there have been rumours about the man up in Norilsk, although nothing seem to have been said more widely than that. They've obviously helped him to keep a lid on it."

I sat back in my chair and took a mouthful of wine. Through the window behind Andrey I could see the lights twinkling around the harbour. It was quite a lot to take in; I was causing ructions at a very high level indeed in the hierarchy. The man was, I knew, a household name within Russia, as well as having a profile internationally.

"So, what should I do, Andrey? You know how things work in your country better than I do."

"Yes." He paused for a moment, looking straight at me, as if weighing up what to say. "Look, I know this is important to you and I know you've discovered a lot of what happened. Obviously, now you want to finish the whole story off. But, and I say this as a genuine friend, with your best interests at heart, you should be satisfied with what you have and leave it now. Trying to make the link I have just suggested will do you no good. I don't just mean in business with Arctic Mining." He paused again and sipped his wine. "This is going to sound stupidly melodramatic, but people didn't stop being killed just because the system changed. At home or abroad. You understand?"

I just stared. I couldn't believe somebody intelligent and worldly-wise was sitting in a bar in Monte Carlo telling me I could be killed for delving back into history.

"But that's absurd, Andrey. That's out of all proportion."

"Yes, you think that and I think that and many, many people would agree with us. It is absurd. But that doesn't mean it doesn't happen. And" - he made a calming gesture with his hands - "I'm not saying that anything like that would happen. I'm just telling you that somebody very powerful doesn't want the events of 1950-whatever-it-was to become general knowledge and he has the power to prevent that in many different ways." He stopped. His expression was deadly serious. He really believed this stuff.

"Alex, it's not a joke. I know you're a man of the world, a metal trader - and that means you're used to dealing with all sorts of people. Good, bad, dangerous - they're all in our business. But this is a different scale. These people have a totally different sort of power. They believe they can do whatever they like and that whatever they want is going to happen. That's just how it is when you reach that level. You and I and most of the people we know are absolutely nothing to them. If this man wants things hushed up and you are the price, he doesn't care. You don't even exist to him. For him, it's a simple equation: does having you silenced pose more or less of a risk to him than allowing you to expose the past? Once he's made that decision, everything else is just pure process."

Beyond Stalingrad

I was shocked, frankly. It's all very well to joke about gangsters and mafia as we did daily when dealing with some of the more exotic of our counterparties; but Andrey was right. However dubious they may be, they were not in the same league as what he was describing. I sat silently for a bit, taking in what he had said.

"And bear in mind," he continued, after a pause, "it's possibly not only you. Your friend Hartmann could be in he firing line as well. He's been no threat in all the time since he left the camp, but now? Now, his name may come to the fore again if you expose what happened."

That shook me again; but he was right, and I had a responsibility to the old man in Hamburg who had been so helpful and forthcoming with his story. I couldn't leave him open to that sort of danger.

1999 Sussex

Chapter Thirty-Eight

"So that's it", I said. My sister Isobel and her husband and Elisabeth's two sons and their wives were sitting around our dining table as well as Emily and me. I had just told them the whole story of Armin's life and death, right up to the conversations I'd had with Andrey in Monaco and Max Hartmann two days ago. "I had hoped to be able to finish the story for you with my plan to put on an exhibition of Armin's pictures, but you can see we can't really do that now. It exposes too many people to too much risk - me included."

George, Elisabeth's second son, was the first to respond. "It's an amazing story. We all knew about his disappearance, obviously, but you've done really well to be able to trace what happened after that. As far as our mother told us, all they knew was that he vanished into the battle" - he glanced across at his brother, who nodded his agreement - "but obviously they didn't know about the rest of it. I think I'm probably quite glad they didn't; it would be pretty grim living with the knowledge that your brother was a slave. Or indeed a murder victim. Actually," he continued, "if you put it like that, I can see why the guy in Russia wouldn't want it to come out. It was that: his father was a common murderer, at least twice, from what we know. That wouldn't sit well with his current position."

"But can you really do nothing? I mean, he has no decent grave - that should not be." Cécile, the French wife of George's elder brother Anthony, was perhaps more religious than the rest of us. "Could we not at least get a priest to mark the place somehow?"

"Cécile, Alex has just told us that there is no way of knowing where the grave is; and anyway, it sounds like it wouldn't be a good idea to try and do anything like that in Russia, in the circumstances," her husband Anthony replied.

"Mmm. Well, perhaps you could put a memorial plaque in the church somewhere here. After all, your families lived here after the war and you all grew up around here."

Beyond Stalingrad

"That's an idea," said Emily, "but who is to say Armin was in any way religious? I would have thought that with what was happening to him, religious belief is the last thing he would have held."

"I tend to agree," said George. "And we all know that neither of our mothers were particularly church-goers. I don't think that would be the right thing to do."

The conversation went back and forth, Cécile arguing that some form of religious mark would be appropriate and her husband and brother-in-law both vociferously putting forward their opposition to that as making assumptions about Armin that couldn't possibly be justified.

Isobel had been silent through all this, and then she spoke. "Honestly, there is nothing we can do. Alex has done a great piece of detective work and now we know the truth of what happened to Armin. But to imagine we can actually do anything? Or even that we should? We can't change anything about what he suffered and that's really the only thing that matters. We know, we can be sure that the next generation knows - your children, you'll tell them" (Isobel had no children of her own) "- and that's the way the memory is preserved. But to try and do anything 'official'? That's crazy. It was a war, people got killed and maimed and made homeless. Children lost their parents and parents lost their children. Armin means something to us, but while you were telling us the story, Alex, you mentioned that they were still discovering thousands of German bodies in Russia every year. And then there are the Russians. And the British, and the Canadians, and the Poles, and the French…….. and all the others. The Americans and the Japanese, the Australians…… In the end, Armin is one man. One man amongst the millions. We can remember him personally, of course, amongst ourselves, but to try and pick out one person from all the casualties, I don't see that we could even expect to do that. I think maybe everybody's getting a bit carried away. We know where some of his paintings are - Alex and I and Maggie have got the ones from our parents' house and we know about the others in Hamburg; they are the memorial. Perhaps we should try and keep those together, but it wouldn't be right to try and single him out of all the millions now, so long afterwards. And pragmatically, as well, if we provoke the guy in Russia, do we not risk stirring all the animosity up again, when actually, from what Alex says, he's in fact been getting help from there?

"Let's face it: Armin was just one of the millions of leaves blown away by the gale."

That stopped the conversation for a bit, while we digested her words. In the end, she was right. What difference would another memorial stone make? I knew Armin's name was on the list at Rossoschka. Maybe the detail was wrong, although one could argue that his life as we knew life had indeed come to an end with captivity. Although, following that kind of logic, perhaps one could say the same of the day on which he was conscripted into the Wehrmacht. That's when the free life of Armin Kuhlmann was shoved into the sausage machine. From then on, like so many others, he was just a pawn in a game not of his choosing.

And that was really it. I made another trip to Hamburg, to visit Max Hartmann; he was understanding, when I explained our decision. I think he felt a great relief that at last he had done what he had promised himself all those years ago in the camp on the day Armin died and made his family aware of what had happened. He'd seen it as a debt of honour, finally discharged. He also told me that he couldn't bear to part with Armin's drawings - they were his only tangible contact with the man who had been his greatest friend - but that he would leave them in his will to the surviving relatives of Armin Kuhlmann; he wanted them finally to come home to Armin's family.

Lightning Source UK Ltd.
Milton Keynes UK
UKHW011851161220
375296UK00001B/32